Thou hast nor youth nor age
But as it were an after-dinner's sleep
Dreaming on both.
Measure for Measure

An After-Dinner's Sleep

STANLEY MIDDLETON

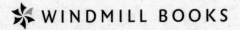 WINDMILL BOOKS

Published by Windmill Books 2014

2 4 6 8 10 9 7 5 3 1

Copyright © Stanley Middleton 1986

This edition copyright © The Estate of Stanley Middleton 1986, 2014

Stanley Middleton has asserted his right under the Copyright, Designs and
Patents Act, 1988, to be identified as the author of this work.

First published in Great Britain in 1986 by Century Hutchinson
First published in paperback in Great Britain in 1987 by Methuen London Ltd

Windmill Books
The Random House Group Limited
20 Vauxhall Bridge Road, London SW1V 2SA

Addresses for companies within The Random House Group Limited can be found at:
www.randomhouse.co.uk/offices.htm

The Random House Group Limited Reg. No. 954009

www.randomhouse.co.uk

A CIP catalogue record for this book
is available from the British Library

ISBN 9780099591955

The Random House Group Limited supports the Forest Stewardship
Council® (FSC®), the leading international forest-certification organisation.
Our books carrying the FSC label are printed on FSC®-certified paper. FSC is
the only forest-certification scheme supported by the leading environmental
organisations, including Greenpeace. Our paper procurement policy
can be found at: www.randomhouse.co.uk/environment

Typeset in Linotron Plantrin by Input Typesetting Ltd, London

Printed and bound by Clays Ltd, St Ives plc

1

The woman searched for the bell, and failing to find it in the patchy darkness knocked hard on the door. No sooner had she stopped than she spotted the button, slightly higher than usual, and unlighted. In the garden wind hacked with unceasing violence through shrubs, tree branches, snapping at twigs, bringing down bunches of still green leaves.

She wondered whether to knock again or ring. There was a light or lights in the hall, red through the glass of the front door. Finally she heard footsteps in spite of the gale, and the door was cautiously opened on a chain.

'Yes?'

Presumably he could not see her face because of her headscarf.

'It's me, Alistair.'

'I'm sorry?' He did not recognize her voice, either.

'Eleanor Franks.'

'Oh, I see. Come in.' His voice sounded dry, unwelcoming; perhaps he had expected nobody, resented the intrusion. He allowed her to pass him, then locked and bolted the door. 'Are you going to take your coat off?' She did so and he carried it away, with her scarf, to hang in an alcove. 'Well, now,' returning, 'I don't often have the pleasure of seeing you.' He showed her into a room on the left, at the back of the building. 'Sit down,' he invited.

The room was surprisingly large, at least twice or three times the length she had expected; its end wall consisting completely of a window, or sliding glass door, in which she and Alistair Murray were reflected, bright and distorted figures in the polished blackness between undrawn curtains.

'Not often I have the privilege,' he said, clearing his throat awkwardly.

She took a chair. The gas fire bobbed in the wind, burning

yellow. He inquired after her health, and she answered reassuringly. There was an odd smell about this quite beautiful room which she could not track down. Perhaps it was damp or the gas. As far as she could recall, Alistair did not smoke. He replied gruffly, succinctly, to her questions how he felt, as if he were lying because that caused less bother.

'Now,' he said, 'before I sit down, can I get you a drink? Coffee, tea, sherry, gin and tonic?' He laughed at his list, and flattened his thick grey hair with his hand. The hair was straighter, less wavy than when he'd been a young man.

Eleanor refused his offer, and he therefore parked himself heavily, holding on to the arms of his chair.

'Well, then.' He bent, not quickly, to retrieve an open book from the carpet at his feet and replace it on the small, polished table at his elbow. 'And to what do I owe the honour of this visit?'

Alistair spoke with slow irony, thinly, breathily for so tall a man. Though his accent was standard, southern English, there was something American about his appearance. Perhaps it was the open-necked, bright check shirt; but he was no cowboy, or square-dance caller, rather the gentlemanly grand-father of a television series who narrowed his eyes and nodded as he dredged up catarrhal wisdom for misunderstood teen-aged talents or beauties.

'I don't really know,' she answered.

'Then how do I begin to find out?'

She sat silently listening to the plop of the gas flames. He must have had an extension built to procure this length of room, though the stone fireplace was exactly halfway down the longest outside wall. The place was bright with the dust covers of shelved books. From where she sat she could see five pictures, all gold-framed, though she could not see what they were. Light was tightly concentrated on the white rug and chairs by the hearth. The large painting above the mantel-piece, a dark oil, was in shadow, its overhead lamp out, its surface tarry, unintelligible.

'I don't know what to say now I've come,' she began.

'I'll tell you then that I'm glad to see you.'

8

'I'm not interrupting anything important?'

'You're not interrupting anything. I was sitting here reading, but if you questioned me I'd have some difficulty recalling what it was. There's nothing I want on the telly, and the Prom's full of stuff I don't want to hear. When I was young Friday night was Beethoven.'

'And Amami,' she said. 'A shampoo.' She giggled, but her face straightened at once.

He shook his head, dazed at her intervention, or not having listened.

'Thus, I am glad to see you.'

The pair sat in glum silence, waiting for the other, uncertain.

'I felt awful,' she said at length.

'I often do.' He guffawed at his own embarrassment. 'Go on. I'm sorry.'

'I don't mean physically. Or not exactly. And I don't think it was because I was lonely. I mean, I am. Often enough. But I don't think that was the basis.'

'No?' He spoke only when her pause had stretched beyond comfort. Gusts rattled windowframes, clashed a door open somewhere inside the house. 'Well, now.'

'Last night in the evening newspaper . . . Do you have it?'

'Yes.'

'Well, you'll have seen it, then.'

'I don't always look at it.' He was trying to remember something from last night's, Thursday's, paper. Finally he shook his head.

'It was the front page. With big headlines.'

Again he frowned.

'I'm sorry. Shall I fetch it? It'll still be in the pile. There are no fires to light here.'

'A young married woman committed suicide. In a car. She had a small child with her. She connected a tube to the exhaust out in the garage. The husband found them. The garage doors were closed. She didn't usually leave her car in there.'

'How old were they?'

'Barely thirty. The child four. There was a photograph of

9

them; that's what's terrifying. The three of them on a garden seat, with the child, a little girl, on the mother's knee. It was a lovely picture, even in the paper. They were smiling. He looked smart, and she was beautiful, and happy, and fair like the baby. It was just the sort of picture you'd like in your album of your children and grandchildren.'

'Why had she done it?'

'It didn't say. You know what the *Post*'s like. Headlines and a picture of the house and this photograph, and hardly any information. Except some neighbour who said that the young woman was always happy and singing about the home.'

He rubbed his chin, rustling the white stubble.

'The photo made it seem worse,' she said. 'I didn't know what to do.'

'No.'

'If I could only have gone round and said a word to the husband.'

'You didn't know them? At all?'

'No.'

'And where did this happen?'

'North of the county. Retford or Bawtry. They lived in a village, it said. Beldonfield, was it? Some such name.'

'It may not have come,' Alistair Murray suggested, 'as a surprise to the husband. He may have known there was something amiss, or the girl may have tried before.'

'They looked so happy. That's silly, because anyone can put a smile on for a photograph, but it did make it feel worse. I suppose it's my age. Fifty-eight's not old these days, is it? It's neither here nor there. But I couldn't get over it. I couldn't concentrate on anything else and I slept badly.'

'Is that usual?'

'Broken, but I have enough.'

'And? Go on.'

'I was worse today. I went about the shops this morning, and there were dozens of women with small children and cars, and I thought that for all I knew they, or some of them, were in the same sort of turmoil as that poor woman. I told myself not to be so silly, that these girls were out shopping, not killing themselves. I was too bothered to cook lunch, and I made myself go to the park for a walk in the afternoon, took the dog. Usually I meet somebody, but today I didn't. Too windy for old people. And I sat at home terrified, so I couldn't even talk to Tina. She lay on the rug and kept looking at me, as if she knew there was something amiss. In the end I jumped up and went out.'

'Without the dog?'

'Yes. I walked about the streets.'

'At nine at night? It's dark. Was that safe?'

'It felt safer than at home. Now that's not right, and I know it's not. I've not taken leave of my senses altogether.' Eleanor smiled, shuffled in the chair, relaxing. 'I tried to write to my niece, but I thought my letter might disturb her, and she's got her hands full, with three young children.'

'Can't you telephone her?'

'Yes. I do. Often. It didn't seem the thing. I tore the letter up and rushed out.'

'Intending to do what?' Alistair asked.

'Intending? No, not anything, really. Just to walk about and stop myself thinking. I know it's not sensible, but anything was better than sitting there going mad. You think I should see the doctor, don't you?'

'Drugs can be useful,' he said.

'I have some. Since Henry died. Tranquillizers.' She pouted. 'I've done all the right things, Alistair. I've joined clubs, I attend WEA classes, I belong to a church in a half-hearted way. I visit people, I take good holidays, friends come to see me.'

'And it works?'

'By and large. Until something like this happens?'

'How often's that?'

'Once a month. Or a six month. It varies. There's no pattern that I can see.'

'And no cause?'

'Yes. No. I saw the photograph. In the ordinary way I'd be able to cope with something like that. I mean I'd feel sad. Who wouldn't? But I'd know this was one case in hundreds, with its own special features, its history, and I'd recover. Not yesterday, though. Not today.'

11

'How long do these attacks last?'

'Twenty-four hours or so. Gradually easing up.'

'And you take your pills?'

'Yes.' She answered now with a cheerful insouciance, like a child who realizes adults cannot fault the reply.

They sat again, not speaking, listening to the boisterous swoops of the wind.

'You'll wonder why I came bothering you?'

'It had crossed my mind.'

'I passed the end of your close, saw the street name.'

He was surprised.

There was a shriek outside and a thump, heavy enough to shake the building.

'What's that?' Eleanor sat straight, hands shaking.

'God knows. Tree down. Tile spinning off a roof.'

'It sounded big.'

'Telegraph pole, perhaps. I'll go and look. Not that I shall be able to do anything about it, at this time of night. You stay here. You'll be all right, won't you?'

'Yes.'

Alistair did not go out by the french window, but by a back door which she heard bang. In the garden, though much diminished by the walls, the ferment of confusion howled on. She walked to the window, but could make out little beyond a patio, a flagged path, an agitation of dark bushes, probably roses. There was no sign of Alistair who was either in another part of the garden, or not using a torch. In the distance she could see street lights behind the complicating geometry of shifting branches. He was taking long enough about it; she wished she had gone out there with him, helping him to do whatever it was he did.

When he returned, still wearing his grey anorak, the silver hair tousled, he held out his hands to her, in apology, to show how dirty they were. She pointed to a scratch on his thumb with a bleb of bright blood, and he babied it into his mouth to suck it clean.

'What was wrong?' she asked.

'A pergola. A couple of rustic poles had come adrift and fallen across the path.'

12

'It sounded as if the side of the house had fallen in.'

'Yes. It's doing some damage out there. I shall be clearing up and tying up all this next week, I can tell you. Excuse me. I'll go and get the muck off.' He held his hands out again.

When he reappeared, without anorak, and hair straightened with water, he said, 'Well, it's time we had that cup of coffee, isn't it? I've earned it.'

'It's time I went home. Tina will wonder where I am.'

'She'd have enjoyed it out.'

'I don't think so. She's thirteen. She was Henry's dog. She's getting on.'

'Coffee?'

'Go on then.'

'I've twisted your arm.' He laughed, and she followed him out to the kitchen where he fiddled with instant coffee. 'How long has your husband been dead now?' The question rang impolitely.

'Two years.'

'I see. Was he ill for long?'

'Not really. Six months. He'd been retired for eighteen months.'

Alistair Murray whistled uncheerfully as he poured from kettle to mugs.

'Do you want a biscuit?' She refused. 'How long is it since we saw each other, Eleanor?'

'You wrote to me when Henry died. It must be six – seven years though. At a concert. They played Sibelius's Fourth. You were there with Janet. Time passes so quickly.'

'I'd forgotten,' he told her. 'I knew it was long enough.'

He had seduced this woman when she was eighteen and he was on leave from the army, and this evening he had not recognized her at his front door. He could drum up excuses that it was dark and she had muffled herself. They sat silently. Eleanor Franks, slim still, well dressed, had not altogether lost the heart-shaped face which had been integral to her beauty. No grey showed in her hair, but the colour seemed natural, or not obviously of a chemical origin. The fine eyes were large, bright, calm, though darkened, faintly wrinkled at the corners. She had kept her figure, the smoothness of

13

the neck, the firmness of lips; her hands had suffered most, in that they were bony, discoloured with liver spots, too thin, chapped.

She spoke about her late husband cheerfully enough, changed her mind to accept an arrowroot biscuit, but sat primly, as if she acknowledged by the posture that she had broken some taboo important to her.

'I don't think Henry was displeased to go,' she said suddenly in the middle of a banal exchange about grand-children. She did not expand, though he waited.

'He couldn't have been very old?'

'Sixty-five.'

'My age now. Why did I say that?'

She laughed, eyes wrinkling attractively, and did not answer. Alistair Murray had barely known her husband, who had made a great deal of money with property and investment. Henry Arthur Franks, a solicitor in his father's firm, had not occupied himself overmuch with legal business. There had been rumours at one time that he had suborned local council-lors to his advantage, but nothing came of the talk, and unfavourable mentions in *Private Eye* were allowed to stand unchallenged. Franks did not need to collect from libel actions; there was easier money to hand. And yet, on the few occasions Murray had met him, the man had seemed monumentally dull, talkative in a conventional way, unin-terested in any but local concerns, uninteresting from his stiff, large-brimmed, old-fashioned hat to his toe-capped shoes. He was not hearty, did not waste time with golf clubs; in no way did he appear arrogant, overbearing, opinionated; nor was he a cold fish or odd or socially inept. Dullness was his all. And yet.

For one thing he had married Eleanor Warrington, a young teacher at that time, graduate of London University, a theatrical whose Cordelia and Beatrice in amateur Arts Society productions had led to prognostications of a professional career. Lively, beautiful, quick, favourite with men and women alike, much courted and fêted, she had become the wife of Harry Franks, her father's partner, a man nearly ten years her senior. It had seemed incredible to all but the girl

14

herself. She gave up her acting, her teaching and devoted herself to family life in a mansion with a five-acre garden; she refused to sit on the Bench, or on committees, or do charitable work. When her sons were old enough to be sent away to her husband's public school, Oundle, she regularly entertained her own friends or her husband's business associates and was treated with the respect due to the wife of a reputed millionaire. Alistair Murray, in love with the student Eleanor, dazzled, had found her brilliantly different from the schoolgirl he had known five years before and was knocked emotionally askew. For her part the married woman did not once invite him to Craigmore for dinner, coffee or a stroll in the grounds; Alistair Murray was to play no part in her life.

'A dark horse,' a friend had ribbed Alistair, making him smart, 'is our Henry.'

'He's rich.'

'You're right there.'

'What else?'

'What else do you need?'

And so it appeared. Eleanor was bought, and grew satisfied with the transaction. It could not be possible.

Men spoke of Franks with admiration.

'He's sharp,' they said. 'My God, he's a fast operator.'

'Dull,' Murray objected. 'A bore.'

They looked him over, and clichés, 'sour grapes', were lined up for use when he was out of the room.

Thus Eleanor had been removed from Alistair's life. He saw her photograph from year to year in the local paper, read the announcements of her sons' engagements in *The Times*, once or twice met the woman herself, who treated him with a friendly carelessness and made no attempt to renew acquaintance. His own marriage, family life, advancement had brought them no nearer, until this evening when like some lonely old biddy from a council flat in a tower block she had turned up tongue-tied by distress at his front door.

At this moment she was perfectly at ease, and was describing a musical she had seen in London last week. Her clothes, he noticed, were very good, as if she had dressed up for the visit, not gone wandering into the streets, as she claimed, driven to distraction by a newspaper picture. He did not understand what was happening and in no way enjoyed his puzzlement.

'I'll get the car out,' he said in one of the pauses, 'and drive you home.'

'You'll do no such thing. It's twenty minutes' walk.'

But she did not argue when he insisted, and he dropped her outside the entrance to the Matlock luxury flats, two streets away from the lime trees at the bottom end of the Craigmore garden.

'Are you coming in?' she asked.

'No, thank you.'

She seemed, how could he tell in the dark street?, relieved.

'I'm sorry to have burst in on you like that. I don't know what made me do it.'

'I'm glad you did.' That was a lie.

'We must keep in touch.'

'Yes.'

Taking her cue perhaps from his lack of enthusiasm, she thanked him again, turned her back at once, and was gone. He waited until she reached her door, heard the rattle of the key and her dog's bark.

The wind blew boisterously where it listed, and he saw not a soul on the streets.

2

Next morning Alistair Murray dawdled over his breakfast toast and coffee.

The gales had blown themselves out wiping the sky clean. He had already inspected damage in the garden and had found himself a week's work which he would not be able to start today as his son had invited himself to lunch. This happened rarely, because although Sebastian often left London it was not in the direction of the north midlands of England, rather New York or Peking or Paris or Melbourne. Alistair, however, saw a great deal of his eldest on the television screen, interviewing notables, laying down the law, knowing more of everything than anyone else, front man to the world. The father was in no way surprised at his son's success, only that it had taken quite so long. He could not see much difference between the thirty-three-year-old, screwing on his frown to harry some president or premier, and the twelve-year-old reporting back, smart in his uniform, on the masters, the lessons, the games field of the local high school. There was no doubt about his cleverness, his quick wit, his incisive mind, but it was that serious face, that frankness under the huge spectacles, the badge of his tribe, that had made him a household name.

Alistair was wondering, vaguely, what to cook, and whether to provide wine. His son had promised to arrive at 12.30, and he'd do that, exactly. They would drink one small glass of dry sherry together and Sebastian would ask about his father's welfare and about his sister, with whom he never communicated, and then explain why he was in this part of the world. He would not be trying to worm information, that would already have been done by his experts far more efficiently, but the impression would be left that Sebastian Murray was in some sense testing out his programme, honing it on the

17

hard surface of his father's provincial cunning. Alistair admitted that this was hyperactive imagination on his part but it kept him amused, made his son's brief appearances tolerable. At two o'clock, and this would be made clear within five minutes of the doorbell's initial ringing, Sebastian would push outside again, stepping into his Merc or Daimler, saying it would not be so long next time, and then disappearing leaving his father to wash the dishes, think his thoughts.

Sebastian knew now exactly what Alistair would put before him: roast beef, no pudding, biscuits and cheese, black coffee, all excellent. The two approved of each other, the father with reservations, the son at the same time wanting to impress the old man, wring from him some expression, however grudging, of admiration. Rivalry between them existed, although in the eyes of the world the younger man, with his newspaper columns, his important appearances on the television, must seem the outright winner. Alistair, a retired director of education, had been successful but never, like his son, a celebrity, and he could not help reflecting that in his Scottish puritan view his son took his pay in fool's gold.

Added to this, thoughts about Eleanor Franks ruffled his calm. He had returned last night in the turbulence of the gale, taken a small glass of neat Scotch, and slept until six, when the milkman woke him. On the drive to her flat Eleanor had been almost cheerful as if despondency had dissipated itself in the talk at his fireside, and on that he mildly congratulated himself. What he could not make out was whether he wanted further commerce with the woman; she was attractive, well-to-do, but she'd done without him for thirty-five years, and that rankled. Her conversation had not impressed, or rather had not approached subjects he was interested in, but he could hardly have expected that, if it were true that she had run out into the street in distress, and had found her way by chance or whim to his door. A likely tale.

Alistair cleared plate, coffee cup and percolator, but before he set out for the butcher's shop sat down at the piano to play Haydn. He chose a C major sonata, rippled through the Allegro, but suddenly in the second half of the Adagio found himself moved, so that he held his breath while his eyes

18

pricked with tears. Here Haydn touched romanticism, cried for the unattainable, but shortly, with a neat brevity that seemed to deny the power of the feeling encaged in a few bars. Sebastian's advent, Madam Franks's appearance had left Alistair vulnerable, with the result that Haydn's modulations spoke through their clouding of eighteenth-century reasonable reticence straight into his throat. He closed the piano lid, not bothering to attempt the opening of the finale which itself would moderately veer into and out of the minor.

Shopping and preparation of the meal occupied him thoroughly. His wife had never been interested in cooking, and had allowed him to take over on Sundays once the children had left home. She knew her mind, and often his, and her death had removed a buttress from his life, which did not on that account then collapse. Wryly he smiled when he remembered Janet and her transformation in thirty-odd years from the pretty Scots lassie to the woman of granite. She had fostered his ambition, had not rested until they had appointed him director in the county where he had lived as a boy, where he had taken his first teaching job, where his father had ministered. Janet had no real interest in the technique of his work, or its difficulties; she entrusted that to him. With her, status was all. She remembered her parents' dairy in Glasgow where one needed to be polite even to people who owed you money, and she was determined never to return to that life. She could be pleasant to underlings, could simper, but it was no more than veneer. She kept sternly out of the way of those who felt they could patronize her husband and his place. Alistair had won his position by hard work, brains, application, proven achievement; the lords lieutenant or, worse, councillors put into power by ignorant voters could not expect her approval. She had died four years ago, just missing what she would have cherished most, Sebastian's apotheosis as a public figure.

At 12.25 the door bell pealed.

What impressed on the television screen about Sebastian Murray was the earnest sharpness of his face. Here one felt was a man concentrating, without thought of his own advancement, on eliciting the truth and having that truth expressed

19

in language without obscurity. No evasions allowed. And this disinterested search was pictured in his features, under the shortish neat hair, with the small frown, spectacled eyes which did not waver, the strong nose pointing, the mouth, now sensual and relaxed, now line-thin and not to be trifled with, the chin aggressive. When one met the man, it was his size which overwhelmed. Alistair stood six feet, but Sebastian six-five, and broad-shouldered with it. One felt he could lean down on other mortals, pick them up single-handed, rattle them like peas in a tin.

Sebastian shook his father's hand.

The two men inquired after each other's health, settled to the sherry neither wanted, while Sebastian explained that he was on his way to Leeds to record a programme with two northern vice-chancellors on the effect of the recession on universities. He looked forward to this, because he knew and admired both men and for that reason would not let them easily off the hook.

'Why not do the programme in London?' Alistair asked.

'Our camera team will film there. Illustrative material.'

'Chosen by you or them?'

Sebastian smiled, stretching out huge legs.

'Who can say? It makes them more careful, that's all.'

'And that's good, is it? Won't they be non-controversial in that case?'

'Knowing them, no. If they give a poor account of themselves, from the point of view of our programme, they'd be edited out. They're competing for their minute or two of publicity against Oxbridge and the bright south. It's tricky for them, I admit. If they convince us that government economies had made such inroads into their institutions that the places aren't worth applying for, they're cooking their own goose and putting off prospective students. Interesting. But you know all about it. As director here you must have been in the same dilemma times enough.'

'I took good care not to parade it in public. Or not from choice.'

They talked thus for twenty minutes, the father enjoying himself. He was much at ease with his son, even if he felt the young man's language was too relaxed for one who had taken a brilliant first in law, followed by prizes in the bar examinations, and who wrote a regular column for *The Times*.

At 1.05 they heard the opening of Radio 4's 'World at One', and drew up to the table. Sebastian congratulated his father on the meal. The pair drank water, because on seeing the unopened bottle of claret Sebastian had poked out a finger and said, 'We won't have that, if you don't mind, Dad.'

'Are you giving it up?'

'Pretty well. I was getting too fond of it.'

'That sounds bad?'

'And it was.'

Sebastian ate heartily, three times the amount his father took.

'If only I could come across cooking like this every day.'

Alistair coughed sarcastically.

'If food's to be plain, it must be good in the first place. Then there's no need to disguise it,' he said.

'Is this what Francesca thinks?'

'We eat out a good deal.'

Alistair rummaged for trouble in the dull sentence.

It appeared at five minutes past two, just as Sebastian hoisted himself from his armchair to leave. They had chatted through the meal, through the coffee, through the walk round the garden. Now Sebastian tried a quiet, throwaway sentence.

'I'd like to ask a favour of you.' He buttoned his coat.

'What's that?'

'Tricky, now.'

'What you'd call interesting?'

Son shook a warning finger at father.

'I'm going to the States and Canada in a fortnight.' He paused as if the information were too difficult to assimilate. 'While I'm there, I wonder if Francesca can come up here to stay at least some of the time with you. I shall be away the best part of a month.'

'With pleasure. If she'd want to.'

'I think she would.'

Alistair neither spoke nor moved.

'I take it she doesn't want to go to America with you?'

21

'No.'

Sebastian seemed to be concerned elsewhere, cut off from his request, bothering himself about his route or where he'd put the ignition key.

'She suggested it herself,' he offered.

'You surprise me. The autumn season is just beginning. I wouldn't have thought she'd want to leave London.'

'You said something that interested her. You were talking about getting old.' Murray had spent two nights and a day in Fenton Square with them on his way to France in the early summer. 'You were saying how your hip joints ached, and how glad you were when bedtime came round. And then you told her that one day you walked along the street, oh, shopping or something of the sort, and you suddenly felt intensely alive, for no reason you could think of. It was, you said, as if a wind blew through you. And you connected it, or compared it with Sibelius's music, odd and spare, unexpectedly rich. Well, she was impressed. Has mentioned it three or four times. I think she'd like to come up to try a glass of Sibelius's spring water.'

'We had *Tapiola*'s gales last night.'

'So did we. Blew a tree over just in front of the house. What do you say? What am I to tell her?'

'I'll be delighted.' Alistair stopped. 'Is everything all right at home? Between you?'

'Isn't that typical?' The son laughed genuinely. 'I tell you. You made a considerable mark on Francesca, and I think she'd like to come up here and ask a question or two. Or she's convinced herself that up here things happen that aren't granted to us mortals in the polluted capital.'

'Not true.'

'She knows that as well as you do. But she asked me to put it to you. And I have. She'll give you a ring, I expect.'

'If she doesn't change her mind.'

'Possible. Always possible.' The big hand gripped, swallowed his father's. 'Thanks for the lunch, Dad. You've lost none of your cunning there.'

'Will Francesca think so, though?'

The large face smoothed itself, the eyes twinkled and Sebastian was out on the pavement. 'Right. Off to preside over the ruin of higher learning, while you rebuild your pergola.'

He waved. Silently, rapidly the Mercedes left the avenue.

Alistair Murray closed his front gate, picked up a snapped twig or two from the garden path, went inside to change into gardening clothes.

When he heard nothing from Eleanor Franks in his next three busy days, he telephoned her, making Francesca's visit the pretext to ask advice. Eleanor sounded glad to listen to his account of the re-erection of the pergola, the clearing up of flattened plants, broken branches, leaves, madly piled rubbish. That was the sort of job she had always disliked at Craigmore.

'Didn't you have a gardener?'

'Oh, yes. But I felt responsibility. I was at home all day, and thought I ought to put some time in out there. I don't think Mr Simpson was pleased, but he humoured me. One of his "boys" cuts the lawns round the flats here. He always speaks to me affably enough.'

Eleanor asked about his daughter-in-law.

'To tell you the truth, I doubt whether she'll come.'

'You mean Sebastian was . . .?'

'Making conversation. Or trying to apologize, at second hand, for spending so much time away from home.'

'Aren't they interested in children?'

'The subject never comes up in my presence.'

'Do you like her, Alistair?'

'Very much. She's clever and beautiful and efficient.'

'Uh, um. What does she do all day?'

'She works a three- or four-day week. She's a solicitor. I think one day, sometimes one and a half, of that's in some charitable cause. Battered wives, is it? I ought to know, but I don't. She doesn't make a big thing of it with me. But I forget so easily. One of these mornings I'll wake up and find I don't know my own name any longer.'

'That's not the impression you give.'

He coughed gruff disagreement, and she invited him round to her house. They consulted diaries; he refused to put her to the trouble of cooking.

'No. I will come after dinner. About eight. To talk to you.'

'That's nice.' She ribbed him, sounding girlish.

'I'm trying to slim, so, please, I don't want any delicious homemade biscuits, or any alcohol. I will take a cup of black coffee if you can rise to that.'

'Goodness, what a puritan.'

His visit fell on the day Francesca rang to arrange her trip. She spoke very diffidently, as though she asked the impossible.

'It will probably be only three days. Friday to Sunday.'

'That's not long.'

'But I have to work.'

'Are you busy, then?' He asked about her charitable activities. She described the three women's hostels for which she acted legally. Yes, they were full. Yes, they could do with twice as many, but neither local nor central government would move in these days of recession and retrenchment. Yes, she gave advice, drew up agreements, attended court. 'I sometimes think I'm living in some barbarous stone-age community. You would not believe how cruelly people behave.'

'Uneducated people? On the whole?'

'By no means. No. Cultured, well-to-do men, pillars of society, at home act like psychopaths. There's no other way to describe them.'

Francesca's voice sounded clear, untroubled, as if she were reading out a list of Christmas presents.

'Why is that?' he asked.

'Human depravity?'

She sighed.

He raised the matter that evening with Eleanor, who looked doubtful, frightened even, passing the question back to him.

'Well,' Alistair stroked his chin, 'her view is likely to be coloured because she sees so many bad cases. The point is, I should guess, that they're only a very small percentage of the total population.'

'These are just the ones that get reported because the wife's had the courage to run out. What about the times where nothing's said? And if these are the serious cases, what about further down the line, intermittent cruelty, occasional beatings?'

'I know.'

'And we are a civilized society,' she persisted. 'You read in the newspapers of soldiers wiping out whole villages, men, women and children, or street after street in Lebanon blasted down by bombardments, or people in South America arrested for their political views and never seen again. And then there are natural disasters: refugees starving under a bit of blanket and an oildrum. That's nobody's fault, and yet . . .'

'Yes.'

'Look, Alistair. I know what you're thinking, that I shouldn't be talking about such things. But that's why I'm glad you're here, so that instead of mulling it over in my mind I can put it into words to somebody and get some sort of answer. So don't just sit there with your "yes" and "I know" and your "well". You're here to talk back to me.'

She spoke almost smilingly, without much emphasis, calm and unfidgety in her manner.

'Oh dear, oh dear,' he said. 'I am in trouble.'

'What about these people then? Would you behave well to your wife and family if you knew you were likely to be murdered at any time or if you were starving to death?'

'I don't believe that I should act very well, no. I'm too selfish.'

'Are you above the average? Morally?'

'I guess not. It's hard to tell. But I'm the ambitious type who got on, in my small way, and I imagine that suggests I'm perhaps more ruthless than the next man.'

'Or more intelligent?'

'Oh, that comes into it, I'm sure, but what I'm saying is I'd use such brains I had to advance myself. That's what I think. Whether that would be the case in these extreme situations you're supposing I don't know. I can well imagine that physical deprivation or weakness or torture would not only knock morality out of my system, but intelligence as well. I'd hardly be a human being.'

'We are civilized, then?' she asked. 'In this country?'

'Oh, yes. In thousands of respects. That doesn't mean we all behave well all the time, but . . .'

'You're very bland, Alistair.'

'Years of sitting on the fence.'

He looked at her, and she seemed at ease, her posture matching the voice. Her questions worried him, not by their content, but because they indicated her own uncertainties. People who stand up in public, for justice or principle, he'd learnt, often do so because of personal deficiency. She saw in the enormous cruelties of the world a reflection of her own despair.

'That's not the way,' she answered, 'that people talked about you. They said you went to great lengths to educate your political masters, and you didn't mind making yourself unpopular.'

'When masters are political, you will always find yourself at loggerheads with one side or the other.'

'They said you were full of ideas.'

'They?'

'People we met. Conservative politicians mostly. They didn't always approve. I often daren't let on that I knew you.' She giggled, shook her head. 'Henry had no interest in politics. Or education. Or even in law. He hardly ever worked in his office. He kept a financial interest, but that's all. He was concerned with his property and his investments.'

'Didn't property become very tricky?'

Eleanor looked sharply at him, drawing herself up. It was some time, an awkward break when he did not know what to fear, before she answered.

'There weren't the easy pickings there once were. That's true. But Henry was shrewd. If he could make a ha'penny he'd do so. It interested him. But not so much as when he was younger. He'd less energy, I suppose. He stood down from three of the boards where he was a director, and did little or nothing at all with Warrington, Franks and Barber.'

'Was he glad to retire?'

'He thought he might be. But he wasn't. We went on a cruise to the West Indies, but that didn't suit him. He'd left himself some "playthings", that's what he called them, but

26

they didn't take up enough of his time. He'd got out of the habit of doing anything but work.'

'Didn't you entertain?'

'Oh, yes. Before he retired, he'd have to go away for days at a time. London or Brussels or to sites. But otherwise every night of the week he'd be home for dinner between six and seven. And we kept up hospitality with the same people. Until he was ill. That came quickly, and he suddenly shrivelled. When I asked him how he was all he could say was "Rotten". And he wasn't the complaining sort. He was glad to die in the end. He used to lie in that big front bedroom at Craigmore, a marvellous room it was, huge, and caught the sunlight all day, and look at me as if he couldn't understand what had happened to him. He'd barely had a day's illness in his life. And there he was, on his back, flat out, in pain, in nausea, not an ounce of strength. The doctors were very good, and we had a nurse in day and night, and at first he'd say, "Ellie, do you think I'm getting better?" '

'Did he know what was wrong with him?'

'I don't know. It seems unlikely, but I don't think he did. He'd seen people die of cancer; his own parents, at least one of his close associates. But for an intelligent, sharp man, he was very, well, simple. About this. Able to deceive himself. At least, I think so. I'm pleased, really. By the end, he'd been ill then nearly a year, he was helpless and in such pain he was glad to die. It was better that way. I didn't want to see him reduced any further.'

'No.'

'He was brave. He really was. But he was beginning to break up. I wouldn't want to keep him like that. And though we had professional help, I seemed tied to that bedroom. I came to hate the house.'

'You've sold it now?'

'No, I haven't. It's let to a television executive. He needs a big place for entertainment, but he won't want to stay for ever.'

Eleanor shook her head. She had talked ridiculously fast as though at a part she'd had rehearsed past forgetting, but which she could not bother to act out.

They drank their coffee, and she talked, hardly asking a question about his family. She spoke well enough, even shaping the short sentences or paragraphs of her conversation, but underlying all was the assumption that her concerns were of as much interest to him as to her. Information and comment gushed, so that while she seemed untiring he sat overwhelmed. She made several attempts to detain him when he said he must go, but he walked out to the hall, lifted his coat down, made straight for the front door.

'It was lovely to see you. Will you bring Francesca round?' At least she'd learnt the name. 'It was good to have somebody intelligent to talk to.' She laid her hands on his arm. 'I've often thought about you. In this gap. It must be thirty-five or -six years since we had any connection, really. All that time. It flashes past, doesn't it? And yet I owe you a good deal. Perhaps I'll be able to tell you.' She reached to kiss him. He touched her cheek formally, but she pressed her lips on his.

'Have you brought your car?' she asked as he broke away.

'No. The walk'll do me no harm.'

'Is it safe?'

'I should think so.'

'Ring me as soon as you get back, will you?'

He promised; with pain on her face she reached up to kiss him again.

3

Francesca drove herself up from London, arriving nearly an hour after her announced time of arrival. Alistair found himself on edge, even angry, though the casserole he had put into the oven would not spoil.

'I'm late,' she said. 'Are you cross? Seb told me that you're furious if people don't turn up when they say they will.'

'He always does.'

'Only for you.'

'Have people lost the art of keeping time, then?'

'Of worrying about it.'

He parked her with a glass of sherry, and retreated to the cooker suspecting that the visit had started badly. As he passed by the sitting room, to lay the table, he saw that she was much at ease on the settee, stretched out, legs crossed, elegant boots shining; she was immersed in one of his books. He wondered which it was. She raised a small left hand to him without looking up. Alistair did not feel comfortable, began to wish he had cooked a more suitably complicated or esoteric meal. Slightly fazed, even annoyed with himself, he clashed about in the kitchen, deliberately noisy.

Francesca ate slowly, complimenting him on his cooking.

'It's all very straightforward,' he said.

'You're quite a byword in our house. For quality. Whenever we've flounced out for some fancy banquet, Seb compares it unfavourably with your dishes.'

She refused a second helping, but enjoyed at her leisure his blackberry and applie pie, thick with cream.

'I see I'm due to put on weight,' she smiled, 'but this is delicious.'

'Have some more.'

'Oh, no, thank you.'

This young woman knew her mind. He began to feel easier.

After coffee, and washing-up, which she allowed him to do on his own, she turned to, almost on, him to say, 'You have high tea, don't you? I think I shall like that. At what time? Now this afternoon I want to go and look at Beechnall. On my own. You shall tell me what I ought to see, but I'm not promising you I shall do as I'm told.'

'That's wasting my time, then.'

'No it isn't. You know it isn't. It makes you think about the town, and about me.'

'I'll go with you.'

'Not today. I'll just get myself lost. I like that.'

He gave her instructions, bus numbers, made sure she had change for the correct fares, and let her go. As the door closed behind her he felt exhilarated, as if he'd achieved something, made himself somebody. Tending the garden lawns exhausted the remainder of the afternoon.

She returned at five exactly as the kettle whistled.

'Have you enjoyed yourself?' he demanded, pleased with her.

'Very much.'

Francesca disappeared upstairs, and again he was kept waiting. When she returned, she seemed not to have changed her clothes, nor altered her make-up or hairstyle. Faintly perfumed, she sat with him to watch the early evening news on television. Only when the weather forecast had finished was she led to the table.

She ate two thin slices of brown bread, thinly spread with honey, and one minute bun. As at lunch she worked slowly through her food, meditatively, as if the mastication of a small mouthful was a full occupation, or gave rise to thoughts which needed constant, insistent care. The movements around the closed lips were delicate, the eyes directed elsewhere.

'What would you like to do?' he wanted to know.

'Sit about.'

'Are you sure?'

Francesca explained how she drove from court to court, or called in on one of the hostels on most days. No, it was not exciting; the majority of her work was not only abominably dull but included a fair amount of hanging about corridors or the back premises of draughty buildings waiting for a case to come up. She represented petty criminals who were stupid, motorists who had the money to defend the indefensible, and ex-partners in marriage who out of lacerated feelings wrangled over settlements. Only rarely did she feel that real justice or injustice was involved.

'The best you can say is that an intelligent observer might conclude that stronger parties, police, ex-spouses, local government officials were precluded by these proceedings from doing as they liked.'

'And in some cases it would be better if they were allowed to do as they wanted.'

'Sometimes, yes.'

She said a sentence or two about her work for the hostels, which he knew she did unpaid.

'Is that more satisfying?'

'Yes. Except I know court cases won't set that world right, not even heal local wounds. And even if they did, there are hundreds as bad that never get near the courts. I'm fine while I'm working, but when I think of the totality of my efforts, it's very little, and I feel low and useless.'

'Would you feel the same if you spent all your time on this work?'

'I'm sure I should.'

She had answered briskly, brusquely, dismissing any attempts at sympathy he might muster.

Alistair inquired after Sebastian, found that she talked with enthusiasm.

'Does he get depressed about his work?'

'Not as yet. He's too busy, for one thing. He's a tremendous Stakhanovite, and takes himself very seriously.'

'And you don't?'

'I didn't say that.' She smiled, in relaxation. 'His column in *The Times* is as good as anything you'll read. And so are his articles for America, which you won't see. But his television appearances take a tremendous lot out of him, and he's not quite sure whether what he's doing is, well, right. The audiences are so large, even for political programmes, compared with those of the quality press, and there is an element of

31

entertainment about it that he doesn't approve of. People want confrontation, not argument from fact or premise. Sensationalism is an important ingredient.'

'You could hardly accuse him of that.'

'He thinks so. It's there. When someone answers your question, there's always a camera trained on you, so that you can frown, or toss your head, or assume an expression of incredulity. "I have to act," he says. "And the temptation to ham it up is constant." '

'Do you think he does?'

'No. He's remarkably restrained, especially if you knew how he pulls faces or waves his arms about at home. He'd be good on stage.'

'He played leading roles in school plays.'

'I bet he did. His mother wasn't too keen, was she? Or so he says.'

'Janet was proud of him,' Alistair answered. 'She admired achievement. What she didn't want was for him to waste hours on ephemeral mummery at the expense of his schoolwork.'

'That's unlikely, knowing him. Seb knows which side his bread's buttered.'

It was a real pleasure for Alistair Murray to be introduced by her into television studios or newspaper offices. She didn't speak with zest; her speech matched her eating habits, slowish, attractive, efficient, neat; he could imagine that she had learnt the unemphatic style in courtrooms or in her office when she had to ensure that her client was somewhere near the truth. Sebastian's voice was more rotund, with a wider range of harmonics; she was flute-like, limpid, girlish, steady.

He asked her what she wanted to do while she was staying with him.

'Nothing,' she answered. 'That's the beauty. I want to sit about. Oh, I'll let you suggest things, or offer to waltz me round if that eases your conscience. But just now I want to tell myself that tomorrow's a blank day.'

'I wouldn't mind being seen about the town with a good-looking young woman.'

'Bolster your ego? Do you ever go back to your office or see your subordinates?'

'No.'

'Is that deliberate?'

'It is. I'd be in the way. Moreover, I'm pretty certain that they're convinced they've made all sorts of improvements since I left, and that would be a source of embarrassment.'

'And have they?'

'They could hardly fail to.'

He described Eleanor Franks's visit and said she had invited him to take Francesca round.

'What do you think?' She stressed the personal pronoun.

'Up to you. It'll be boring, I expect.'

'To see your old flame?' Her eyebrows rose whimsically. 'Let's leave it, shall we? I don't know how long I'm staying for, so it's no good arranging things days ahead. I'd like to kick my heels.'

'What was all that about Sibelius, then, and my new lease of life?' he asked.

'Sebby told you, did he?'

'He did.'

'Yes. I was quite taken by what you said. I'll admit that. But it's not for a shaking-up I've come here. The very opposite. I'm busy every day. And I'm starting to take work home for Saturdays and Sundays. Well, Sebastian's often away, and I thought I might improve the shining hour. But it won't do, really. Or so my husband tells me.'

'But he can't find time to take you out.'

'That's not true.'

'You're getting on all right? Together?'

'Seb said you asked him that.' She laughed, to set him at his ease. 'I think we are. We're both pursuing our careers as hard as we can, and this is interesting and tiring. You think there ought to be a child or two about in the picture. I'm not so sure. I know you're going to tell me that clever, privileged people ought to have families, but I'm not convinced in myself. I think now one can say that. In your day a woman would have been judged, have judged herself even, as odd, not quite human.'

33

'You might change your mind?'

'Yes. Or make a mistake.' She tidied her position in the chair. 'And then it would be a case of a nanny and au pairs, and you wouldn't approve, would you now?'

'I'm a pragmatist. I'd look at the products.'

Soon after ten Francesca went to bed with an anthology of modern poetry. When Alistair woke in the early hours, he saw that his daughter-in-law had the light on in the room, but next morning she said she had slept well. She insisted on doing his shopping, saying that Sebastian had told her that his father would not use a deep freeze, but preferred trudging round the cold streets every morning.

'So I shall relieve you,' she laughed.

'And deprive me of my morning's occupation.'

'You could do with a change.'

'Does Sebastian say that as well?'

'I'm not his parrot.'

Over coffee they perused, he offered her that old-fashioned word, the evening paper of the previous day to see what the theatre or cinemas offered. Francesca had seen all the films on offer; the National Theatre production at the Royal she had enjoyed months back when Ralph Richardson had appeared in it in London.

'And here was I, thinking you were worked to death, never out enjoying yourself.'

'Once or twice a week, and partly by way of Seb's business. You'd be amazed how much you can get through.'

Immediately he began to detail for her the cinemas of his youth. His suburb alone had four, each with a change of programme in mid-week. He described the odd-job man with his paste pot slopping round to recharge the posters for the Thurs-Fri-Sat performance.

'A big picture, a supporting film, the newsreel and forthcoming attractions,' he boasted.

'A cinema organist?'

'No. Only in one big plush place in the city.'

'Ice cream?'

'In tubs. And Sloan's Liniment on sale for necks in the front row.'

'And were the films good?'

'Almost invariably rubbish.'

They laughed together, as he gibed at talk of falling standards, and made up their minds to try an amateur production of *Twelfth Night*.

'Shakespeare's perfect play,' he said. 'We shall be disappointed.'

Her face twisted as if in physical pain.

'You don't mean it.'

The next morning she went out again on her own.

' "I'll go see the relics of this town." '

'Sebastian,' he said.

'Yes. I once understudied the part at school. We girls did the lot.'

'And you didn't know that was the name of your future husband.'

She put out a hand to touch his arm. Outside the sun was bright, the wind spreading a thin wash of cloud over blue sky. On her return she found him at the piano. She poked her head round the door.

'Bach,' she said. 'May I come in?'

'If you can put up with the wrong notes.'

Francesca sat by the table, knees together to listen.

'What's that?' she asked, as he ended.

'The E Major, Book Two.'

She refused his offer of a drink, and asked him to play it over again. She thanked him, said, 'I must have heard it before, but I don't know it. Would you do it again?'

'I could do with the practice.'

In all she had him play it over five times, and then they talked about stretto and countersubject, in an innocent way, as if they were adolescent students and excited by the trappings of knowledge. They were both delighted that she had never heard of either Ebenezer Prout or his mnemonics.

> ' "John Sebastian Bach
> Sat upon a tach
> But he soon got up again
> With a howl," ' he sang. 'C Minor, Book One.'

35

'Play it for me, please.'

He took the first book from his stool, and tripped through the Fugue. They joined together to sing the final entry into the Picardy third, and sat pleased as punch.

'You'll never get any lunch at this rate,' he said, but refused her offer of help. She asked for ink because she wished to write up her diary for yesterday. He unscrewed the lid to peer into the bottle.

'Plenty left.' She filled her fountain pen. 'I'm surprised you use an old-fashioned implement like that.'

'Oh, no. It suits my style of bad handwriting.'

'Do you know,' Alistair said, 'that every time I buy a bottle of Quink I can't help wondering if it's the last I shall ever buy. It's the same with clothes. If I get a new suit or shirt I think it'll do me to the grave.'

She rebuked him jovially, telling him he'd live to be ninety-five, but he noticed she shuddered. For a few minutes she sat writing in an armchair before she sidled into the kitchen.

'Yesterday hasn't taken much time,' he said.

'I've not quite finished, but I just wondered if you'd been in touch with your old flame this morning.'

'I tried twice while you were out, but there was nobody at home.'

'I was just consumed with curiosity.'

'Why was that?'

'I don't know. I was putting down the bits and pieces of yesterday's doings when I just had to know whether you'd spoken to the lady. It doesn't seem important now, but it did then, five minutes ago. Perhaps because you'd spoken about dying.'

'I don't see the connection,' he grumbled, moving about with his saucepans.

'No more do I. But it seemed absolutely vital and I leapt up to find out. I don't understand myself.'

Over lunch she told him she had spent an hour at the Shire Hall.

'Busman's holiday,' he said, serving potatoes. 'What was it?'

'Preliminary stages of a murder trial.'

36

'Interesting?'

'It can't be other, can it? Some young man, eighteen, had murdered a woman old enough to be his mother. They'd had sex. He looked a pathetic figure.'

'Was he backward?'

'No. He was an A-level candidate in one of your ex-schools. But physically he was a poor specimen, with a bad cold. He looked incapable of anything more violent than a coughing bout. I found myself looking round the gallery for his parents.'

'And did you pick them out?'

'At least two lots. I don't know.'

'And were the barristers any worse than the London variety?'

'Not that I noticed.'

She remained silent for a time, and asked him after the meal to walk her round the local streets. They donned scarves, for the cold brightness of the sun.

'Just before we go, ring your Eleanor, will you?'

'Why?'

'To tell her I'm here.'

Alistair, surprised and displeased at this interference, which seemed both out of character and mischievous, obeyed. He was not sorry when his call went unanswered.

'Nothing doing,' he told her.

'Is she usually out at this time of day?'

'I haven't the very slightest idea.'

She caught the asperity in his voice, and immediately walked over to him.

'Oh, dear. I've annoyed you.' Francesca looked him straight in the eye; he did not deny her statement. 'I'm sorry. I thought perhaps you wanted to get in touch but didn't think you should while I was about.' His frown blackened, but though she meditatively licked her lips she did not quail. 'I've never seen you look like that before, Alistair.' The use of his Christian name jolted him. Sebastian never used it, nor had anyone at work. These days tiny children called their grand-parents by first names, and it had an attraction, if at a distance, to him who had been brought up to show friendship

37

to colleagues by referring to them with a bare surname. 'I'm not doing very well, am I?' No fear cracked in her pleasant tone.

'Let's forget it.'

They went out, through the garden, into the street in a rush, with no leisure for commentary on plants or plans. After five minutes his expression had softened.

'I'm sorry I annoyed you,' she said.

Again a stab of impatience thrust into him. The damned woman seemed to have no sense of when to leave ill alone. She was talking again. He barely listened.

'Old people should not be interested in sex,' he said, in the end, bailing her out. 'The eleventh commandment.'

Now she laughed, took his arm, smartened her step.

'Steady on,' he ordered, 'no jogging allowed.'

'Nor yomping.'

They felt friendly, and he was pleased with himself, but she saw what she had not known before, that he must have been formidable as a director of education, or, for that matter, as a father.

Now he talked pleasantly of the district which had been first developed in the eighties and nineties of the last century. Huge houses had been built on the hills, some streets laid privately, and the whole developed for businessmen, lace manufacturers, surgeons, lawyers, administrators, monied ladies over the last ninety years. Roses grew tall in the heavy red clay, dahlias, Michaelmas daisies, chrysanthemums; the limes, sycamores and horsechestnuts in the streets were old, thick-trunked, forest trees.

He described some of the inhabitants: a knight, retired from selling wine, who lived in his mansion about two months a year; a company director who tried to balloon across the Atlantic and to live for a week buried deep in the sand at Skegness; a bachelor professor of engineering who occupied a palace with sixteen bedrooms. On the corner of the drive of a hidden building a chaste notice proclaimed that the place was for sale. The old lady who had died there a year ago had left nearly two million pounds, almost all to charity.

'How had she made it?' Francesca asked.

'Her father and grandfather. They were manufacturers who had presumably invested wisely so that the daughter lost nothing in the recession. She never married.'

'Did you ever see her?'

'Occasionally. She'd drive out. Not recently; she was ninety-odd when she died.'

'Was she very unattractive?'

'No. Not at all. She seemed an old lady all the time we've lived here. That's twenty-five years. We came when Sebastian was seven or eight.'

'Why didn't she marry, then?'

'I don't know. Perhaps she thought nobody good enough presented himself. Or perhaps her parents thought so. The Marshalls were big noises hereabouts. I'm only guessing.'

'Did you know her father?'

'Only by name. When I came back here as director, that's when we bought this place, he was dead. My father had some dealings with him, over some charitable or church matters, and gave a favourable report.'

They stopped at the top of a hill, the ascent had been steep, to allow Alistair to get his breath back, and began to go down the other gateway, pointing out that the metal was worked into patterns more usual in lace, the business of the first owner.

'It's good,' she said.

'Yes, it is. And it's a kind of symbol of the nonconformity you'd find hereabouts. Lace and iron don't seem very similar, and yet, there they are, on the old chap's say-so, in a very satisfactory design.'

'Perhaps it was the blacksmith who suggested it? Or an architect, knowing how he made his money.'

'Possibly.'

'What was his name?'

'Crane. You'll still see the signs up in the Lace Market. Thomas Crane and Son. He was a Scot, I think.'

'Do the family live here, then?'

'No. The son retired to Bournemouth or Brighton. Fifty years ago. Forty. I've no idea whether there are any descendants.'

'They've just disappeared from your scene?'

'To the best of my knowledge. But that's not saying much. Daughters marry and change their names.'

They looked along the drive to the house, nearly a hundred yards back from the road. A wide flight of baronial steps led upwards to a balustraded terrace, on which they could see two pieces of statuary, naked gods and goddesses. Enormous windows stood behind the patio and one could make out two turrets, the first green copper-topped, the second almost hidden among trees.

'It must be large,' Francesca ventured.

'Much more so than it looks from here.'

It seemed an ideal film set, for ladies with cloche hats and long cigarette holders, large eyed and flat-chested, kempt and beautiful, as gentleman friends in grey trilby hats raced up and down the steps, shouting at each other or flourishing walking sticks in an elaborate dance routine. This afternoon in October sunshine one could easily imagine that palm trees flourished in the gardens.

'The rates must be high,' she said.

'Colossal. It's inside the city.'

'And wouldn't one need servants to run it? Aren't the kitchens likely to be in the basement down a great flight of stairs?'

'Not so. It's modernized. It will be very up-to-date.'

'Who lives there now?'

'Some television executive. I imagine there are offices and perhaps studios, even. It's owned by Eleanor Franks. She lived there while her husband was alive. Craigmore.' Alistair pointed to a small wooden nameboard, black with gold letters, fastened above the postal box on the gates.

'But she hasn't sold it?'

'No.'

'Why was that?'

He shook his head.

'A source of income?' she suggested. 'And appreciating in value all the time?'

'I wonder if it is. Or if she'd need it.'

Francesca looked her fill, advancing a few yards along the drive, and returning made some remark about extravagance.

'I don't know,' he said. 'If you sold your London house, you'd be able to buy this. And with your incomes you'd easily afford the upkeep and the rates.'

'But all the empty rooms? What should we do with them? Why should we want them?'

'Ostentation.'

'So that's what you think of us, is it?' Francesca asked, laughing at him.

'You have to spend your money somehow.' He looked at her wry face. 'You could fill it with your battered wives.'

'There'd be better buys for that.' She offered no explanation, but as they continued under the high stone walls, the multitude of trees, she murmured that she could see the place hung with fairy lights.

'The horse carriages would manage this hill,' he said, 'but they'd be in terrible trouble on the other side.'

'Would there be no cars when it was built?'

'1890s? The odd one, I suppose. But Crane would be old-fashioned.'

'His son?'

'You're right perhaps. I don't know.'

'Did they not attend your father's church? They were Scots, weren't they? Presbyterians?'

'Not much. High days and holidays. I think I can just remember the old man turning up for some service and all the fuss there was meeting him and escorting him to his seat. He was good for a generous subscription.'

She deliberately asked no questions, he decided, about Eleanor Franks and her family, and though he was relieved he felt she had given up too easily. He had always liked a pinch of opposition, not prolonged but needing effort to quell.

That night they attended, in Francesca's car, a poorish performance of *Twelfth Night* which sent them home silent. They sat moodily over a cup of coffee, he rehearsing in his mind the speeches of Orsino, a part he'd never played, poetically strong but feeble humanly, an alter ego. She seemed caught up elsewhere.

41

'I think perhaps I shall go back tomorrow,' she said, offhandedly enough as she turned to go to bed. He thought she had made her mind up that minute.

'That's not been a very long stay.'

'No. But it's done the trick. I want to get back to work.'

He nodded, refusing to argue or voice his disappointment. In some way he had let her down, had learnt nothing about her, and had revealed the rough side of his nature. The failure did not please him, but he kept his mouth shut.

4

In the night after Francesca's departure a murder was committed not twenty yards from Alistair Murray's front gate.

He had heard nothing, as he told the policemen who appeared early at his door next morning. He had gone to bed at a quarter to eleven, not as late as usual, had read for half an hour and slept well. Twice during the night, at 1.30 and four, he had been to the lavatory, but had heard no sound. This was not surprising as he slept at the back of the house.

The policemen were forthcoming. Between one and 1.15 a taxi driver had been stabbed to death presumably by his fare. The driver had made a fight of it, but had stood no chance against a man armed with something the size of a butcher's knife. The murderer had run across the road, and for some reason had turned into Murray's gate; there was a sprinkling of blood on the path.

'Why would he do that?' Alistair asked.

'He may have heard someone coming.' The earth behind the front wall under the rowan was slightly scuffed as if he'd stayed there restlessly. The policeman had brought in the morning's milk and the *Guardian*, allowing no one up the path. They then looked, with his permission, round the house, the outbuildings, the garden.

'You don't think he's hiding here, do you?' he asked, unlocking the tool shed.

'No, sir. But we don't want to leave anything to chance.'

The garden seemed full of policemen, and part of the road was sealed off with tapes and red-and-white witch-hat bollards. An inspector appeared about ten o'clock to ask if his men might go over house and grounds again, and sat down on invitation to a cup of coffee.

'Are you hopeful?' Alistair asked, producing chocolate biscuits.

'Hopeful and careful in this job. You have to be. Chap phoned in, wanted a taxi from the city centre to St Jude's. Gave a name, Ward. Could mean anything, or nothing. There's no telling whether he intended the murder from the word go. Taxi driver was a young married fellow, Pakistani, quiet, no enemies, family man, hard-working.'

The inspector had already let it be known that he recognized Alistair. 'I remember your name sir, A. S. McM. Murray, Director of Education, on those labels we used to stick in front of the textbooks at the grammar school. A. S. McM. Murray.'

The man tried, obsequiously but with resolution, to make Alistair recall some shout, rattle, creak out of the ordinary from the middle of the night, but without success.

'At four the street must have been full of policemen, musn't it? And yet not a murmur. The doors were all shut, and the loo's at the back here. Did nobody hear or see anything? Have you no witnesses?'

'Yes, sir. A Mr Whittle over the road saw the two fighting in the street, and phoned the police immediately. We had men on the scene within five minutes, but the driver was dead by then, and the murderer disappeared.'

'He couldn't have been far away.'

'Five minutes is a long time, sir. Presumably he lived somewhere hereabouts, and he'd be home and inside.'

'Wouldn't he be splashed with blood?'

'Very likely.'

'Wouldn't his wife or somebody notice?'

'Possible. That's not to say anything, really. There's one hell of a house-to-house inquiry starting up there by St Jude's, but there are hundreds of houses.'

'It's a decent district, isn't it?'

'Yes. A bit mixed at the bottom end.' The inspector bit with strong teeth across a chocolate biscuit. Not a crumb fell. 'You'd be surprised what curious characters we'd turn up even on a posh avenue like this.' The policeman looked him over humorously, not quelled by his job.

Murray did his morning chores, tried to read but failed. Once again the policeman appeared in his garden, but did not disturb him. He telephoned Eleanor Franks, and found himself unanswered. He wondered if she had gone away. By the afternoon, when he turned out for a walk, the street was clear except for one or two pedestrians who had stopped to stare at the chalklines on the road and the two towers of piled bollards. Nobody called on him; a cordon of polite behaviour kept him clear from friends and acquaintances.

The next morning Francesca's short note of thanks arrived. The visit had done her good; Sebastian was preparing to go abroad; she'd now have to make a big effort to catch up in the office.

Sweeping leaves from his lawn, Alistair saw a young uniformed policeman patrolling the road. The officer stopped at the gate, greeted him, saluting. No sir, they hadn't caught the man yet, or hadn't when he came out but sometimes things blew up quickly, unexpected developments caught you on the hop if you weren't on the qui vive. Alistair looked at the fresh face, rosy with health.

'Keep your eye open for us, sir,' the policeman asked.

'You don't think he'll come back to the scene of the crime, do you?'

'You never know. In our business we can't afford to take chances. And if we know you're on the alert for anything out of the way, well, it's one more factor to the good.'

'I shouldn't think he's likely to come here. He might be recognized. The inspector told me that somebody over the road actually saw him.'

'You never know. Keep a weather eye open for us.'

The policeman stepped on, leaving Alistair satisfied, almost convinced that he was part of the force, protecting law and order. This must be what they meant by 'community relations'; he stood spellbound by his gate, noticing the turning of the leaves.

Inside, on impulse, he replied at length to Francesca, describing the murder in detail, the police searches, the conversations with inspector and constable. He enjoyed the exercise, making out that she had left for dull London just as excitement burst here. He wrote so long at his desk that he was nearly an hour late for his lunch, and by that time felt ashamed of himself. A family grieved; fatherless children would never be the same again; a community was outraged, and here he wrote it out to catch the attention of his daughter-in-law. Nevertheless he posted the letter before he spent the afternoon clearing up in the garden.

Nothing happened in the next few days, during which he received neither letters nor phone calls. Though he ventured into the town centre, spent time at the library and at the office of records he met nobody he knew. The streets were thronged with hundreds of people, all unknown to him, all intent on business or pleasure that was in no way his concern. This seemed to happen to him at intervals: for a period the postman brought nothing, the neighbours never appeared, the telephone was silent, the streets were either deserted or full of strange faces, and even the newspapers, the radio, the tele screen were barren of interest. He had learnt since his wife's death to expect this, to put up with it, singing the opening sentence of a tenor recitative from *Messiah*: 'He was cut off out of the land of the living; for the transgression of my people was he stricken.' Then he'd settle to his piano, or some laid-aside book until the world came back to him with a livelier titbit.

He had decided on a bonfire, burning the heaps of hacked-down plants too woody for his compost. The stalks, twigs, attached leaves had been standing in the dry days and caught easily. He packed on the newest, greenest waste and a column of smoke rose thickly straight into the air. At the same time, he turned one of his compost heaps, not working hard at it, slowly dismantling its brick enclosure row by row and rebuilding round the re-established pile. Now and then he would turn to his fire, lifting it, or padding it round with fuel. His hands were black, his wellingtons clogged, but he enjoyed the steady pace of his labours, the sense of achievement, the necessity for watchfulness.

His neighbour, a Mrs Montgomerie, walked down her garden, which ran at right angles to the end of his plot. A young woman, fair-haired, in her late twenties, with three youngish children, she often asked his advice about horticultural problems. Not that she spent a great deal of her time there; the majority of the work was carried out roughly at the weekend by her husband, a gynaecological consultant, who crashed about the garden with energy. A big, bucolic young man, with a ruddy face, he loved to prune, or uproot, or dig with violence. Alistair thought the man would be completely happy if once a year he could set about his garden with a bulldozer, flatten everything, mature shrubs, ancient apple-trees, the lot, and then single-handedly wrestle with, replant the replacements. Montgomerie would call out cheerful greet-ings but did not stop work, except when he removed his fisherman's hat to wipe his spectacles or forehead with a square of dirty handkerchief, big as a sail. Alistair named him the demolition man.

Katherine Montgomerie advanced.

Alistair peered at her, jabbed his fork into the ground in readiness to make for the fence and exchange a word or two. He had not seen her for some days; the family would not have been away now her eldest son was at school. She would perhaps have some interesting snippet about the murder, or remind him of the cutting of a double philadelphus he had promised her, or ask what Sebastian was about. She would be disappointed that she had missed Francesca.

He waited for her to reach the spot where for some yards she'd have a clear view of him. His bonfire suddenly crackled, heaving up a pillar of grey smoke. She did not turn her head at the expected place, but marched on looking straight ahead.

'Hello, there,' he called.

The salutation went unheeded. She kept her face straight before her, stepping on. He wondered what she was about. From her upright carriage and rapt expression she might have been counting out steps or broadcasting seed in the biblical fashion. More than likely she was about to feed the birds or add some mite to her husband's untidy heap of rubbish. She obviously did not intend to stay out for she wore a light summer frock, a pretty biscuit-coloured affair with flapping, decorated hems. Now she had disappeared behind the thicket of lilacs, high privet and holly that rampaged at the end of her garden round a place of chaos. After a few seconds, time for her to reach the boundary hedge, turn about and walk straight back, she reappeared in the gap.

'Good afternoon,' he shouted.

She paid no attention, though she must have heard.

Katherine Montgomerie was an odd young woman, he had already decided. Alistair, descended from canny Scots, invariably spoke with caution to strangers, but Mrs Montgomerie observed no such restriction. Once, leaning elegantly on the fence, she had said, loudly enough to be heard two streets away, 'Sometimes I could kill my husband.'

'Why's that?' Alistair did not know offhand whether to be shocked or amused.

'He hasn't the remotest notion of how my time is spent. He comes in when he thinks fit, expects to be fed, or me to be ready to go off to the theatre or a restaurant at half an hour's notice. And when I say "What about baby-sitters?" he'll answer, "Ring up Jane, or Molly or Debby. They're always ready to earn a few bob." And if I ask him, "Why can't you give me some notice?" he looks at me as if I've taken leave of my senses. The trouble with doctors is that they get their own way at work too much.'

'But his patients must die sometimes.'

She looked startled, pretty and anxious.

'Not often. In his speciality. He'll have his disappointments, I'd guess.' Her anger reasserted itself. 'I don't suppose he notices.'

'Is he good at it?'

'Yes. He's clever, and quick, and has a nice, confident way with the women he sees. A pity he's used his supply up by the time he comes home.'

'Not the confidence.' He'd chaff her back to good humour.

'I tell him he might know how to deliver children, but he doesn't know what happens to them afterwards.'

'Oh dear.'

'You side with him, don't you? I might have known.'

She had flounced off.

On another occasion she had told him that she was inefficient, couldn't cope with her daily round, didn't know how it would end. She had then turned on him, demanding advice, shrilly.

'Is your life harder than that of other women?' He had finally come out with that.

'I've three children. That's a full-time occupation. Or it is if you look at it as I do.'

'They'll soon be off your hands and at school.'

'Soon? It doesn't feel like it.'

Though Murray was uneasy about her remarks, he had concluded that she was, in fact, much on top of her job, and loosed off these verbal sallies out of a frustration which sprang from surplus energy. There ought, however, to be a more tactful method, he decided, than making neighbouring old men uncomfortable.

Today she continued up the garden; he saw the flash, heard the click of french windows as she went inside. He pulled up his fork, pitched into the compost heap far too violently so that within minutes he had to stop, to lean over catching his breath. Recovering, he wondered, idly because he had no intention from the start of doing so, whether he ought to knock on her door, ask if anything was amiss. She wouldn't receive that too kindly. Half an hour later she was hanging out washing on the top lawn, shouting cheerfully to her cleaning woman, roaring away in her car.

His telephone rang; he pulled off gloves, made for the house, but the caller gave up just as he reached for the instrument. His wellingtons had deposited rectangular cubes of earth along the kitchen. He methodically cleared the mess with dustpan and brush and, deciding not to go back into the garden but to prepare his lunch, began to pull at his boots. The struggle puffed him so that he stood in his stockinged feet, holding on to the washing machine with grubby hands, sixty-five years old and at a loose end.

5

The fugal opening of Beethoven's C Sharp Minor Quartet crept, compelled from the speakers in Alistair Murray's living room, as he sat stirring his coffee, without milk and sugar, to cool it. He could imagine the players, foxy, at the alert, disciplined, not only speaking the distanced order of the master's present mood, but utterly aware of the explosions of high spirits to come, to be flung into the audience's faces. Beethoven, chronically unhealthy, getting on in years, dashed and threatened, caught napping by his love for a nephew most would have abandoned, found himself huge with creative energy, whirling the world round his head like a child with a balloon on a stick.

Old man Beethoven was nowhere near his age, Alistair decided, at least ten years younger. He grinned as he scalded his lips and tongue with the preliminary skirmish, looking about him for a surface he could not disfigure with the hot china. Placing the cup at his feet on the carpet, he reminded himself that in his wife's day he would have done no such unmannerly thing. But he was pleased with himself; he had left the wilderness.

First, he was to have dinner that evening with Eleanor Franks at her flat. The letter inviting him had come from Shropshire where she spent a few autumn days with a sister, whom she disliked. He imagined her sitting in her bedroom, scribbling this sentence of confession before mincing downstairs to continue the polite domestic war both publicly deplored and privately enjoyed.

Secondly, Francesca had phoned him yesterday, past eleven o'clock, just before he went to bed in a delayed answer to his letter about the murder. She was now on her own, like it or not, but not displeased with the state. Sebastian had gone off to America where he'd record an hour-long interview with the

President; he was terrified, she said, because he was convinced they'd hog-tie him, not allow him the questions he wanted, warn him against crafty supplementaries, leave him liable to erasure so that the result would be flat and anodyne. The idea of the visit was to put to the President the questions an intelligent Englishman or Englishwoman would want to ask. Francesca had mercilessly pulled his leg; let's suppose he trapped the President into an admission that he would just as soon blow up 10 Downing Street as the tents at Greenham Common or either or neither, what would be achieved? 'The trouble with Sebastian,' she hectored, 'is that he allows himself to think parliamentary elections and world wars are won and lost on the say-so of clever clogs like himself on television.' Alistair demurred. 'Oh, no,' she answered. 'I know he wouldn't say that in so many words, but what annoys me is that he won't admit that the only one to get anything really valuable out of it is himself. He shows off his face and his reputation in the square public eye, and this raises his price. But he won't have it. He's offering service, he says, in that people are able to evaluate the worth or honesty of leaders by whose decisions their lives are governed. When I ask him what about the large majority of voters who are not watching him, but goggling at some soap opera or comedian or singer, he says that they, in fact, will come on his ideas later, third or fourth hand, without even knowing his name, and so are influenced.'

Alistair, every cheerful minute precious, asked if she saw anything in the argument.

'I don't,' she said. 'And I don't want his head turned. He's clever, and presentable, and writes well, but he's not likely to turn the world upside down. He's not a subversive, and he's not a genius.

'Won't it do the President some good to pit his wits against somebody as quick and clear as your husband?'

'If he takes it seriously, he'll prepare himself. And he'll have plenty of skilled negotiators or propaganda experts who'll tell him what he can let out, and what he can't.'

'But it will be the way Sebastian places his questions, springs them on him, if you like.'

51

'The President will know exactly what questions are to be asked, and how far Seb can go, believe you me.'

The pair talked on animatedly until midnight, when Francesca, hearing the chimes of his grandfather clock over the phone, called a halt. Alistair felt lively, young as the new day, marching out into his garden, reminding himself in the starry darkness that the President was some years older than he. It did him good to realize the high quality of opposition his son grappled with at home.

He was listening now to the fourth movement, 'andante ma non troppo e molto cantabile'; the violins sang, overlapping, above the plucked cello, and he mused on the extraordinary sweetness of Beethoven's spirit. This great soul, this invalid, this volcano could speak peace to his audience, not quiescence but a delicacy, a contemplation of silence through sound. There seemed a simplicity, no, that was wrong, a directness about this Atlas of a man, this colossus of a mind. Alistair remembered the music master at his old school telling him, they'd just listened on shellac records, with steel needles and constant winding, that he wished he believed in life beyond the grave, because then, 'Haydn, that superb musician, would have heard this, and realized that his lessons had not been wasted.' Then, typically of old Hurtwood, had added, 'At least, I think he would. You can never tell.'

Alistair's mood had made him receptive. He wanted both to sit in thrall to Beethoven and march about the house, the world. From outside he heard a long-drawn-out cry, in the baritone register, a level vowel delivered without force but impelling its way inward at a break in the quartet. A man pushing a pram, not unsmartly dressed, though he wore wellingtons under his trouserlegs, a weather-beaten fifty-year-old with his thick hair combed down with Brylcreem from a centre parting, called for 'Rags'. On his way to the rows of terraced houses on the other side of the main thoroughfare at the walled end of the park, he could not resist plying his trade. The pram always seemed full, his takings bundled under a sheet; nobody hereabouts would pay any attention to the low howl, the constant, watchful, sly scrutiny. Perhaps once he had struck such treasure, or believed he could,

amongst the affluent that he came this way *en route* for his
real profit or loss, and shouted, as any sucking dove,
penetrating the length of garden, shrubs, walls and windows,
the silence between Beethoven's sublimities, to make his little
presence known.

Alistair returned to the quartet.

He had spoken to Katherine Montgomerie, again as she
walked down the garden, jovially quizzing her why she had
ignored him a few days before. At first she appeared puzzled,
frowned attractively, established by hesitant questions exactly
the time of her preoccupation, and then brightened on
discovery.

'I know, I know now.' She sounded jubilant. 'I was reading
and I'd come to an exciting point, and I just put back the
pleasure by strolling out. I didn't know I was so caught up.'

'It must have been a marvellous book.'

'No, it wasn't. Not at all. It was a spy story. Oh, what was
the thing called? It's being made into a film. I think I saw
that in the *Sunday Times*. I'll forget my own name next.'

'Have you finished it?'

'Yes. The same day. And took it back to the library. I
sometimes go twice a week.'

'It must have been spellbinding.'

'Not really. It was quite good. I wish I could . . . You
must have thought me mad or rude to go barging past you,
especially when you called out. I'm sorry.' She did not sound
so. 'Now you mention it, I do remember coming out, made
an errand of it, teabags on the compost or something.'

'And I thought it was something serious.'

'But it wasn't.'

'I nearly came round to find out. You would have been
cross to have your reading interrupted.'

A book of poor quality, its title unmemorable, had so
fastened on the imagination of this young woman that she
could temporarily lose contact with the world, as represented
by her elderly neighbour, crashing about with his bonfire.
Beethoven now ripped into his powerful last movement,
discarding illness, his solitary squalor, his disappointments,

or rather made them the origins, the energies from which his great dance leapt, cavorted, swept the low world aside.

Alistair stood to listen, in the grip of the racing music, the fine October day, his garden replete with golden leaves, pleased with himself, his friends and relations. He cleaned and put away the record, pausing to read the sleeve, to add to his small sum of information, and made for his garden.

That evening in his bath he pondered a problem, whether to go by car or foot to visit Eleanor. By such he occupied his life. He did not like the notion; there ought to be better. In the end he walked to her flat, swinging his stick, singing snatches of Beethoven.

Every window in Eleanor's flat was ablaze with lights, and he was not the only guest. An elderly couple draped themselves on the large, multicoloured settee, substantial soft drinks at the ready. Mr and Mrs Lennox-Smith were introduced, Eleanor's sister and brother-in-law who had returned with her from Shropshire; he wondered why she had made no mention of the pair in her letter.

'We shall eat straightaway, if that's all right with you,' the hostess told him, handing him dry sherry.

'I'll come out and help you,' the sister offered.

'You sit still.'

'And that puts me into my useless place,' she grimaced to Murray.

He did not remember meeting Eleanor's sister before, and imagined that she would have been married and away from home during the war. Both Lennox-Smiths looked ill, old and pinched; good clothes do not disguise wrecked bodies. Smart shoes and brand-new spectacles mock pallor, wrinkles, eaten-out cheeks, thin hair.

They talked, but with effort, making little attempt to accommodate Murray to the drift of their remarks. The excitement of a brilliant room, the promise of food and company stirred them to conversation, but it seemed to matter little what they said. Two elderly people touched on autumn weather, and travel, and then oddly ignored their fellow-guest as they argued slowly about a holiday a neighbour had spent in Kenya. They acted out parts, aware of the audience, but

54

not expecting interruptions. At dinner they ate sparingly and drank only water, and at 9.30 asking to be excused they left for bed.

'I wonder if it will be foggy tonight,' Mrs Smith said, as if it made a difference.

Murray mentioned the television forecast, clear skies, the possibilities.

' "Season of mists and mellow fruitfulness," ' Lennox-Smith intoned, a grimace of embarrassment across the lined face. 'It's what we should expect.'

They left the room and Eleanor called to her sister that she'd give her a hand upstairs. Murray was left alone, listening to the faint rise and fall of voices from the other side of the door.

When Eleanor returned, after a considerable interval, she sat down exhausted. She seemed near tears, and motioned him towards the drinks table.

'Are you all right?' he asked.

She nodded, recovering. 'Ned usually comes down because they've forgotten something.' She spoke as if the sentence excused her silence. After she had named her drink, she took it, held it in front of her, still unspeaking. Lennox-Smith made no appearance.

'Sorry,' she said at length, blowing breath out. She sipped, smiled, wriggled more comfortably into her chair. Alistair waited. 'We have to put Lizzie to bed between us.'

'What's wrong? She looks very ill. And her husband for that matter.'

'She's going to die. They aren't sure when, but it will be a few months at most. Cancer.' She sucked breath in. 'The big C. She's had three major operations.'

'Does she know?'

'Oh, yes. She ferrets the truth out of them. She knows she's a hopeless case, and it makes her very down sometimes, but more often than not she's more concerned with what's going to happen to Ned. He's not strong; he's diabetic amongst other things. It's knocked him out.'

The door opened; Lennox-Smith crept in.

'Hullo, Ned.'

'Has Elizabeth left her reading glasses here?'

'No. They're in a red case on the dressing table. I put them there myself.'

'Thanks, Eleanor.'

'Is she all right?'

'Yes. She thought she might read for a bit.'

'Good. What's she tackling, then?'

'*Mansfield Park*.'

'Great.' A generous, encouraging smile crossed her face.

'Thanks, Eleanor. Good night. Goodnight, Mr Murray.' He closed the door as stealthily as he had opened it.

'Would you choose *Mansfield Park* if you were dying?' She asked the very question he would have put to her.

'I've no idea. I can't conceive what it must be like. I think I'd be constantly overwhelmed with the thought that I'd soon not be here. Unless there was bad pain, when I might be pleased to let go. But I can't imagine any book or music or work of art offering anything but the most fleeting relief. It's a condemnation, really, of all the things I've stood for, isn't it?'

'No.' Eleanor said the word firmly. 'Art is to occupy those who are alive, even art that's concerned with dying. Then it's death as judged by the living.'

'We've all got to go.'

'But we don't concern ourselves with it much. Not seriously. We think we do when people we know die, or we read in the newspapers about earthquakes and massacres, and see Lear or Oedipus on stage. But we don't.'

'It's perhaps as well.'

'People don't die so suddenly,' she whispered, surprising him with the lowering of her voice. 'Jane Austen was scribbling album verses, and three days later she was dead. I thought we'd half tamed death till all this happened.'

Alistair waited.

'Liz and I have never been very close. She's twelve years older than I am for one thing, and always seemed grown-up. And when we met, we didn't exactly hit it off. She didn't approve of Henry. He was far too successful for her liking. And he stood no nonsense from her.'

'What did her husband do?'

'Ned? Public school. Regular army. He was badly wounded in Italy, and then joined an estate agent. He's one of the nicest men. His father had a great deal of money, I guess. He was a stockbroker, the father, I mean. They're comfortably off; lovely house.'

'Family?'

'None. Their one daughter died. She was twenty-two, killed in a road accident.'

The two sat, caught up in their own thoughts.

'They've had a comfortable life by and large.' Eleanor spoke without much conviction, perhaps expecting him to argue the point. When he made no observation, she pressed on. 'She's been ill for two or three years now. Internal operations, mastectomy, chemotherapy. I didn't really know how bad she was. I think it was all starting about the time Henry died, but she didn't say much. Too busy comforting me. My sister has the proper sense of proportion, I'll say that for her.' She laughed tinnily. 'I travelled about and didn't see much of them. I knew she was ill, but I hadn't cottoned on how badly. That's odd, really. They didn't mention the word "cancer". Some weeks ago, Ned phoned to ask me to go over and told me the position. I was shocked. It was not long before I came running into your house that night.'

'You never mentioned it.'

'No, I didn't.'

'You talked about a young woman who'd committed suicide.'

'I know I did.'

Eleanor answered harshly, as if defying him or defending herself, but she settled herself again, smiled companionably at him.

'Anyway, Ned told me that she was talking about a trip over here, to come back to see the places where she was young. I went over and made arrangements. I'm not sure we've done right. Her doctor didn't know, either, blew hot and cold.'

'She really wanted to come?'

'Why do you ask that?' Eleanor almost snapped.

'People get things out of perspective, especially when they're ill. What I mean is, she could have said it once, just a bit of time-filling conversation, and her husband took it up seriously, because he was at his wits' end.'

'I see. I think she meant it. I may be wrong. Anyhow, we had her brought over by car, it's only a couple of hours, but it's too much for Ned on his own, and it knocked her about. She's been here four days now, and hasn't been out of the front door.'

'But she offered to help you serve dinner?'

'Yes, she did. Lizzie will put on her show. She'd have carried things in and done well. That's one reason why you're here, to try to jolt her back.'

'Is it possible?'

'Possible? I'd like to fill her time in as profitably as she can take it. She didn't get up today until three o'clock. God knows how she'll be tomorrow. The journey here nearly finished her off, and sitting making polite conversation to you might well have half killed her.'

'I wish you'd warned me.'

'What difference would that have made? You'd have been more uneasy, that's all. No, I wanted you there leading off about Vivaldi and eleven-plus selection and pruning appletrees.'

'I thought they were ill, but I'd no idea they were as . . .'

'I'm hoping, Alistair, it did them good. To talk to somebody new, who'd no idea how desperate they were, who wouldn't shape himself and what he said or did because they were as they were.'

'And when will they look round the town?'

'Depends. This evening may have knocked all the stuffing out of Liz so that she'll have to spend all tomorrow in bed. I'd also like to give Ned a good rest while he's here. He's plenty coming to him.'

'Perhaps I could offer them a meal, and take them out somewhere.'

'When are you free?' Her voice struck lively; she leaned out to touch him in her relief.

'Tomorrow. The day after. The one after that. You see

how she is, and give me a ring on a morning when she seems better.'

'I will.'

Eleanor stood, took him into her arms, kissing him full on the mouth. She pressed against him almost furiously. The embrace was openly sexual, surprising him. No sign of desperation showed; she made herself blatantly clear. He felt afraid, trembled but gently returned her kiss. Her tongue burst into his mouth, but then she withdrew herself, sat down.

'Give me another small gin, Alistair, if you please.'

Her voice demonstrated normality, sounded warmly social, but no more.

They talked for an hour about Francesca's visit and Sebastian's plans. She made no attempt to detain him when he said she must be tired and that he must find his way home.

6

The Lennox-Smiths were not well enough, it appeared, to visit Murray immediately, but four days later Eleanor rang to announce that she thought Lizzie had recovered sufficiently to try it.

'It's very short notice,' she apologized.

'Quarter to ten. I'll manage to get you lunch for one. I'm efficient, you know.'

She issued instructions, detailing what the Smiths enjoyed, what was forbidden to Ned. He took a note, but could have as easily dictated it to her.

'No wine. Orange juice for Liz. Water for Ned. And cups of brutal, democratic tea afterwards.' The literary phrase put him on guard; Eleanor did not feel easy.

'And the trip out?'

'Oh, yes. We'll have to see. It wouldn't have to last long. No more than an hour at most. I'll make inquiries of her and let you know.'

They arrived at a quarter to one on a sunny day that had begun with sharp frost, bringing down the leaves. Their progress into the house was slow, but disguised by Elizabeth's performance as she pointed out treasures in his garden. The rooms were warm and they sat gratefully, the women beautifully dressed, carefully made up. All were well, Ned claimed, or at least not grumbling; it was most kind of Alistair to bother himself with old fogies. The man wore a well-cut tweed suit, a sporty shirt and tie, an expensive raglan overcoat.

When Alistair inquired about a trip out after lunch he met awkwardness; obviously Eleanor and Ned had discussed this, and had decided against any sort of expedition. Liz, on the other hand, grew excited, waving clawlike hands.

'There's one place,' she said, 'I'd really like to see again.'

Her smile of real pleasure disfigured her face. 'Ned will be able to guess.'

Her husband shifted in embarrassment.

'Elm Avenue,' he said, naming her birthplace.

'Not really. We didn't stay there for very long.'

'Stockwell Crescent,' Eleanor guessed.

'No.' Liz straightened herself. 'St Peter's, Shenstone, where we were married.'

'It's quite a way out. All of twenty miles,' Ned objected.

'We'll see.'

Eleanor put an end to argument, and Liz offered Alistair snippets of information. They had been married the summer the war started, when her father had bought the Old Rectory at Shenstone, partly to mark his success in investing money and partly because the Munich crisis had frightened him into thinking that a village would be safer than a city from German bombs.

'It was a lovely Georgian brick place,' she twittered.

'It was falling down,' Ned muttered, military as his polished shoes.

'I loved it.' Eleanor.

'Were you married there?' Alistair asked her.

'I was married in a register office.'

'That's what they call it,' Liz said, 'nowadays.'

Murray realized he had trespassed on unpopular ground.

The luncheon cheered them again with bland food and talk. Over the soup the Lennox-Smiths talked about skiing; over the chicken Eleanor described a farmer out at Shenstone who had terrified her in spite of frequent presents.

' "Ha'e one of these 'ere doneys," he'd say, offering a turnip. "I'll clear the di't off an' cut you a square or a finger. It'll be sweet as a nut." '

'And what was behind it all?' Ned inquired, guffawing. 'The usual?'

'Goodness of heart,' Eleanor told them. 'But he sounded so rough, and he had one eye bigger than the other, and his working clothes were ragged and filthy. I'd never come across anybody like that.'

'And what did you do?' Alistair.

'Answered him like a prim miss. "No, thank you very much, Mr Warton." He'd press me. I only took one thing, an apple, and I threw that away.'

'When I knew you you lived in Lucknow Drive,' Alistair said.

'Oh, we kept the town house. And moved back when petrol got short and things seemed safe.'

The Lennox-Smiths did not talk at any length, but enjoyed themselves, now and again initiating a topic and once or twice laughed aloud. It cheered Murray to see Elizabeth ravelled for a few seconds in pleasure. They opted, to his surprise, for he had thought Eleanor was pulling his leg, to drink tea, and he settled them with his best china service in front of a gas fire. They chatted about pictures; Smith had just bought a Henry Moore drawing and a small Kitaj painting.

'I never buy as an investment,' he warned. The man was standing again, as if the effort of lowering and raising his bones from a chair deterred him. He coughed dryly, covering his mouth with a clenched fist. 'I buy what I think I can live with.'

'Do you ever make mistakes?'

'Now and then.'

Elizabeth started into a stumbling anecdote about a Lord Leighton oil that had been in the family for years. Ned had refused to hang it, but had kept it in good order on the same grounds that he preserved shopping lists or postcards for years: 'Somebody might find them interesting at some time. You never know.' She even attempted, recognizably, a parody of her husband's voice. He looked both miffed and delighted, reaching out once to touch her on the shoulder.

Outside in the kitchen Alistair, washing up, asked advice of Eleanor.

'What about going out this afternoon?'

'I don't know. It's been marvellous so far. They've forgotten themselves for an hour. But I don't want to push our luck. How long will it take to Shenstone?'

'Half an hour.'

'That means we could be there by three.'

'Easily.'

'Half an hour there. And we'd be back by four or just after. But it's so cold.' Outside, the sun brilliantly smartened brickwork, trees, fallen leaves. 'It will freeze again tonight.'

'We could come back here for another hour or so.'

'No, Alistair.' She waved her teatowel, Irish linen with Lincoln Cathedral in green. 'We mustn't overdo it. You don't know how close they are to,' her mind flapped like the cloth, haphazardly, was restored to limp stillness, 'absolute exhaustion.'

The Lennox-Smiths had decided on the ride.

'There's no rush,' Alistair said, but he was aghast at the length of the preparations, the long hobble to lavatories, the vacillations, the physical difficulties of pulling on a coat, the mental obstacles to tying a neckerchief or scarf satisfactorily. They joked about their disabilities, but their groans were not spurious.

Alistair rang the rector about the key, and consulted a map with Eleanor.

'This is a lovely car,' Liz told him, tucked finally away into the back of his 3500 Rover.

'Too fast for me,' Ned, sadly.

'I always liked comfort in a car.'

Traffic was scant; the sky ice blue scored with vapour trails, the sun steadily bright on the oaktrees, the birches which still kept their leaves.

'We couldn't have picked a better day,' Eleanor, navigating. 'It's perfect. Slow down, here. Do you remember that, Liz?'

'What, darling?'

'That bridge. You were furious because I wouldn't go across it.'

'Why was that?' Ned.

'God knows. I hated being taken for walks.'

'As I remember you, you'd be balancing along the parapet.'

'Did she ever fall in?' Alistair.

'I expect so. Cut knees and torn stockings all the time.'

Eleanor made him drive slowly into the village, and then to draw up outside the low wall of the Old Rectory. The house was in excellent order, newly painted, and a cloth-capped gardener swept up leaves from the well-kept lawns, wheelbarrowing them over towards a bonfire.

'They haven't heard of compost,' Alistair said.

'He's in his shirtsleeves on a day like this.'

'What Daddy,' Eleanor answered, 'used to call "in his hot blood".'

'Can you remember your room?' Liz asked.

'I think so, but I seem to think I changed. Didn't I go into your room when you left?'

'The trees look quite different.'

'You're talking about forty years ago. More. You can get a fair amount of growth, even on new trees, in that time,' Ned told her.

The exchange was animated.

'How far is the church?' Alistair asked.

'The other end of the village street. As soon as we're round the Hall garden we'll see it. We walked back from the wedding. Do you remember, Ned?'

'Yes, I do. I wasn't reckoning on that. Nobody had told me.'

'Don't be ridiculous, Ned. Of course we had.'

Eleanor nudged Alistair, motioning him to drive along. He drew up, parked where the road had widened by the lychgate, and waited. The passengers in the back sat silent. The sun glowed redly on the rustic bricks of a cottage, washed the new rectory into pallor.

'It's warm in the car,' Ned barked. 'Really comfortable.'

'Do you think you'll manage it up to the church?' Eleanor asked her sister. 'It's quite a stretch.'

Elizabeth hesitated.

'No,' she said at length. 'Perhaps not.'

'You go, Ned,' Eleanor ordered. 'You can tell us if it's changed.'

'Well. I mean, er. I shan't insist on . . . You know.'

'Go in with Mr Murray, Ned.' His wife. 'I'd like you to do that.'

'Fair enough. Right you are, darling.'

'Have you not been back since you were married?' Alistair asked.

'Oh, yes. We often visited the parents. When Ned was abroad in the army, I spent a lot of time here.'

'Right sir.' To Ned. 'Let's get the key.'

The two men made speed along the short gravel drive to the rectory, made conversation with the rector's wife, returned, waved as they passed the car. Eleanor, Murray noticed, still occupied the front seat; for some reason he'd expected her to move back with her sister. They seemed not to be talking.

With some difficulty Alistair unlocked the door of the porch and the south door. Inside it struck icily cold, in spite of slats of sunlight through the west window.

'Smells damp,' Ned muttered.

They walked along the main aisle to the chancel steps. The wood of the roodscreen was polished, dust free.

'Nice little church,' Alistair said. 'Well looked after. Has it changed much?'

Ned kicked at the heel of his left shoe with the toe of his right.

'Don't remember. They all look the same to me, these places. How old's this?'

'I looked it up in Pevsner. Fourteenth century.'

'Thirteen hundred and something. Six hundred years.'

They tramped through the chancel, peered at the locked organ console, stood in front of the altar. 'Must have come up here. Can't remember, though I was sober enough. Lizzie looked beautiful, her hair was light in those days, and bushy. Women used to have waves, some of 'em, looked bloody silly.' He ducked as if apologizing to God. 'She was magnificent. Beautiful.'

'I'm sure.'

'Forty-five years. That other one was there, she was bridesmaid. Still a little schoolgirl, but arsing about as usual. Knew it all, then. I could tell you a thing or two about her to her discredit.' He laughed, a sound out of character with his appearance. 'Still, she's a friend of yours, and it's not good enough to talk scandal in the house of God, is it?' He laughed again.

They had returned to the roodscreen and faced the nave.

'Where did the family sit?'

'For the wedding?'

'No, on Sunday.'

'Did they come? I never did. And the army took their house over, and then old Warrington sold it not long after the end of the war.'

Now they examined tablets along the wall of the south aisle, two knights, three clergymen, a child and a pious lady.

'What will your wife want to know?' Alistair asked.

'About what?'

'About the church. What questions will she ask us?'

'Search me.'

'I wonder if there's a pamphlet.'

They found one on a table by the door, at the price of fifty pence. Searching for coins, they made the sum up between them, dropped them into the receptacle. Both produced wallets, folded treasury notes to slip into the contributions box.

'Funny,' said Lennox-Smith, looking back again. 'It is. Where did you get married, Murray?'

'In Glasgow, though I was teaching in London at the time.'

'Your wife's home?'

'Yes. She had a job in Richmond. That's where we met.'

'Scot, eh? Are you? Alistair Murray?'

'By descent. I was born in Nottinghamshire. A son of the manse.'

'Unnh.'

Lennox-Smith had stepped back now to the middle of the church, where he stood, hands in pockets, staring up at the roof.

'Can't even remember the name of the parson.'

'Easy,' Murray called. 'Thirty-eight. Albert Edward Goodchild, MA.' He tapped the framed list of rectors on the wall. '1929 to 1948.'

'Don't remember him?'

'Didn't he give you some advice?'

'If he did, it was wasted.' Ned guffawed again, made for the north wall. 'Goodchild, that's a right sort of name for the job. You'd think I'd remember. I wore my uniform. I was in the regular army.'

'Before the war?'

'Yes. It was an important day, and here I am, can't remember a thing.'

Lennox-Smith shrank inside his overcoat. During the five or ten minutes inside the church, Murray had glimpsed the smart, confident man his companion must have been at one time. Not that he himself would have cared much for the square set of the shoulders, the barked clichés, the sense that if one had been at the right school, in the right regiment and kept one's head down, it would all turn out for the best in the end. Present arms. Eyes front, sergeant, please. And now age, old wounds, disease had the man hobbling round at his dying wife's command, scratching about for reminders of his wedding day. Damn it all. It was already damned.

'Do you think we should go now?' Murray asked in a softened voice.

'Suppose so.' Still Ned looked about up to the roof beams. 'Mustn't let the ladies get cold.'

'No. Liz has a blanket.'

Lennox-Smith drew himself together.

'Shan't see this again,' he said. Unless Liz has put something in her will about being buried here. You never know.'

He sniffed hugely, marched for the closed door.

Outside afternoon light leapt like a smack in the eye.

'God,' Ned called, 'it's bright out here.'

'But not very warm.'

Lennox-Smith looked back, searching again, fidgety.

'We were photographed there in the porch. Still have them, somewhere. Nowadays they let you take pictures inside the church. I suppose it's influence of flash. Don't like it much.' He took two or three smart paces before relapsing into the old man. He regained confidence, poise. 'Then we all traipsed off, Liz and I in front, rest in a caterpillar behind. That's what they do in Scotland, isn't it?'

'I've no idea.'

'Saves a bawbee. I felt a bit of an idiot, but Liz enjoyed

67

herself. It was her idea; she'd seen it somewhere else. Always trying something out.'

'You'd come down this path?'

'Presumably.' They walked together. 'You have a son, haven't you? Something to do with television?'

'Yes. And a daughter.'

'How old is she?'

'She'll be thirty this year.'

'Emily would have been thirty-seven. That was our child.'

His face showed no emotion, though the end of his nose had reddened in the sharp air.

'You go back to the car,' Alistair said. 'I'll return the key.'

All three sat silently when he returned, straightfaced, in discomfort, as if they had quarrelled.

'You're not getting cold, are you?' he asked, switching on the engine.

'That lane,' Eleanor pointed, 'goes right round the church-yard. You could drive slowly along that, and then back the way we came.'

They made the circuit in silence; the ruts in the shadow of the hedges were frozen still. Alistair drew out on to the main road, but stopped again in front of the Old Rectory gate. Gardener and barrow had disappeared but the heaped bonfire sent up a cottony pole of smoke against the pale sky. Nobody offered comment.

'Shall I press on?'

As they hummed along the road, Ned Lennox-Smith broke the awkwardness with another question about Sebastian. Alistair told them what little he knew about the present American jaunt, and Eleanor immediately enthusiastically gave voice. When Alistair described Seb's visit to India, Lennox-Smith provided gruff information of his own, as he had served out there. As they discussed the influence of television, its expensive and roundabout ways, its importance in society and Sebastian Murray's own unique niche, the talk flew livelily and the journey, even the last part through town and the beginnings of evening traffic, seemed short. It was not until he drew up outside his bungalow, offering them further hospitality, that he realized that Elizabeth Lennox-Smith had not once opened her mouth.

He turned. Liz smiled at him, wrapped almost to the chin in a tartan blanket. Her face seemed small, an insignificant yellow triangle under a complicated hat.

'Are you all right?' he asked.

'Perfectly.' That put him into his place.

'We'll go in for a cup of tea.'

'No, thank you, Alistair,' Eleanor answered. 'We've been out long enough. We've thoroughly enjoyed it, but it's time we were making tracks for home.' She spoke quite evenly, not quickly, as if fitting words together like easy jigsaw pieces.

He did not argue, and on arrival helped Lennox-Smith to take Elizabeth into the house, where she collapsed into a chair, still clutching the tartan blanket. She looked exhausted, but roused herself sufficiently to send her husband for a glass of water and to thank Alistair. He made for the door and as he was letting himself out Eleanor, flitting past, called out a distracted farewell. Standing on a neat path between a newly cut lawn and tidy shrubs, he felt lost.

7

Alistair Murray heard nothing from Eleanor until the beginning of November, when the weather had turned milder.

He had suffered a heavy cold that he could not throw off, and had spent some time writing an article, allegedly light, on the tribulations of an education officer. This was written at the prompting of an old friend for the internal magazine of a metropolitan authority, with a half promise that it, and others like it by chief constables, finance officers, administrative executives, heads of housing or leisure services, directors of welfare, even Lord Mayors and chairmen of councils, might appear as a hardback book.

Whether it was the blocked nose, the headache, the sneezing that hindered him, he found great trouble in ordering his thoughts. He had often lectured his underlings on the importance of putting down plainly exactly what they meant, and had prided himself on the brevity and clarity of his official minutes, orders or reports. Now he did not know what he wanted to say. He could easily have completed his quota of words with a few old chestnuts about councillors who wished to appoint some BSc to a teaching post because he had one more letter after his name than his rival with a mere BA, or the occasion when a group of parents angry about the closing of a village school had flooded his office with a ton of letters on the very day after he had left for an educational conference in America. These anecdotes, suitable enough for after-dinner speeches to people who wished to keep him sweet, now seemed unfunny, demonstrating a pretension to omniscience. Aspirate-dropping politicians, educational psychologists, parents hot under the collar, lunatic schoolteachers had all added to the tally of ludicrous error, but then so had he. His whole career was shot through with misjudgement, mismanagement, support of wrong causes, failure to assist decent men and women, he considered, and yet he was still praised as one of the most successful directors of education in the whole country since the war. He could not see why he had made such a name, except that favourable publicity or circumstances had helped him, and his pleasant but utterly serious committed manner and approach had led people, political masters or paid subordinates alike, to act more sensibly on this account. In so far, he warned himself, that he had had any influence at all.

Thus his article ought to warn of the many devil's temptations, sketch the compromises that could be accepted, and clearly set down those that could not, demonstrate the part humanity must play, philosophy, belief and character, and all within a framework of reminiscence, glowing vignette, even a modest confession of weakness. It did not. However he attempted it, it resulted either in a ragbag of self-exalting stories or, worse, a sermon, a puritanical and dull exhortation, high-minded enough, but with little relevance to the wear and tear, getting and spending, learning and forgetting that had rattled on daily in a competent administrator's office.

Snuffling, his handkerchief soaked in hateful eucalyptus, he struggled and gave up morning after morning. He was getting old; at one time he'd have had his two thousand words out of the way and on to his secretary's typewriter inside a couple of hours. He had been able to think then, judge, compose with wit, in control. Now all he could do was stumble, sneeze, clear his throat and trembling brush the rheum from his eyes.

In depression he told himself that he had never been as incisive, as sharp-witted as he now remembered. At his work he had become used to flirting with fear, and even encouraged himself to courses that roused apprehension, so that by the end of his time he had muddled or burst triumphantly through so many times that he confidently expected to emerge on every occasion. He had, it is true, grown slower, more liable to delegate, and his period of retirement, with decisions only about garden and shops, had made him that little less enterprising, more prone to hesitation.

These were sentences formed in his mind, arguments

71

clearly marshalled for himself, but carrying no emotional charge. He did not believe them. With something of his own obstinacy he forced himself into his study where in three sessions, two mornings and an afternoon, he completed the article and put it into the drawer of his desk not to be reread until Friday, four days' grace. He staggered downstairs, one o'clock on Monday, to watch November rain, from the west and thus not cold; too exhausted to cook, he cut a piece of cake and made instant coffee. With a pang, he heard himself groan out loud: 'I want to die, I want to die.'

That was not the truth either, more of a dramatic metaphor, but it set him back. This voice had spoken from inside himself, as from an oracle's cave. He did not like it. The sensible propositions he put to himself did not convince him; he could only give voice to words that might sooner or later speak exact truth.

He made himself walk out whatever the weather, but the afternoons were short, and on cloudy days it grew almost dark by 4.30. Whether he chose to stroll in a park, on to agricultural land, or in the centre of the town, he could not rid himself of the thought that he had come across an Alistair Murray who had not existed before. Hills snatched his breath from him; his hips ached after four or five miles, but he did not feel old. From time to time he could have dressed up and barged into the dancehalls of his army days, except that they no longer existed; he wondered if he could recall the complicated steps that had once won him admiration, or even shuffle through the basic routine. He'd be tired in no time, but in his head for a few unthinking seconds he was the smart young man who'd pleased and chased the girls.

When he fetched the article from the drawer, he found it bearable, but rewrote it, and posted it away before he had time for twenty-second thoughts. Released, he scribbled a long letter to Francesca, making fun of his pretensions as a writer, and describing the Shenstone trip. Disappointingly, he had heard nothing from Eleanor, not a call, a note of thanks, an invitation to do more. By now she would have returned the Lennox-Smiths to Shropshire, and gone off to please herself. A phone call from Sebastian, reporting a most successful time in the United States, seemed curt and dry, like the daylight getting itself over and done before it half satisfied the observer.

'Are you sure you're all right?' he queried. His son laughed at him. 'What's so funny?'

'You're as bad as my mother was.'

Alistair kept his mouth shut, and his son pursued it no further. Sebastian was off to probe middle-class mores in Scandinavia at the end of the week.

'Do you know anything about it?' his father asked.

'I shall before I start. We've experts galore instructing me.'

'Why not save money and use them, then, and library film?'

'You clearly don't rate known front men as highly as my employers, thank God.'

Sebastian fancied he'd have part of Christmas Day and Boxing Day at home, but he had promised to visit a children's hospital to distribute gifts in the eye of the camera.

'They usually choose comedians to do that,' his father said sourly.

'A different face.'

Alistair knew his son would be successful, in that he'd let the youngsters make the headway. This childless man would perfectly act the father to the underprivileged, the disabled, the diseased, stirring Christmas cheer and tears. Back at home, his own father would watch, be moved, marvel, trying but failing to mock.

He had walked through a park, finding nothing of interest except a group of junior schoolboys playing football on a full-size pitch. Nearly all the players were concentrated in the penalty area at the far end, hacking at the ball which never moved above five or six yards before hitting a pair of legs or another flying boot.

'What's the score?' he asked the goalkeeper at the unoccupied end.

'Three–one.'

'Who's winning?'

'We are.'

The swarm of boys had staggered with the ball towards the centre spot where their advice or abuse grew shriller.

'Look out. They're coming.'

'Ah. He'll blow the whistle.'

The refereeing master obliged.

'How did you know he was going to do that?'

The boy leaned, propped by one straight arm, on the upright.

'He always does.'

'Are you keeping awake there, Terry?' the master shouted, warning Murray off.

'Yes, sir.' The boy's voice was all humility.

'Keep them out,' Murray advised, walking away. The child took no notice but, picking a lump of wettish mud, rolled it into a ball and hurled it upfield. He seemed so small in the man-sized frame of the goal, but kept to his own way, strolling up and down, whistling, once turning a cartwheel.

The young teacher had not recognized Murray, had probably been appointed to the authority after the ex-director left. Just as Murray was about to quit the park by the lower gate, a shout announced four–one. One or two tiny figures, chests out, clenched fists raised, imitated scorers on television. The figure in the raincoat stepped away.

On the road uphill, taking the pavement by the park railings, he caught up with a young woman pushing a pram, laden on top with a baby and a sitting child and below, on a rack, with plastic carrier bags.

'Heavy work.' Pleasantly.

'You can say that again.' The mother almost stopped. 'The next bit's worst. It really is steep.'

'I'll give you a hand.'

She looked him suspiciously over, dabbing a cigarette into her mouth.

'Go on, then.'

He put his left hand down to the handle and they sped off. The child sitting stared with unsmiling eyes.

''Owd on, our Tone,' the mother commanded. 'Now this mester's helpin' us we're gettin' a bit of speed up.'

The smoke of her cigarette was acrid, biting into his chest. Ungloved fingers next to his on the handle were nicotine-stained, grubby, short-nailed, ugly.

74

'This'll keep you fit,' he said.

'Oh, ah?'

'I try to take a walk every afternoon. Not when it's raining, of course.'

''Ave you got a car?'

'Yes.'

'I wish I had. Wouldn't half save me legs.' She grumbled about her varicose veins, the difficulties of getting two children and a pushchair on and off conductorless buses, the battle in the supermarket.

'Does your husband own a car?'

'Yes, a banger.'

'Couldn't you persuade him to drive you down on Saturday morning to shop?'

'I like to live a day at a time.' He waited for an explanation which she did not give. They reached the top of the hill. 'I've got to cross over here. Thanks fo' the push. Ta-ra.' She made quick steps on the Belisha, looking with violence both ways twice.

He hated the shortening of the days, which could be brilliant at mid-morning and pitch dark at the beginning of his six o'clock meal. At one time he enjoyed winter evenings at home, but now he hankered after daylight. Warmth and electric bulbs meant time wasted listlessly in front of the television.

His preparations were under way for high tea, when the telephone rang. Turning down the gas stove he was delighted to hear Eleanor.

'Are you still alive?' he asked.

'Yes.'

'I've not heard a word from you.'

'No. I've been over in Shropshire.'

'How are they both?'

'Alistair, Liz has died.'

His legs trembled; his back froze. Minute aches squirmed in neck and shoulders.

'Oh, Eleanor. I'm so sorry. I really am. How's Ned taking it?'

'I wanted him to come back with me, but he wouldn't.'

'There's no family, is there?'

'No. They had a daughter, Emily, who was killed. In a road accident.'

'She was the only child?'

'Yes. There were a couple of miscarriages before Emily was born.'

'How does he seem?'

'He's taking it well. There's less for him to do. He's had his hands full.'

'I knew she was very ill, but I didn't think . . . It seems so . . .'

Eleanor described in a flat little voice how she had taken the Lennox-Smiths back home, how her sister seemed much better for a couple of days but had then been violently ill with haemorrhage and nausea, had been rushed into hospital and had died thirty-six hours later.

'It was quick, at least,' he said.

'Not quick enough. She was awful.'

'I thought they could . . .'

'They didn't.'

Eleanor's voice trembled.

'Would you like to come round?' he asked.

'No. You come and see me.'

'When?'

'Tonight.'

'I'll walk over.'

'That's good. Then we'll get drunk.'

He tried to talk to her, but she stopped the conversation ruthlessly, cutting him off in mid-sentence. For a few minutes he stomped up and down his kitchen, uncertain of his whereabouts, duties, even his wishes.

After the meal, he bathed, donned a dark suit and carefully locked his house, which he left lighted. He needed to go back indoors for his umbrella, as it was now drizzling. The streets were, as he expected, deserted.

Eleanor in a bright housecoat looked cheerful as she opened the door.

'Am I late?' he asked.

'We didn't stipulate a time, did we, so how can you be?'

She took his coat and brolly away and returning congratulated him on his suit. 'You look really nice. Very dignified. A man of the world.' Her breath smelt of gin. She led him to an armchair where he chose to join her in gin-swilling. 'I've already started.' Her voice was steady, her movements quick and controlled.

'Your health,' he called, raising his glass.

For twenty minutes she talked about her sister. She confessed that they had never been great friends in that Liz had been so much older and utterly conventional. 'She was *the* Tory lady in person.'

'What do you vote?' he interrupted, crudely comic.

'Conservative. Always. But you know what I mean. Don't be awkward.'

The three of them had arrived back in Shropshire and as the journey had tired Liz she had been put to bed. Next morning she had appeared well, rose earlier than usual and, suitably swaddled, had taken a turn in the garden to see what had happened in their absence.

'She talked quite a lot about you,' Eleanor told Murray. 'And the trip to Shenstone. It seemed a treat, an event. It had nothing to do with nostalgia, as far as I could see. It was as if she'd been to some Taj Mahal or Blenheim and had no connection with our living there.' Eleanor looked about her as if for the presence of a critic who would take issue with these conclusions. Her movements were so definite he was reminded of the framed cards that had hung on the walls of at least three of his father's congregation claiming that Christ was the guest of the house, 'the unseen listener to every conversation'.

'She had two really good days,' Eleanor continued, 'when she seemed stronger, freer from pain. And then the collapse in the night.'

'Had she overdone it?'

'I wondered. But Ned and I were most careful to see that she didn't overexert herself, physically at least. I don't know.'

Elizabeth had hung on for a further day and a half in hospital, in misery, agonized, beaten out of her wits. 'She hadn't an ounce of strength on the first day, and when she

77

moved as much as a finger she was in torment. She hadn't the strength to scream, but she whimpered, like a dog. I don't want to see anything like that again. She was a decent woman, not without ideas in a limited way, but this had knocked all humanity out of her, my God, it had.'

Murray felt himself crouching, braced against the onslaught of Eleanor's banal outburst, remembering his own wife.

'Were you there when she died?' he forced himself to ask.

'Yes.' Eleanor threw her arms about, for no reason that he could see. 'They rang us fairly early on the Monday morning and we went down. They said she wouldn't last long. She seemed unconscious, or half there most of the time. We tried talking to her, but it didn't make much difference. They must have drugged her. She was breathing very heavily; it seemed noisy. I went outside and asked the sister how long it would be, but she said they couldn't tell, not exactly. They were very kind to us, gave us tea and biscuits, and were looking in on Liz all the time. She opened her eyes once, when Ned was talking to her. She recognized him, I think, at least he hopes she did, and tried to say something but it was only a murmur and when we asked her what it was she drifted away.'

'It must have been terrible for you. And Ned.'

'Not as that first day. Then it was hell. No, she wasn't with us, and though the sound of her breathing was nasty, she'd no idea and she wasn't uncomfortable.'

'What time did she die?'

'About midday. She just stopped living. Eased away. And then she was lying there with her mouth part open. There wasn't much difference between being alive and dead. I fetched the nurse in, and she said, "She's gone," and a doctor came. We kissed her. She looked so thin, and they took us out to the office.'

'You went back home?'

'In time. I cooked us an omelette. Ned was ever so good, poor fellow. Very steady, but he kept holding my hand as if he was frightened something was going to happen. But he bore up, and talked to the undertaker and the rest of it.'

'Will he manage?'

'He'll have to, won't he?' She relented. 'A woman will

come in every day to look after the house and prepare his lunch. Give me your glass.' He had not finished, but she refilled hers. 'People die. You know that. Especially at our time of life. But I put it to myself like this, that up till now there hasn't been any minute of my life where Liz hasn't existed, whether I've thought about it or not.'

'I don't understand you,' he answered.

'It doesn't matter.' She seemed elsewhere. 'Or does it?'

They talked about Ned's future, about Christmas, about Sebastian and in silences between, which were not uncomfortable because he expected healing from them, coming to terms. He did not mention Janet in spite of himself. They drank gin, but not desperately. At ten o'clock she offered to make coffee, and walking across threw her arms round him, kissed him full on the mouth. He was not altogether surprised. They kissed deeply.

'Turn the main lights off,' she ordered.

In warm chiaroscuro, one decorated standard lamp glowing, she pulled him to her, handling him intimately and with hunger. She stripped herself with an efficient dexterity, her body in the half-light young and attractive, and made love on the carpet, her head on an orange oriental cushion dragged down from the settee. They groaned at each other, and she kept up an amorous babble, until both were satisfied.

She eased him from her.

'Oh, I needed that,' she said. She looked about for her housecoat. 'Don't you get cold.'

He dressed in a daze while she was out of the room preparing coffee. It seemed improper to put on his tie or his shoes, but he retrieved her lace-trimmed french knickers and bra from the floor, laid them tidily on the settee.

When she returned carrying a large tray, she ordered him to switch the lights back on, and pouring coffee said, 'You'll have to stay the night. I can't send you back at this time half drunk along dark streets. It's asking to be mugged.'

'I'm sober,' he claimed.

'You're staying.'

He did not argue, drank one cup of coffee as he would have done at home, refused biscuits. She sat matronly; although she was naked under the housecoat she kept it buttoned in decorum down to her calves, her slippered feet together. She had combed her hair. The rings on the third finger of her left hand flashed gorgeously against the pale flesh.

Eleanor offered him a single bed or a share in her double. The single, she warned, had not been warmed. She found for him a pair of pyjamas, once her husband's, but now worn on occasion legs and arms rolled, she giggled, by her. She had slipped on a vulgarly decorated short nightdress while he was in the bathroom.

They clung together, gin fumes heavy. He had not shared a double bed for more than twenty years; Janet had bought, after a consultation, of course, of sorts, two single bunks, which still stood side by side in his bedroom.

'There's no sense,' the Scottish voice undulated in sweet reason, 'in keeping one another awake unnecessarily.' He wondered why she had not insisted on separate rooms.

He slept well tonight, though he woke often as usual and twice made his way out to the lavatory. To dress without shaving left him mildly unsettled, but he ate his breakfast and set off for home at twenty minutes to ten in triumph. The rain had disappeared, clouds stretched silvery and he knew himself a different man.

The old fox, the administrator, let himself into his front door, glanced over three uninteresting letters, undressed with leisure and took to his bath. To wallow in hot water at a quarter to eleven in the morning broke every rule of his puritan upbringing, but he needed to relax, to stand away from himself. He had made love to a woman, and thus far committing himself, now noted a twinge of fear with his pride and pleasure. What would Eleanor want from him? Had he acquitted himself well enough for the physical relationship to continue? Did he want it to? What privacy must he relinquish? Did she intend marriage, and what would that entail? Who was he?

Stepping down from the bath, he posed naked in front of his mirror. His body had not sagged into blubber; the hair on his chest, though grey, grew darker than that on his scalp. He turned head, trunk to assess legs and buttocks, and not dissatisfied plugged in his razor. The mirror light wickedly etched wrinkles round his eyes, ruined his forehead, but his skin this morning at least looked healthy. He dragged on gardening clothes, and singing 'Prepare thyself, Zion', ran out to the kitchen, to a large mug of coffee and a folded *Guardian*, deciding that he was pleased with life or himself.

8

Alistair telephoned Eleanor twice in the afternoon, twice in the evening and failed to contact her. She had said nothing about going away, and he wondered where she had hidden herself. Their lovemaking had happened so naturally, with such grace, he informed his doubts, that she could not just disappear from it. He imagined a beautifully got-up Eleanor on a Christmas shopping spree in London, or amongst well-to-do friends living the life to which she had accustomed herself, drinking cocktails, exchanging confidences, filling in her diary, parading herself at the theatre, in and out of taxis, straightfaced or laced at *têtes-à-tête*, attractively outgoing at parties. She had literary friends, acquaintances amongst academics, City tycoons, actors; she wrote regularly to a well-known composer, recently knighted, to the wife of the Governor of the Bank of England, to a young social worker in Shropshire, to her MP as a friend, to a man in prison. She did not of necessity need him. Jealousy tapped; he laughed at himself, or tried to, failed, pitched into the final clearing of leaves from his garden.

Three days on, the weather mild and damp, he bustled about his garden, ostensibly clearing up, but in fact doing nothing useful except exert himself to temper his disappointment with Eleanor's silence. He was brushing his path with vigour when he noticed a man staring at him over the gate. He stared back. The man seemed familiar.

'Good morning, sir. Keeping yourself busy, I see.'

'There's always something in the garden.'

'I suppose so. I've not got much. My lawn's the size of a postage stamp.'

Alistair had recognized the voice. Odd; his eyes had failed him, but the ears had dutifully worked. There stood the police inspector who had questioned him about the murder.

'Just having another glance at the scene of the crime?'
Alistair advanced to the gate, leaned on his broom.

'No. My day off. To tell you the truth, I've just been for
a haircut.' Certainly it was newly plastered down with bay
rum. 'I like to stretch my legs. Don't often get the chance
these days.'

'Are you any further on with your investigation?' Alistair
asked, waving towards the spot on the road where the murder
had taken place.

'Progressing, you might say. Progressing.'

'You'll get him in the end, you think?'

'That's always a possibility.'

'It's a long-drawn-out campaign, isn't it? Incident room
and door-to-door inquiries?'

'That's the way we do it. It flushes 'em out in the end.'

'I see.'

The inspector cast a pale eye over the garden, then swivelled
to sniff loudly at the road.

'It looks peaceful enough here, now,' he said. 'A bit rural
with all these big trees.'

'Out of the way, though. Isn't that why the man would
choose this spot? Ask to be put down here if he intended a
robbery?'

'Very likely.'

'How long will it take you to find him?'

The inspector came a long step nearer, put both hands on
the gate, almost sacerdotally.

'You needn't shout this round the houses,' his voice had
softened and deepened, 'but we know who he is.'

'Does he know you know?'

The policeman's head jerked back.

'What do you think? We've got no evidence, or not enough
to make a court case yet. The woman he's living with is
covering for him.'

'Has he got a criminal record?'

A hesitation, a narrowing of the eyes accompanied by a
gloved hand tapping on the gate.

'Yes. Of a minor kind.'

'Will you drum up enough evidence in the end, do you think?'

'That remains to be seen. I mean, there'd be some who'd say it's best left as it is. He knows how he stands with us, and won't try it again.'

'Not unless he's a psychiatric case.'

'I don't think he's that. He's got a useful job. We don't have the expense of keeping him in prison. He's not likely to go over the top again.'

'So you won't press?'

'Press? Of course we shall press. If we don't get a conviction, the public think we do nothing, and are that little bit more edgy.'

'Why did he do it?'

'Drink. Temper. Bravado. Having the knife to hand.'

'And he won't repeat it, you think?'

'No. We've frightened him all right.'

'And his woman? She'll continue to cohabit with a murderer?'

'That wouldn't be unusual.'

'Wouldn't she be afraid? For her own safety, I mean?'

A Jaguar drew up at the curb behind the inspector, and Eleanor, dressed picturesquely and carrying a resplendent handbag, glided round the back of the car, watched in admiration by both men.

'Visitors,' the inspector said, viewing Eleanor with satisfaction. 'Keep it under your hat, sir, what I've been saying.' He made a double semi-military salute in their direction, was away without hurry, steel-tipped heels clacking, down the street.

'Who's that?' Eleanor inquired as Alistair closed the gate behind him. He explained. 'And what have you got to keep under your hat?'

'They think they know who did the murder.'

'What murder is that?'

'Goodness, where have you been?'

They walked laughing together into his kitchen, where he told the tale. At the end of his exposition, during which she had sat on a high stool warming her hands on a coffee mug, she asked why the policeman had told him to keep the conversation secret.

'Because he knows I won't.'

'You're not to be trusted, then?'

'Nobody would sit mum on that bit of tittle-tattle. Moreover, he can remember when I was director of education. My name appeared at the front of his schoolbooks. He even remembered my initials. And he thinks I move in influential circles.'

'Don't you?'

'Not any more. But the police will now let it be known to the right people that they've traced the murderer. So if there's any outcry, you can never tell these days, persons of authority . . .'

'Ex-directors of education.'

'Exactly . . . will put the word round that all's well.'

'How funny.'

'Not really. An important part of their job is public relations. It's not easy for them.'

'You don't think it's some chatterbox, bursting to tell you something he shouldn't, but incapable of keeping his mouth shut.'

'That's a possibility.'

She laughed again, as if she did not trust his judgement, but went on to ask him if he'd mind looking after her house in the next few weeks while she was on holiday abroad.

'I'm going to stay with friends in Portugal. They invited me. It's warmer. I've informed your allies the police; I also took the liberty of saying you would keep your eye on the premises for me.'

'You won't be here over Christmas?'

'No. I'm not altogether certain how long I shall stay. If I get bored I shall go elsewhere. There's nothing to keep me in England.'

The sentence was delivered casually enough, but it smarted in his ears.

'Not Ned?'

'No. He'll be well enough looked after.'

She described her friend's villa in the Alentejo, bare country without shade, sweltering in the summer with beautiful, deserted beaches. He could not make out whether she approved of the place or not; she rhapsodized, she blamed, blew hot, cold, lukewarm.

Suddenly she left her stool, with a flourish of wristwatch.

'I must rush. I've a hairdressing appointment.' She handed him the keys of her flat. 'I'll leave the Portuguese address and phone number for you.'

'Shan't I see you again before you leave?'

'I'm afraid not. London tomorrow. Richmond for a few days.' Janet had taught there. He remembered her digs. 'Then Portugal. Easy now the dog's dead.'

'Are there plants to be watered?'

'No. My cleaning woman will see to that. There aren't many, anyway.'

'Do you want your correspondence forwarding?'

'Not really. There'll be nothing important. And if it is, I don't want it chasing me slowly round the backwaters of Europe.'

Eleanor put strong arms about him, kissed him warmly, sisterly on the mouth, slightly rearranged her hat and fur collar with the help of the kitchen mirror and was off towards the door. He followed her along the garden path, out into the street, where she was into the Jaguar and away, raising her left hand as she smoothly accelerated. His jacket faintly retained her perfume.

Disappointed, he returned to his chores, but only fitfully, dodging from one useless exercise to another so that he was glad when it was time to prepare his lunch, a nothing, cheese omelette with frozen peas. There was little between him and Eleanor, except a small sexual adventure, to be enjoyed apparently, and then forgotten. He sourly wondered what more he wanted. Any talk of marriage would have terrified him, but this, this. Biting his lip, he washed the dishes after he had eaten (her cup was unmarked by lipstick), played the E Major Prelude and Fugue from Book Two without interest, walked round every room in the house, decided he'd clean the windows on the inside ready for Christmas, but before he began that had a second shot at the Fugue.

Cleaning windows exhausted him, and he had not half finished them when it became too dark to continue. Somewhere about in this city Eleanor Franks chatted to shopkeepers, to her coiffeuse, packed her cases; tomorrow she'd be in Richmond, next week in Portugal. He'd been once to Lisbon, for a conference. She had signed, sealed, delivered herself over to him, and had immediately gone gadabout. He rang her flat for Ned's address, and she spoke with warmth, promising to call on him immediately she returned. Slightly reassured by this reception, he wrote, painfully, saying then crossing out what he did not mean, a letter of condolence to Ned Lennox-Smith. When he'd completed and posted it, he decided he would buy a Christmas tree, and the decision seemed to cheer him, until he told himself he'd in all probability spend the day itself writing letters. Stoically, he concluded he could do worse.

Almost immediately he had decided how he would waste the evening, Francesca telephoned to ask him to spend Christmas with them. He could drive down the motorway at his leisure a day or two before, and return as soon as he liked after Boxing Day. Delighted, he did not immediately accept.

'I'm not quite sure what I am doing,' he havered.

'Ho, ho,' she answered. 'The ladyfriend?'

'No.'

'What's she doing then? Your Eleanor?'

'She's in Portugal from next week until some time in the New Year.'

'Lucky her.'

Francesca cut the conversation short, excusing herself that she must now phone one of her women. He stood in the hallway disappointed in himself, in his grudging reception of her kindness, certain he could have made her evening, or the next hour of it, by an enthusiastic acceptance. Without doubt, he would go; they both knew it, but he had to vacillate, reveal his awkwardness, get his own back on the hard world at the expense of a vulnerable Francesca. 'Murray, you're a bastard.' He said it out loud, surprising himself. With a flurry he dialled his daughter-in-law's number, ready to confess, apologize, make reparation. Engaged.

He had not taken six steps from the phone when it rang. Relieved, he turned back to hear Katherine Montgomerie, his neighbour, asking him if it would be possible for him to baby-sit that evening. Their usual girl had cried off at the last minute; now she'd been ringing round the wide world getting nowhere, and he was her last hope. Otherwise, she would not be able to accompany her husband to some grand dinner of gynaecologists and obstetricians.

'Do you think I'll be any good?'

'They're all in rude health, and tired out. You shouldn't hear a squeak from them.'

'When do you want me?'

'We'd like to leave about seven forty-five.'

'I'll be there.'

'You're an angel.'

'I shall need to ring my daughter-in-law. I intended to, later in the evening.'

'You do that. Our girls spend half the night chattering to their boyfriends. Frank sets it down to expenses.'

He chose a book, Angus Wilson's *The Old Men at the Zoo*, put last week's unread *Listener* with it, added, after he had buttoned his overcoat, Fodor's *Guide to Portugal*, and arrived five minutes early. Katherine Montgomerie in evening dress, with a small tiara, welcomed him in a hall ablaze with lights.

'They're all in bed,' she concluded after a fusillade of thanks.

'And asleep?'

'Jeremy's not. But he won't be long.'

She showed him the doors of children's rooms, led him round lounge and kitchen, told him he'd easily hear sounds from upstairs. The house was spick and span in the extreme with no signs of toys, mess, infantile occupation. Mr Montgomerie arrived in braces, asking his wife to supervise the tying of his bow. He thanked Murray in a superior, absent-minded fashion and muttered to himself all the way upstairs.

Katherine laughed, said her husband was invariably nervous before he had a speech to make, but had no doubt he'd outstrip the rest. 'I'd like to talk to you some time,' she concluded.

'What about?'

'One or two things. I wish he'd hurry up. I've been ready for a quarter of an hour, and there he is.'

She went upstairs for a last look at the children. Husband and wife came down resplendently together, lost none of their brilliance when she took to a fur cape and he to a white scarf and overcoat.

'The hotel number's by the phone in case of emergency.' She smiled, touched him on the arm. 'You've saved our bacon.'

'Enjoy yourselves.'

The foyer seemed suddenly empty as the door closed behind them, its amplitude needing bright figures and young voices. Murray essayed a turn about the ground floor: hall, kitchen, breakfast, dining, sitting rooms. He took to an armchair in the latter, door ajar as instructed, curtains drawn, furniture dark, chair covers and carpets freshly laundered, large abstract prints on the pale walls. This would photograph well with big spaces broken into interesting shapes, all highly desirable and expensive but nothing quite as expected. Katherine was, he decided, a lady of parts. The room was at exactly the right temperature. He opened *The Old Men at the Zoo*, and making himself read slowly admired Wilson's adjectives in the first paragraph, and then, like some examiner of quality, the verbs. In this edition, on this initial page, an apostrophe was missing, and it jarred. Had the writer deliberately abstained? Murray roused, looked further; there were at least three in occupation on page three. Oh dear. An error. He shifted on his hams in the comfort of the chair. What did it matter? It made no difficulties in understanding. And yet, yet. Annoyed and at the same time perversely pleased with himself, he read the paragraph out loud in penance, in enjoyment.

The door opened. A small figure in pyjamas faced him.

'Hello,' Murray said after an interval, heart thumping.

'Hello. What are you doing?'

'You're Jeremy, are you?'

'Yes. You're the baby-sitter.'

89

'That's so.' He could hear his father's Scottish intonation in the answer. 'Do you want anything?'

'I like to come down. I always come.'

'To see who's looking after you?'

'Yes. It's usually Marie. She gives me a biscuit.'

'After you've cleaned your teeth?'

The boy grinned wickedly at Murray's quickness on the moral uptake. He changed tack.

'She sometimes reads me a story.'

'I don't mind doing that. You fetch a story you'd like.' The child turned. 'Wait. One story, now. One. And short. I'm not reading *War and Peace* to you.'

Jeremy nodded with old-fashioned courtesy. Murray recalled the freshness of daffodil shoots on a wet morning of early spring.

When the boy returned, with one slim booklet about a fireman rescuing a fox terrier, a prosy saga interleaved with gaudy pictures, he clambered without hesitation on to Murray's knee to hear the recitation.

'Can you read?' Murray asked as Jeremy was settling.

'Yes, but not properly.'

'How old are you?'

'Six and a half.'

'It's a good thing to learn to read.' Murray pointed to Angus Wilson splayed open by his chair. Slowly, clearly, making sure the boy could see the illustrations all the time, allowing him to turn the pages, Murray began *Rex's Evening Out*.

'Thank you,' Jeremy said on completion. 'Would you read it again?'

'Just once, and then it's bed.'

The child snuggled briefly against him, but sat straighter for the performance. When it was over, he slipped to the floor, held out his hand and invited Murray to accompany him upstairs.

'Is that what Marie does?'

'Sometimes. She doesn't read as well as you.'

They went, Murray at the rear, up the stairs, into a room on the third storey, lighted from the corridor outside and by a small lamp on the dressing table.

'That's the toy cupboard,' Jeremy pointed, 'and that's the bookshelf.' He returned the story and clambered into bed.

'Do you have an animal or something?'

'No, thank you.'

But he clasped to his chin a small square of blue blanket. Murray made no remark on this.

'Do you have a kiss?'

'Yes.'

Murray bent, kissed the forehead.

'Do I leave the door open?'

'Yes, please.'

'Goodnight, then, Jeremy.'

'Goodnight, Mr Man.' The boy giggled.

Murray made his way out, spent time on Angus Wilson, on a book review that annoyed him, on a description of Eleanor's part of Portugal, on the ten o'clock television news, on a map. When the Montgomeries arrived at a few minutes after midnight he was back with *The Old Men*.

'Have they been good?'

'Perfect. Not a squeak.'

'Didn't Jeremy come down?'

'Yes, but the rest was silence.'

The three drank coffee in the kitchen. Mr Montgomerie did not settle, bundled himself restlessly about the place, twice out of the room.

'Good speech?' Murray asked in one of these absences.

'Marvellous. He really grips them.' She glanced about. 'He's not like himself.'

Murray, pleased by this striking young woman's compliment to her husband, nodded.

'It takes it out of him, you know. He won't sleep.'

They accompanied him to the front door. As he walked along the deserted street he wondered why he had seen so little of Jeremy and his siblings, who must play somewhere on the far side of the house. An interesting family, he concluded, with the powerful, nervous father, the social mother, the boy who knew what he wanted and how to achieve it; he ought to have been more interested. A taxi drew up. Murray stood back in the shadows as a young woman emerged, paid the driver, and clacked towards one of the houses opposite his own. The Whittles' daughter, he decided, but did not move out of hiding until the place was clear.

Mrs Montgomerie rang next morning to thank him again. By that time he had already telephoned Francesca to accept her invitation.

'I'm glad,' his daughter-in-law had said.

'I ought to have told you so last night. It would have saved money.'

'Why didn't you, then?'

'I'm a bit of an old curmudgeon.'

'Well, come and enjoy yourself.'

She put him on to Sebastian who said the right thing, but sounded, in spite of overt cheerfulness, preoccupied.

'I see you're busy. I'll ring off,' Murray said.

'I'm not. I'm kicking my heels.'

'Read a book, then.'

'Which one?'

'I can see I'll get no sense out of you. I'm delighted to come and stay. Tell Francesca so for me, will you? The words stick in my craw.'

His son gently ribbed him for a few minutes; neither was sorry to end the conversation. Sebastian's last words were: 'Are you in your dressing gown? No? Well, I am.'

Outside now it was cold, but northerly winds had blown the skies clear, and to observers behind glass in centrally heated rooms the sunshine sparkled. Murray took down his overcoat and made for Eleanor's flat. As he opened her door he heard the sound of a vacuum cleaner. He introduced himself to the cleaner.

'I'm coming in Tuesday and Friday, as usual,' the woman said. She'd be forty at the most, but wore a flowered, full apron as a badge of her work. 'I said to Mrs Franks that with nob'dy here it won't get di'ty, but she'd have me in. I worked for her when she lived in the big house.'

'There'd be a lot of work there,' he said.

'There was a lot of us to do it.'

'You liked it at Craigmore, then?'

'Work's work, wherever it is.'

As if in reparation of her rudeness, she offered him a cup of coffee, dark brown, strong as iron.

'I bring in my own milk.'

'I'm sorry,' he said, blowing and sipping, 'I didn't get your name.' She had not given it.

'Mrs Mills.' She made the announcement with paradoxically grudging aggression, perched on a chair arm, swinging laddered tights.

'You were working for Mrs Franks when her husband was alive?'

'Yes. Not that I seen much of him.' She gulped her coffee, wiped her lips with the back of her hand. 'And not that I liked what bit I did see.'

'I hardly knew him. We met just once or twice.'

'I could tell you something about him, if I had a mind. She's different altogether. A lady. Always was. How she could come to marry him, and stop married to him, I don't know. Money, I should think. He'd plenty o' that.'

'Was he generous with it?'

'Not to me, he wasn't. Not that he'd any reason.' She returned to her mug again. 'Couldn't keep his hands to himself, that was 'is trouble. My mother warned me, when I started. She worked there for years. That's how I got a job.' The woman spoke over the surface of her drink, from behind her hands. 'Put one, I know for certain, in the family way.'

'Did he look after her?'

'Well, she didn't seem short. She married a man from up our road.'

'And he accepted the baby?'

She looked over her cup with incredulity. 'I've no time to be sittin' here. I'll never get done.'

Mrs Mills leapt up; he said it would be sensible if he called in on a day other than those when she appeared. She mimed acceptance and he immediately quitted the flat.

As he sauntered along the street, wasting the newfound hour, he wondered why the woman had raked up this ancient gossip. He could find no sensible answer, but remembered Eleanor as a schoolgirl throwing herself at him sexually, unskilled but enthusiastic, trusting and abandoned. He had not come out of it well, he decided; she had loved him, in an exuberant desperation, until he had begun in the end to think seriously of her, but by then he had left it too late. He could not make head or tail of such behaviour now, but it was long enough ago and the hurt had all but healed.

At home, he began the chore, which lasted out the rest of the day, of writing his Christmas cards, adding a sentence of information here and there, asking a question, cursing the address book he had not kept up to date. Ironically smiling, he dispatched Christmas robins and no verses to Eleanor's empty flat.

9

On Christmas Eve he travelled by train to London.

Platforms and trains seemed only moderately crowded, and he was surprised at the strength of his pleasure when he saw a decorated tree at St Pancras; that partially quieted his dissatisfaction with the station bookshop which offered nothing of interest, whereas twenty or thirty years back he would have been hesitating between half a dozen paperbacks he wanted to read. Francesca had told him to make his way towards Bloomsbury by taxi, but he refused this expense, and after five minutes in the warm wind outside, he decided against walking along the Euston Road and returned to take his time on the Underground.

Francesca was waiting for him in the flat she and Sebastian had occupied for the three years of their marriage, and which they were considering ditching, now that her husband coined so much money, for a house in Chelsea, or Hampstead, or even in the country. Alistair mocked his son, taunting that they did not want to leave, that it was merely a lively topic of conversation, because the world had ideas about investment in bricks and mortar.

Sebastian had eyed his father with polite suspicion.

'We shall surprise you one of these days.'

Now pleased with himself that he had worked the lift, Alistair rang the doorbell.

Francesca kissed him.

'Why didn't you ring from the street?'

'I wanted to get here on my own.'

Her eyebrows met, as she made no attempt to relieve him of his suitcase.

'Come in, then, Mr Independence.'

They had a Christmas tree in the hall, hung with splinters of light, redolent still of the plantation.

She parked him in an armchair and, rushing out to the kitchen to make tea, told him to find himself a book.

'I should like to listen to the carols from King's College, if I may.'

'What time's that?' she called back.

'Three, is it?' He was surprised she did not know; she handed him the *Radio Times* in a binder.

The room was large, the wide window overlooking bare trees and the houses on the other side of the square. The chairs and settee were huge but there was space round them and the tables. Multicoloured books filled the long wall opposite the plainly beautiful hearth and mantel, ruined by a gas fire. A silver tree now occupied one corner, surrounded by gaudy packages.

Francesca brought in the tray, poured.

'Don't let me forget your carols.'

'I shan't. Don't you listen, then?'

'I've heard them. Aren't they on the telly sometimes? I shall have to go out. Last-minute shopping.' She laughed, perhaps at her own incompetence. 'We've one or two friends coming in this evening to keep you amused.'

'And out of bed.' He enjoyed playing the bear.

'No. Shan't be late. Kick them out at eleven. Sebastian will need to be up and about first thing tomorrow for the children's hospital. That's where he is this afternoon. Planning it all. He's a bit apprehensive, if you ask me.'

'He'll be all right.'

'He'll be very good. The authorities are making a change, putting a serious face on.'

'Is that sensible?'

'He won't be as well known as television comics, you know.'

She lifted her cup. In no hurry, she showed him his bedroom, instructed him how to turn on the radio in the music centre, how to work the volume control, and donned a coat with grey collar matching an astrakhan hat.

'Is it cold out?' she asked.

'No. Very mild.'

'I shall not be much more than an hour.'

She sang 'Good King Wenceslas' as she left, and returned

laden before the end of the carol service. At 5.30 Sebastian
arrived quietly, shook his father's hand and the three sat
down to thick pea soup, cold meats; all decided against trifle.
Sebastian spoke cheerfully about preparations for his visit to
the hospital; he would do his round with slightly older children while a knockabout comedian dealt with the youngest
patients.

'What's he like?' Francesca asked.

'Very good. And very funny. Marvellous eyebrow play.'

'You'll have your work cut out,' his wife warned. Alistair
tried to put a face to the comedian's name, and failed.

By the time the first guests appeared at eight, the younger
Murrays had bathed, changed clothes, had polished all
outward and visible signs of grace. Musak drifted from the
concealed speakers; bottles and glasses sparkled; voices and
laughter were loud. The men shook Alistair's hand; two called
him 'sir'. One shining wife, champagne glass in hand, asked
him if he lived in London. When he explained, she expressed
surprise saying she had thought Sebastian came from
Scotland.

'His grandparents did on both sides. So did his mother.'

'And you were, are, not a minister of the Church of
Scotland?'

'No. I was a director of education.'

She began to question him, with almost puppyish enthusiasm, how she should educate her sons, now aged two
and four. She and her husband had pretty well decided on
the private sector. When he replied that it depended where
she lived and what the neighbourhood comprehensive was
like, she asked where he had sent Sebastian.

'He won a scholarship to the High School.'

'That's a public school?'

'It is now. Direct grant, then.'

'Would you do the same now?'

She listened intently as he outlined what he wanted from
a school for a clever son. Were her sons bright? She thought
they were.

'Did you feel guilty?' she asked.

'Because I sent my son to a private school?'

'Because he had advantages that others were denied.'

'He won a scholarship from an authority primary school. His mother had been a teacher. We had plenty of books in the house. These were advantages, yes.'

They were joined by another couple who captured the young mother with chatter about a squash club. Within five minutes Alistair had been deserted, but he was glad to be relieved of the bright, banging voices.

Francesca, not content for him to sit on his own, wheeled up a second pair, this time a barrister and his wife. The man, sallow, neat, spoke with extreme clarity, as if the merest pleasantry carried a weight of legality; the woman, who looked older than her husband, had listened to the afternoon's broadcast from King's and criticized their style, asking for something more abrasive.

'You'll get that tonight,' her husband warned. They intended to go to midnight mass. 'I don't know why we bother,' the man said. 'We don't get on with the vicar, the choir's hopeless, and the organist's got a wooden leg. They keep pressing Sue to play for them, but she won't.'

Murray learned later that the wife had been a professional pianist.

'Why do you turn out?' he asked.

'We were both brought up in agnostic families. Mine was apathetic, Sue's more militant. Now we attend because friends do, not regularly; it's interesting. Pretty well as you might find a visit to the law courts worth your while now and again.'

'But,' Murray pressed, 'why don't you go to a place with good music or good preachers, if there are any?'

'You're right. That's what we ought to do.'

'Why don't we?' Susan asked.

'I wonder if it's because seeing something happen at its most humdrum gives you a better insight into its nature.'

'You're not interested in religion,' his wife said dismissively.

'You think not?'

'Well, are you?'

'I'd say so.'

'You surprise me.'

They laughed together as if this small exchange had been practised, burnished so that its significance lay in the performance.

'An interesting couple,' he told Francesca next morning.

'Very bright,' she said. 'He was an academic for a bit, but he's making a great deal of money now. Took silk a year or two back.'

'Will he be a judge?'

'Sebastian thinks he's doing too well for that. Financially.'

'He's not a marvellous talker.'

'No, but utterly clear. As though he knows what you are thinking as well as his own mind. He's very incisive in the courts, and weighty, and quick. He doesn't waste a word.'

'And would you say he was interested in religion?' On Francesca's startled expression, he recounted the conversation. She considered it.

'He'd see the advantages of making an occasional appearance in church. And Sue's very ambitious for him.'

During the evening all the guests paid their respects to Murray. No one drank heavily; within his earshot people discussed an exhibition of photographs, a television serial, a film he had not heard of, and the imminent death of a politician–journalist. Again Murray had not realized that the man was ill. Everyone relaxed, but within limits of decorum. It seemed something like a stage play. By ten minutes past eleven the last guest had gone, and the glasses collected and stacked in the washing-up machine. Sebastian disappeared for bed.

Francesca brought her father-in-law in a pot of tea just after eight next morning, telling him not to hurry. At a quarter to nine Sebastian poked in his head to wish his father a happy Christmas, and said he was just leaving.

'I'll watch you.'

'Good.'

'Will you be back for lunch?'

'Late lunch.'

His son seemed twice mansize.

After breakfast Francesca asked what he wanted to do, and he decided on a walk if it kept fine.

'You're in for cold lunch, except for Christmas pudding and the veg, so I'll come with you.' They made speed round empty streets, took a turn outside Regent's Park, remarking on the weather which was grey and clement. Francesca stepped out in a lively fashion, sometimes talking, but not invariably. They met no one they knew. When they arrived back her cheeks were healthily pink.

'Time for coffee before television,' she said, pulling off her coat with elegant energy. Alistair occupied himself with coffee pot and china while she bustled about in the kitchen.

'Don't you move,' she called back at an offer of help. 'Just settle yourself down to watch your son.' Time ticked slowly on. Francesca joined him, elated, on the edge of her chair.

Alistair sat ill at ease, robbed of his breath until the programme began, and then he lost himself.

Sebastian, sober-witted, coaxed talk from the children. The comedian was droll, sympathetic, exploiting the situation, while Sebastian acted as a catalyst. The patients, who had no idea who this quiet man was except that he had connections with omnipotent television, came out with their stories; one boy, in care now that his family had been wiped out in a fire, had fallen three days before Christmas in front of a car and broken both his legs. He spoke with cheerful stoicism. A girl, disease unnamed, refused to call out greetings to her home, but at the last minute summoned Sebastian back so that she could whisper a message. He returned and kissed her; she picked up and hugged a doll, and there existed peace on earth to men of goodwill. Alistair brushed off a tear; Francesca glanced up and away. A group of nurses sang, 'O little town of Bethlehem', the comedian fell beautifully flat on his face under the eyes of an unsmiling baby; the matron, Sebastian, the comic and four small girls gathered arms full of super-balloons to release them in front of a Christmas tree. It looked perfect, so that viewers believed they had donated and shared the Christmas cheer.

'Do they rehearse all this?' Alistair asked when the hour was over.

'To some extent. They must. But you can never be sure with children what they'll do and say next.'

'Sebastian seemed at home.'

'Yes, he just about got it right.'

'He likes children?'

'Knowing next to nothing about them, yes.'

'Do you ever think of having a family?'

'You shouldn't be asking questions like that, now, should you?' She held a hand up prettily to check his answer. 'We think about it. Inconclusively. Does that disappoint you?'

'You're a bit of a terror, young woman.'

They cleared the coffee cups, retired to the kitchen, and were tasting dry sherry when Sebastian returned.

'What was it like?' Sebastian asked, abashed.

'Superb. I felt like crying.'

Alistair nodded, throat full, He put out his hand to his son. Over lunch, he asked Sebastian if he had been moved.

'You're too busy. I was. The kids can dart like quicksilver, or refuse to budge. But the cameramen we had are out-standing. Jerry O'Brien doesn't miss a trick. He reads what's coming next. I only hope Tom picked the right pictures. Was Les funny?'

'Very. But within reason. And you were just right, darling.'

'Only just?' He was pleased now.

They ate without speed; he told them that the little girl who at first would not wish her family Merry Christmas would die inside a year.

'Does she know that?' Alistair asked.

'God knows. She wanted to be on telly. So they said.'

The telephone rang at the end of the meal. Sebastian dashed out. The others waited in silence.

'I hope,' Francesca said soberly, 'it's somebody to tell him how good he was. He's jumpy if they don't. Wonders where he's slipped up.'

'I'd have thought he'd more self-confidence than that.'

'Yes, and no. His nervousness makes him. He's very gifted.'

She broke off as he returned, much at ease.

'Lydia. To say how much she enjoyed it. She cried and her children laughed at her.'

Lydia Powys, the actress, Francesca explained, a new

101

friend. All afternoon the telephone interrupted their present-giving and receiving, their comatose comfort, the exchanges after each congratulatory call. Alistair instructed himself that he would never have wasted any part of Christmas Day ringing up friends on such flimsy pretexts. This clever son of his had joined a society which kept itself stable only by constant resort to mutual admiration.

At 5.30 Sebastian burst in to ask if they'd like to call round at the Barclays' later in the evening.

'Who'll be there?' Francesca.

'Don't know. I'll make inquiries for you. We can always come away.'

'Would you like to go?' she asked Alistair. 'To see the rich?'

'That's kind of you.'

Sebastian had already swept through the door to accept. Francesca complained that it meant she would have to dress up, but he could tell she was pleased.

'You men don't know how lucky you are. As long as your shirt's clean, that'll do.'

'Don't tell your husband.'

'Tell him what?' Sebastian asked, also delighted. They explained, and Seb extemporized for them a paragraph or two on a man's art of clothing himself inside strict limits, as opposed to the delicious licence allowed to women. It was well done; sixty years back it would have made a brilliant literary essay: how high wit is mirrored in small by the way we patronize the rag trade.

Francis Barclay owned, managed and sold property and lived in a large house in Highgate where a dozen people talked in the great spaces of his drawing room. Alistair was installed in an armchair, against his will, for there he felt cut off from the company. At least for a time he would have liked to stand, but both host and hostess had insisted. Sarah Barclay was small, dressed in tropical colours, a peacock; she made a fuss of Murray, congratulating him on Sebastian's performance that morning which she had not seen herself, but which her children, one at Oxford, one at school, and both hard-boiled, had pronounced worth the hour spent on it. Alistair asked if her guests were mainly television people, and at that Mrs Barclay scrutinized her guests as if she were uncertain who had been invited. He found the performance ridiculous; she peered to satisfy some craving on her part for the dramatic. In the end she said that no one but Sebby worked on TV.

She pointed out a man from the Foreign Office, a business executive of the Murdoch papers, a Cambridge professor, her cousin, a millionaire supermarket owner, all with wives talking to others' husbands. Conversation was sober, even dull; Murray wondered if the very successful spent their spare time being or acting out mediocrity.

Sebastian nodded solemnly at conversation from a young woman in glasses; Francesca in a group of three seemed more animated.

'What do you think of it all?'

A stocky young man with hair plastered down, and light, overlarge horn-rimmed spectacles, presented himself at Alistair's chair. Murray tried to guess his age; he looked like a schoolmaster, willing to lay down the law on entropy, *The Times* crossword or England's chances in the Calcutta Cup, but not old, merely old-fashioned.

'This suits me,' Murray answered.

'Good, good. In what way?'

'It's not noisy. People have half a chance of hearing what's said. When one gets to my age one finds it increasingly difficult to distinguish between conversation, or commentary on the television, and background noise or even music.'

'Is that so? I never thought of that.' The man blew his nose, straightened his back, and patted the oiled fair hair. 'My name's Mark Lambley.'

'Alistair Murray.' He tried, managed, to rise with difficulty from his chair, held out a hand. 'Sebastian Murray's father.'

They shook hands.

'You're staying with them over Christmas?' Lord Lambley said.

'I am. They thought I should.'

'And you're enjoying it?'

'Oh, yes. They try to take me out of myself.'

'I see. And that's good, is it?'

Francesca had spoken about Lambley once or twice; he was a tragic figure, she said. He owned estates in Northumberland and the West Country; the sixth baron, he had qualified as a barrister, did not practise now but regularly attended the Lords where he had won a name as a sensible committee man. Three years before he had been involved in a motorway accident in which his wife and his heir had been killed, together with a family of five in the other car. He had crossed the reservation at high speed, in a place without a barrier. The police thought that he must have dropped asleep, a quite unaccountable lapse on his part, for he drove as he did everything else, neatly, unshowily, with full control. When he came round after the accident with bruises, cracked ribs and superficial head injuries, he remembered nothing and the death of the seven people broken to him struck him senseless again.

Now the man stood stiffly, saying his piece, wine glass in hand. He lived within five minutes' walk of the Barclays, had been out to a hotel for Christmas lunch having spent the morning in bed.

'Is that usual?'

'No. I'm an early riser. But I've no family and no commitments.'

'So you didn't see Sebastian's programme this morning?'

Lambley shook his head, in a daze. As Alistair described it, he could not be sure that the other was listening.

'I don't patronize the box much, except late at night.'

'Sebastian and Francesca hardly watch it at all. It surprises me. I mean, it's his living.'

Lambley asked about Murray's work, then questioned him closely on education. This stiff, little man with his plummy voice, his set of head, was intelligent. Education, he thought, was one of the subjects they could treat adequately in the Lords; they had time to examine all the prejudices and old wives' tales which underlay the simplest discussion of any educational change. What did Alistair think of the Burt scandal? Was there any truth in his views of inherited intelligence? The pair of them grew animated; Alistair wished he had kept his reading up. Lambley pressed, a good man.

Half an hour, threequarters passed quickly. Lord Lambley separated by crossexamination anecdote from ascertainable fact; Alistair level with him, suggested new approaches, criticized current proposals, showed how money could be saved, roughed up the government. He felt on top form, with the energy and grasp he remembered from the days of his monthly strategy meetings with his subordinates. He and Lambley together could make substantial progress.

Francesca came across, but listening for five minutes made no attempt to intervene. The host silently filled their glasses, and left them alone. Alistair Murray, MA, MEd, was a young man again, on the watch to kill catchpenny schemes or blast election-winning slogans, willing to wound, the expert, tough in argument, uninhibited in thought, but matching his language to a rigour that demanded complete absorption from the listener.

Lord Lambley, Francesca reported in a letter, had said it was the best hour he'd spent for months, that he'd learnt more than from days with official reports, civil servants, union worthies. 'That's where real knowledge is, and too often hidden, with the big provincial authorities, when the political in-fighting is not so wild it stops all sense, and where schemes are large enough to attract the occasional talented man, such as your father-in-law. I wished I'd met him before when he was in the job. It's the fuddy-duddies or the pouter pigeons I come across far too frequently.'

After the conversation, Murray exhausted, found an armchair near enough to a conversational group to feign interest. He stared at his drink, and, he was uncertain, may have dropped off for a short doze. Nobody seemed to have noticed, and when he came round the cluster knot nearby had enlarged itself. A bearded man, later discovered to be an accountant, claimed that the greatest poetry 'teetered on a narrow ledge between high rhetoric and disaster'. Rhetoric declared itself, excluded itself by its nature, vocabulary, syntax from the perfection of great verse; he instanced Shakespeare and Yeats. A poet and publisher sourly said it was impossible to generalize. Some magnificent poetry was simple, without the formality of rhetoric, even close to the order of prose.

'I can't think of any,' said the accountant.

' "Since there's no help, come, let us kiss and part." '

'Not my idea of the greatest poetry.'

They argued, quoting Milton and Pope. One young woman, auburn-haired, suddenly reeled off a passage of Racine, without embarrassment, not raising her voice, but silencing the rest. She held her hands with fingers out straight and spread harshly wide. When she had finished, she stepped back, literally, from their congratulatory noises, explaining that if they had been educated in France they too would have heads full of Alexandrines.

The argument about poetry disappeared; groups broke and re-formed. Francesca swooped from time to time on Alistair to check health and spirits, then darted away. At about 10.30 they were all shunted off to eat in another room; the buffet supper laid out would have fed the five thousand.

By the time, well past midnight, that guests prepared to leave, Murray almost staggered into his overcoat, and slept most of the few minutes in the car. He made straight for bed, but woke after a short nap, excited, taken out of himself. This dozen, fifteen people, not spending Christmas Day at home, and yet not dining out, had talked of poets, computers, scientific theory, the theatre, judgments in law courts, a scandal, a death with polished zest. He had been amazed how, once they had broken from one cluster, they re-formed, stumbled on their next subject, and then immediately distinguished themselves. It seemed a different world from his own, with no extremes, undrunk, the real interest implicit in the thrust and counterthrust of speech. And in the middle of it all, stubby Lord Lambley, like a well-dressed schoolmaster, crossexamining him with such aplomb that the old Murray, the A. S. McM. Murray, Director of Education, resurrected himself, became a power in the land.

It was a different society from any he had met. True, Francesca had hinted to him that all they bothered with was gossip about people they knew but who had not been invited. That was not so. People seemed knowledgeable, erudite even.

Alistair tried to recall, but could not, who had outlined C. S. Lewis's poem about Simon Magus finding Helen of Troy a housewife in Antioch and restoring her lost memory. Had she, did he say, been taken up to her father, Zeus? He could not remember, nor whether the poem had been written, or published, whether it was a legend from antiquity or a modern parable. And yet this paragraph of narrative had transported him into a zone beyond his so that he had felt as he'd felt now and then as a schoolboy, on the brink of some novelty beyond the temporal, near some life-lifting, -shifting strait of discovery. He had been too clever, crafty, cautious or worldly as a grown man at his work; the minor brilliances, glimpses into the ineffable, had been, properly, lost. They would have been useless, even though he never in the rough-and-tumble of the pragmatic lost his idealism, his puritanical foundation for his many practicalities.

Alistair turned, tossed.

These were people who earned their living as he had done, spent the majority of each day to provide a roof, Westmorland slates perhaps, for the family, fine feathers for the beautiful wives, expensive schools for the children, cars, holidays and villas abroad, and yet, on Christmas Day, without unduly raising their voices, and presumably without preparation, they had worked this little miracle, allowing him back to the earth-dispelling hints he had received as a child, and had childishly put aside or found wanting, or in adulthood nonexistent.

It could not have been alcohol. He had drunk one gin and two American dry gingers. They, too, these smart men, these dazzling women, had been unexpectedly temperate, hardly touching their glasses of wine. It kept him awake until past three o'clock, and then sleep was broken by unpleasant bright dreams.

In the mild afternoon of Boxing Day the three took a walk round the streets, called in on an elderly couple, who crowed delight to see them. They stayed for threequarters of an hour, when Francesca withdrew her men. The retreat surprised; conversation and laughter were flying, but when the visitors were in the street, she explained that it would have taken too much out of the old people.

'Half an hour's long enough. We gave them the extra quarter for Christmas. They pay for too much excitement.'

Both the old people had draped tartan rugs over their knees in a room that had seemed overheated. The furniture, admirable early nineteenth-century, was wonderfully preserved, polished; drink abounded, though the hosts did not partake of it. The couple looked well, but frail, with skin almost transparent and hands bony.

'How old are they?' Murray asked. They had rushed at the last minute into the visit without explanations.

'Let's drop in on the Generals,' Francesca had said, and husband and wife had laughed out loud as they retraced steps. 'They're called Fletcher, really,' she'd instructed her father-in-law. 'He's a retired general, and she's a novelist. They're lovely.'

Now back in the street she answered Murray. The old man was eighty-eight, and, Francesca was not sure, no one dare mention it, his wife, Antonia even older.

'Does she write now?'

'No. Her last book was published before the war.'

'I've never heard of her.'

'One, *Rain in the Pyrenees*, had quite a vogue. You might still find a copy in a second-hand bookshop. She had a great deal of money.'

'From writing?'

'No. From her family. But she knew Lawrence and Frieda.'

'Does she talk about that?'

'She hardly says a word, as you noticed. Neither of them do. But, yes, she'll come out with a thing or two. She actually saw him writing.'

'In England?'

'I'm not sure. I think they first met in Germany, before the fourteen-eighteen war, when she was only a girl. The family travelled a good deal.'

'When did she marry?'

'In the thirties. She'd be quite old. They had one son. He took us to see them in the first place. He's a friend of Sebastian's. He's a linguist. Teaches Hungarian at London University. Rum and clever. Did you notice their Cézanne?'

'I didn't.'

The room had been dark, not uncomfortably so, and two lamps had been lit above the mantelpiece, but pictures were mere rectangles of shadow. He had noticed that they had pictures, but winter afternoon light, and that partially blocked by heavy red velvet curtains, does nothing even for masterpieces.

Murray, on his return home, often thought over this visit. The old people, who did not move from their chairs once the visitors were inside, were clearly fond of Francesca and Sebastian, who both talked vying with each other about the television appearance on Christmas Day, the Generals had not seen it, the visit to the Barclays (Antonia knew his mother), their Christmas presents, their recent late nights. Murray was encouraged by Francesca to give his account of the murder outside his front gate; it hardly seemed suitable, but she was importunate, and the eyes of the Fletchers were bright; their heads nodded. Though they said nothing, they wanted more, and in bloody detail. Francesca prompted him. The inspector who knew the murderer made an appreciated appearance.

In this low key it seemed exciting, excitable, even feverish on recall.

The threequarters of an hour had passed like lightning, so that when Francesca issued marching orders Murray needed to empty an almost full glass. The Fletchers struggled to their feet, shook hands, their faces wrinkled into smiles.

'Francesca comes every week,' Lady Fletcher whispered. 'She's such a good girl. We thought as it was Christmas, she might not have time. . . .' The old voice trickled dryly away.

'Do they ever go out?' Murray asked in the street.

'To the chiropodist, that sort of thing.'

'Not to see their son?'

'No. He visits them regularly. We can't get them to visit us. All they need is a taxi; it would only take five minutes, but they won't.'

'Are stairs and lifts beyond them?'

'No. Not if they made up their minds.'

'They've both had very exciting lives, very full,' Sebastian said. 'They've travelled all over the world, had friends everywhere.'

'And that suffices?' Alistair surprised himself with the word, lifted from one of his father's sermons.

'I doubt that,' Francesca answered. 'They're both very tired. Everything's too much for them. They just want to sit and be looked after and keep out of pain.'

'Old people quarrel sometimes,' Sebastian said. 'Even take to blows.'

'I think they're past that.'

'Can you get them to talk? About Lawrence, for instance?'

'Not really. If you ask questions, they understand you perfectly well, you saw that, and they'll answer "yes" and "no", but I'm never sure if I'm asking the right questions. Sebastian tried to talk to them once about Mountbatten, they knew him well, but really he got nowhere. One needs the qualifications and riders and detail. That's the beauty of conversation. You don't get it.'

'Were they good talkers? They must have been?'

'I imagine so. But . . . I don't know. William, their son, hardly knew them when he was a boy. Sir Frederick was away at the war, and Antonia was never still, it seems. Now they sit all day like firedogs. They're not even hungry; that's why they're so thin.'

'They were really pleased to see you,' Alistair said.

'I don't know why. We must upset routine. It's a shame.'

'It could be worse,' Sebastian said. 'They're rich enough to keep a housekeeper and her husband living in. Otherwise it would be a nursing home.'

Francesca shook her head, and directed them along the streets at a cracking pace. Once back in the flat, when she had gone to make tea, Sebastian spoke solemnly.

'I admire her for going. She doesn't like it. It leaves her thinking that life's meaningless.'

'And it isn't?' Mischievously.

'It doesn't do to think so at her age.'

'She worked really hard at conversation with them.'

'It's like painting a picture for somebody nearly blind. You need to lay the colours on thick.'

'Put me in a home.'

'Eh?'

'When I'm past it.'

Sebastian saluted comically. 'I'll see to it personally, guv'nor.'

Lady Fletcher telephoned that evening to say how much she had enjoyed the visit and meeting Francesca's father-in-law. Lord Lambley also rang with the details of a piece of research on dyslexia he thought Alistair might like to read. It had been a privilege to meet Murray.

'I hope I'm as sharp and energetic when I'm his age,' he said. 'He really made me aware of my shortcomings.'

'I didn't know you had any.' Fran laughed at his lordship. Alistair stayed one more day, left for home in the morning soon after Sebastian had returned to work. He refused to allow Francesca to drive him to the station.

'I shall miss you,' she said.

He wondered whether to believe her.

10

Alistair Murray back at home spent a good part of his first morning at his desk writing to those to whom he had not sent Christmas cards. At eleven o'clock he was interrupted, to his delight, by the telephone and Eleanor.

'Where are you ringing from?'

'Home.'

'Not Portugal?'

She had returned yesterday; in due course she would tell him why. He invited her round that afternoon.

When she arrived she seemed on edge, and showed this, examining his rooms to see whether he had made any attempt to dust them. She accepted a cup of China tea.

'I'm glad to be back,' she announced.

'Were you homesick, then?'

'I was not.' She looked out through his window to the grey flatness of the sky, the darkness of branches, the dullness of evergreens. 'Not for this.' She replaced her cup and slightly reorganized her sitting.

'Come on,' he teased. 'You're making me curious.'

'Have you ever watched films on late-night television?' she asked, matching him in social facetiousness. He gave no answer. 'They always seem to be set in most beautiful surroundings, and you know quite well something horrible's about to happen. That's how I felt.' She looked up brightly. 'Except it wasn't particularly beautiful.'

'But warm.'

'Warmer than it is here. Certainly.' She looked about; judging perhaps the straightness of his pictures or the state of his window glass. 'The couple I was staying with were old friends. He was a business associate of Henry. They invited me over for Christmas, oh, last September.'

'You've stayed there before?'

112

'Yes.' She was in no hurry, reaching out for her cup, stirring sugarless tea. 'They were in a state. Their name is Mayor; he's in his early seventies, she a bit younger and they've been married for forty-odd years. Now they can't bear the sight of each other.'

'Was this sudden?'

'Comparatively. They've always seemed close. Devoted, you could say. I mean, I don't know. It's over a year since I saw much of them, and that wasn't for long.'

'Had they invited you over, do you think, because of this development?' he asked.

'It did occur to me. But they didn't say so. She wrote to ask me. I doubt if they'd agree to anything now. A daughter and her husband were going to be there, but something happened to prevent them.'

The pair sat quietly until Alistair noticed with relief that her cup was empty, at which he eased himself out of his chair. She allowed the replenishment, but was in no hurry to begin again. She squinted at the nearest row of books as if it were important that she read the titles on the spines.

'What form did their disagreement take?' he asked in the end. 'I mean, was it obvious?'

'From the first minute.'

'How?'

'They quarrelled, and complained, about the slightest thing. As soon as I sat down to lunch Charles said, "There's a damn great stain on this cloth." And Miriam said, "What do you expect, with your dirty habits?" And nastily. That could have been friendly, joking, but it wasn't. And they'd ignore each other. Refuse to pass the salt. Or contradict, for no good reason. And they were rude. He called her a silly cow before I'd been in the house ten minutes.'

'And this isn't like him?'

'I was never very fond of Charles. What he wanted came first. He was very selfish. But she didn't seem to mind, or notice.'

'But she does now?'

Eleanor knitted her brows in suspicion. 'She seemed uncomfortable, uncertain. Not that she said anything outright to me, but I felt she was on the edge of confession. I thought, for instance, several times she'd been crying.'

'Are they ill?'

'I wondered about that, and asked. They say not. They're fine, given their age.'

'Financially.'

'Well off. Charles made a packet, and they've never thrown it away.'

'Dying?'

'What do you mean?' Eleanor sounded startled.

'They realize they're getting on, that life won't last much longer.'

'Do you ever feel like that?' she asked.

'Yes.' Alistair stroked his chin. 'I think back twenty-five years, and it seems hardly any time. In another twenty-five I'll be ninety.'

They paused. She had put her empty cup away from her, and sat, schoolgirlishly, with her hands between her knees, rucking her dress.

'I don't know what it was. I didn't know whether to stay or come home. I thought perhaps they wanted to be rid of me, that having visitors upset them. They had plenty of local help. I don't know. It baffled me.'

'What made you decide to leave?'

'It was so unpleasant. I also thought it might press Miriam into saying something, but it didn't. I just made my excuses and they offered token resistance, and that was that. But I keep worrying that I shall hear something horrible. That isn't like me.'

He looked her in the eye.

'You came to see me because . . .' he began.

'Oh, yes, yes, yes. But I get over things.'

'You've not had long to recover in this case.'

'Did your father talk like this to people?'

'Like what?'

'Cold. Get your story straight. Be consistent. Don't waste my time.'

'Is that how I seem?'

She did not answer but reached for her cup.

114

'Is there more tea?'

'I'll make some fresh.'

'No. If there's any left, I'll . . . that'll do.'

He poured, passed the cup over.

'You think I'm unsympathetic?' Alistair asked.

'Not exactly. You sound like a parson. That's why I asked you. No, that's not right. More like somebody trying to deal gently with an unreasonable child, but who knows it will all end with a smacked bottom.'

'Uhhm.'

They sat silent again, not comfortably, shifting on their hams, without giving the impression of moving.

'You don't think I'm being silly, do you?'

'No. You seem an eminently sensible woman to me. On that evening you first came in, it was not unreasonable to try for help. No. I can't say anything here because I know so little about your friends. It could be that they had heard bad news, about their health, or their investments, didn't want to spoil your stay with them, but couldn't cover their disappointment, or fear, and didn't realize how uncomfortable it made you. Or were so worried they didn't much care. On the other hand it may have been some minor disappointment, such as their daughter's non-appearance. Is she the only child?'

'No. Two sons. Both married, with families.' Eleanor straightened herself. 'You don't think it was me, Alistair, reading into it something that wasn't there?'

'Why should you do that?'

'Because I'm unstable myself?'

'Are you?'

'I don't think so. But that doesn't mean anything, does it? I wouldn't know.'

'Well.' The long-drawn-out word hung between them. Eleanor straightened herself, smiled much at ease, as if pleased by his puzzlement.

'Is there anything I can do, do you think?'

'Ring them up. To thank them for their hospitality. Or have you done that?'

'No. I intended to write this week. But I suppose I could. That's a good idea.'

115

'It's no use getting in touch with the daughter, is it?'

'I hardly know her,' Eleanor answered, 'and in any case I don't want to upset her for something that may be entirely my fault.'

'Yes, I see. How well do you know the Mayors?'

'They've been acquaintances for years.' Suddenly her face lit up. 'He once made a pass at me.'

'Go on.'

'Nothing to go on with. I wasn't very keen on him before. It means nothing now. He's probably forgotten. He couldn't keep his hands to himself.'

'It wasn't serious?'

'On neither part. He was a ladies' man, always trying it on. Henry was rather like that.' She offered the information without embarrassment. 'But thanks, Alistair. You've told me what to do, and I'll do it. I ought to have thought of it myself.'

She did not stay much longer, hugged him as she left, and hurried out, saying she felt relieved, would not now neglect things. He watched her progress towards the garden gate, and turned away puzzled, uncertain of her motive, wishing he had solved the problem there and then, if it existed. Indoors he sat himself at his piano, leafing over music before he started on the Italian Concerto. He did not play well this morning, and resolved to spend some hours of careful practice. Repeating an awkward phrase, twice making a hash of it, he stood angrily and walked about the house, straightening pictures, poking at books.

He heard nothing of Eleanor for a week, and that seemed typical of the woman. She arrived in crisis and then silence followed, as if the rehearsing of her problem had eliminated it. January under high pressure was frosty with fog, outlining the trees and bushes in the garden with white rime. Mrs Montgomerie invited herself over one morning to question him furiously about schools for her children; she sounded flustered and angry because, he guessed, she would feel guilty if she decided to withdraw her children from state schools, but was quite determined that she'd pay if that procured the best education. She harboured no doubts about the brightness of her children.

'What does your husband say?' Alistair asked.

'He won't give his mind to it. He thinks if they've anything about them, they'll make their way in the world.'

'And you don't?'

'No. Do you?'

There was something rugged about Mrs Montgomerie, for all her quick attractiveness. Alistair, reminded of his wife Janet, who never wavered once she'd made her mind up, apologized for his own indecision.

'I can't give you any real answers,' he said. 'It depends on the children.'

The house seemed quiet on her departure; she had spoken strongly, as if she stamped her foot, and he felt slightly uneasy.

In the same foggy week he sent his regrets to the Education Office at County Hall, claiming he was not well enough to attend a party on the retirement of an inspector he had appointed. He wrote a letter to the man, but knew quite well that health had nothing to do with his absence from the junketing: he hated the idea of being a nobody, or patronized or ignored in the very places he associated with his days of power. He tried to laugh at himself, but could not. He missed the busy life still, had not replaced it. His books, his music were no surrogates; neither could he live through his son's success. With decent weather he could just fill in his days, pottering in the garden, the streets, at the stove, the keyboard. Perhaps he ought to travel; he'd consult Eleanor about that. Twice a week he went to the public library, though a good half of the books on his shelves remained unread.

He stood at his front door on Saturday morning, listening to two women who tried to convince him that the world approached its violent end. They flashed texts at him, or the shorthand equivalent, John 1, 14, as if they were arguing with colleagues equally learned in biblical lore. The roofs of the houses on the other side of the road could barely be seen in the grey murk. The tips of the women's noses were red with cold, and their cheeks pinched. The older of the two wore fingerless mittens as if to make access to the soft-bound Bible she held in front of her chest easier. The coats and hats were not new; they themselves, as one fiddled in her pocket for a handkerchief to wipe the dewdrop from her nose, were unattractive, not well educated, but polite and perseverant, unabashed, not to be moved, fanatics by choice if not by nature. He envied them.

'I think you are wasting your time on me,' he told them.

'The Bible tells us to go out into the highways and hedges and compel them to come in.'

The pair set off into a rigmarole about the end of the world, the atom bomb, Armageddon, with quotations from the Book of Revelations in which the kings of the earth and the great men and the rich men, and the chief captains, and every bondman, and every free man hid themselves in the dens and in the rocks of the mountains.

Alistair cut them short, brusquely offered to buy their two magazines, but said he would not read them. He could not resist asking if they minded. They did not; they had obeyed their Lord. With short politeness, he closed his door, but rushed to the window to see the women walk the garden path, carefully latch his gate, and then stand in the street in earnest parley with another of their associates, a man in a brown trilby.

On a morning like this he ought to have invited them at least into the hall, but feared he would never have got rid of them. Did they pause from missionary duty to take lunch? Or did these apostles combine fasting with proselytization? Sometimes, he remembered, they took their children round with them, ever encouraging their offspring to speak peace unto the heathen. 'Out of the mouth of very babes and suck-lings,' he quoted against himself. Was that from the Psalms? He had a vague recollection of learning it in elementary school. His vagueness annoyed him; he'd consult one of his father's concordances. His father would have had no trouble with these back-door prophets, would have matched them text for text, and with Greek and Hebrew for good measure. But why should he, Alistair, feel annoyed that he could not

118

blister these women with his own certainties of faith or scholarship.

He telephoned Eleanor, made contact with her help, Mrs Mills.

'She's out.'

'For long?'

'She won't be back for lunch, she said that. I shall be away after two.'

Alistair was about to ring off, when the woman said, 'She's not been very well. You know that, don't you?'

'No, I didn't. I saw her, oh, just over a week ago, and she didn't say anything.'

'Perhaps she didn't want you to know.'

'What's wrong with her?'

'Listen, Mr Murray, if she didn't see fit to tell you, it's not my place to do so.'

'I see.'

He thanked her. For nothing. Later in the afternoon he contacted Eleanor herself.

'You're not very well, I hear?' he asked.

'No.' She posed no further queries.

'What's wrong?'

'Heart. Angina.'

'Is this new?'

'No. I've had it for some time, but it's been worse recently.'

'Can they do anything about it?'

'I carry my tablets. If I get the pain, I sit down. It's a warning, and I reach for my trinitrin.' She laughed. 'It's a disease of middle-aged men and old people.'

'What are you doing with it, then?'

She did not answer; he felt he had erred.

'Are you worried?' he asked.

'Not unduly.'

'Well, I am.'

She made no demur when he invited himself round to see her later that evening, even sounding amused.

'I'm not likely to die,' she said.

His words of comfort bumbled, so that he felt ashamed.

Alistair dressed carefully, as a bridegroom coming out of

119

his chamber he told himself, half remembering another psalm from his youth, but rang Eleanor's bell in uncertainty. She put him immediately at his ease. The room was warm, bright, comfortably pretty as money could make it; Janet, his own wife, would not have countenanced such fancywork. Eleanor had been reading, the book lay open, but he could not make out its title. She smiled, moved quickly and efficiently, poured drinks for them both and began to tell him how well she felt. Relieved, and in return, he tried to explain or account for his distressed shock at Mrs Mills's blunt sentences. Eleanor interrupted.

'She loves to be the bearer of bad tidings.'

Briefly Eleanor outlined the progress of her illness, explained laughingly that she did not venture out into north-east winds or run upstairs, always had tablets handy; she produced a phial from a small bag in her chair, like a conjurer.

'Can they do anything about the condition?' he pressed.

'Don't tell me that you haven't looked it up in Black or Wingate?' He had. In both. Her sharpness reassured him. Her doctor had spoken of surgical advances, but she was not keen, and the GP, though optimistically expansive, had been vague. She crossed her ankles elegantly, informing him that 'atheroma' was the Greek word for porridge.

'And does that comfort you?' he snapped.

'Sorry, I'm sure.' She adopted stage vulgarity. 'Scholarship always butters your parsnips, in my book.'

They talked for an hour, then drank coffee, and at nine o'clock she gave him his marching orders.

'I'm going away again tomorrow, so it's early to bed.'

He took her in his arms, but when she had kissed him, she pushed him away.

'Remember my delicate state of health,' she said. She seemed excited, in a way he could not understand, like a daredevil rider shouting as he rounded a dangerous corner.

'Where are you going this time?'

'Bournemouth.' She laughed. 'The refuge of the aged. The northeasterly's temperate there.'

As he put on his topcoat, disappointed to be bundled out, he asked about her friends in Portugal.

'Did you ring them up?'

'No.'

'I thought you were worried. Have you heard from them?'

'No.' Nonchalant.

'But you . . .?'

She stopped him by turning her back, almost rudely, and walking two or three paces towards the door.

'You take these things too seriously, Alistair. It was just a mood on my part. You've lived too long on your own.'

She had opened the door, switching on the lanterns outside on the patio.

'I'm sorry,' he said.

Eleanor stood back, but near the edge of the door, making it difficult for him to lean over and kiss her. He tried; his lips made contact with the parting in her hair, and she withdrew no farther.

'I'll send you a comic postcard,' she promised facetiously.

'Look after yourself.'

'I'll do my best.'

He stood outside, in the chilling fog, dismissed.

11

The dismissal was confirmed a week later.

Raw weather, with wet snow, drizzle, unbroken grey skies, daylight half darkness piled misery over slimy earth, branches constantly lined with raindrops, wet roofs, clogged or swirling gutters.

Eleanor Franks sent him, inside a envelope, a picture card, a Tate gallery reproduction, pleasant piece of Victoriana, a young woman shelling peas in a yard at the back of her kitchen. A waterbutt swelled in an alcove beside a brush; the sill of a low window, not a foot from the ground, was crowded with six potted plants. Frederick Walker, *The Housewife*, 1871. Jugs and plates and creeping ivy.

Her message wasted no time. He would, she hoped, be pleased to learn her news. She was engaged to be married. David was an old friend. She had to tell him first, but he'd hear the details on her return next week. Love.

Love.

He had recognized Eleanor's handwriting, and had walked with pleasure into his study where he had seated himself at his desk, taken his time over the choice of one of three ivory openers before slitting the envelope. Wry-faced, he had wondered why she had picked this: *The Housewife*, 1871. He looked for irony in her, in himself but found none.

He turned the card and the message clubbed him. It was not necessary to read the words one by one, to piece the meaning together. One glance of the eye fastened on to the crucial statement, 'I am engaged to be married.' Breathless, caught out, fingertips caressing the polished wooden margin of his desktop, he sought inside himself for strength, found nothing but physical weakness.

He seemed incapable of rising from his chair, even of breathing smoothly. On the blottingpad lay the card, but now his eyes were so wet he could not make out the writing. Not that there was need. Eleanor had snatched herself from him for a second time. As a schoolgirl, she had been at his beck, and he had despised her even as he took pleasure in the enjoyment of her body. As a student, she had deliberately forgotten the enthusiasm of two or three years before, and had been unfriendly, at best distant, rebuffing sexual advances, giving the impression that she had more interesting beaux or times in London. He had not desisted, writing to her while she was away, taking his second job in London where she was. He had read of her engagement to Henry Arthur Franks in a cutting from the *Daily Telegraph* his mother had enclosed in one of her weekly letters. The marriage had taken place a bare month after the announcement.

Alistair had not written a congratulatory letter, nor had they invited him to the wedding. Not long afterwards he had become engaged to Janet Brown, whom he had met in a teachers' dramatic society, and when he returned a few years later as an assistant director of education to Beechnall, he found that the Frankses moved in different circles from his own, though they lived close by. When he left on his appointment to the directorship of education in Hertfordshire only four years on he had seen Eleanor perhaps a dozen times, and spoken to her, pleasantly enough, on three or four occasions. After three years he had been strongly pressed to apply for the directorship here in his native city; they needed a young man, a strong man, a man of ideas, a modernist, a realist, a pragmatist. He himself was doubtful, for he had just begun, not without storms, to make his presence felt in the job he presently occupied. His wife had no such qualms. The new position was better paid, promised more prestige, and to be professional head of the educational service of a large urban authority, and that at the age of forty-two, was what he deserved. She had lived with him in Beechnall, was prepared to return there in triumph with him, but only because he was the outstanding candidate for the job. Janet burnt with his ambition. He applied, impressed the huge interviewing committee, which included the few enemies he had already made, both by his grasp and his nerve. They appointed him, but only after argument, and by a narrow majority.

Alistair had wondered, despising such speculation, whether he had sought the job to fulfil his wife or to catch the attention of Eleanor Franks by the only means he knew. He had failed, as he was bound to, in the latter; the director of education was about as important to her as the milkman, and less useful. They met rarely; his hurt died; he forgot her in his press of business.

And now she had knocked him flat again.

As he sat at his desk, incapable, he reminded himself of that newspaper cutting which he had read on the Tube on the way to school. The swaying of the train, the swift changes of personnel, the noise, the acrid reek of cigarette smoke had kept him alive. He had opened his mother's letter expecting her usual three sides of boredom, church and neighbours and father's dignified tantrums, but had found instead four lines of killing newsprint. He had worked through the day, half crazy, had attended a meeting at five and a class on educational statistics at 7.30 and nobody had remarked on his appearance or behaviour. Inside, he knew himself poisoned, unmanned, beyond reason, felled by a putrefying lesion.

Now, fingertips braille-reading the non-message on the edge of his desk, he forcibly reminded himself that he had recovered from that first blow. You got over it, he hectored. Not only had he mastered his misery, he had looked round, found and married the right woman, the neat, blue-eyed Janet Brown who'd made a success of him swiftly and elegantly, presented him with a position in society, a brilliant son and a self-regard that needed to be earned.

Janet often quoted when he was down a snatch of Anglo-Saxon from her university course: 'That passed over, so may this.' The little woman had managed him, and his talent, matched him to place and hour, accompanied him to Buckingham Palace for the CBE she had deserved more than he, the recipient.

There was no Janet this time.

He staggered up from his desk and examined the picture again. The artist had learnt perspective in order to handle

124

roof tiles, a drainpipe, flagstones, wickerwork, and colour so that grey matched beige and countermanded small yellows and reds and whites. The housewife. Eleanor could preside over a new household, in this town, or elsewhere, with David, whoever he was.

Alistair walking towards the window talked sense to himself. He had not expected to marry Eleanor; she had not suggested it, and he would have regarded even a hint with suspicion. She had money, would have called the tune, dragged him away on cruises, dispersed his books, made no concessions to Bach. How was he so sure? He was a man of character, not to be pushed around by women's whimsies. Janet only had the courage to put into plain language what he wanted for himself. What did he hanker after in this Eleanor, who ignored him for thirty-five years and then knocked on his door with some cock-and-bull story about photographs in the newspaper?

Eleanor represented what he had failed to win. He took out a piece of white card and wrote down: She is what I can never have. In Greek letters, for some reason he could not recall he had written *boukephalos*, ox-head, Alexander's horse, Bucephalus.

> Does the imagination dwell the most
> Upon a woman won, or woman lost?

She is what . . .

The sentences did nothing to ease his headache, eyestrain, the trembling in his legs, the cramp in lungs. He stood again, skimmed the card towards the wastepaper basket. It fell pitifully short, as he expected, and in anger he thumped his clenched fist on the desktop. Pain split and crippled his hand. He looked at the unmarked flesh.

He rose from his desk, struggled into his raincoat, tied a scarf and sidled out of the front door. Only when he had taken a step or two towards the gate did he wonder if he had dropped the catch at the back. Irritably he stalked round the house, pulled and pushed at the knob, found the place safe, and shuffled for the road. Cars passed; one was parked, its owner considering piles of papers on the other seat, a clipboard resting on his driving wheel. A silver pencil was poised. In this office on wheels somebody did something useful, or made his living.

Murray walking uphill made his way to the main road which skirted the eastern border of the residential park. Up there buses braked, traffic jams coagulated at rush hours, shops were small and vulgar and lively and, on the other side of the hill, Victorian–Edwardian terraces of workmen's houses presented garish paint on windows and doors to the dull road. He rummaged in his wallet for his recently issued bus pass, and made for the centre of the town.

The fountains played heavily into rectangular basins on which one or two cartons floated. People bustled, not talking, with destinations grimly in mind, past two winos who lolled across a seat. Buses seemed sluggish; the sound of the Council House clock banging out the threequarters echoed with extraordinary power as if in a stifling cave. He used the gents' underground lavatory, still fierce with the morning's disinfectant, looked for a wall mirror to examine his face for misery, but found none existed; he read a police notice about the disappearance of a child. Back on the face of the earth, he retraced his steps, the only man with nowhere to go.

He turned out of the Council House square, crossed the road, walked down a narrow pedestrian street, paused at a stall to buy himself three new biros. The woman, making no conversation, tested the pens before she handed them over, and with the change twisted her face into a short grimace of acknowledgement. The purchase had eased his pain, but only momentarily. He stamped out into a broad area, flagged and cobbled, with a tree flourishing where once heavy traffic, trams, trolleys, buses, jams of cars had dominated the main road southwards. A young woman on her knees was drawing with chalk a picture of dancing clowns on the flagstones. Nobody paid attention and he went out of his way to drop a coin into her receptacle; she did not look up, or speak, but continued her shading. It was not raining now, but the skies threatened to obliterate her picture. Grimly, beret pulled down squarely to her ears, hands mittened, she worked on.

He felt again in his pocket, found a second coin, lobbed it towards the first and fled, ashamed.

More than a quarter of a century before, just before he had been appointed to the directorship in Hertfordshire, he had applied for a similar position in a northern city. His chief had drawn his attention to the advertisement, had encouraged the application, had made inquiries on Murray's behalf amongst officials and politicians in what was his native place. They wanted, it appeared, a youngish man of ideas, who would introduce a scheme of comprehensive education; there would be opposition, and the new appointee would have to be administratively outstanding as well as persuasive. No errors allowed. The retiring director had hung on too long, frustrating his political masters by his inertia. Now they wanted dynamism, change, but all bound to common sense, brass, solidity.

'They pride themselves on their hard-headedness,' his chief laughed. 'But they couldn't shift Walter Weardale, and now they're baying for new blood.' Murray considered the extraordinary metaphor, but decided against comment. The old man prided himself as a kingmaker, wanted to send his young men out to positions of influence. 'The opportunities are very great. They're a rich authority; they're getting richer and they want to splash out. I wouldn't recommend anybody for this job, Ally, but you've got your head screwed on. You'll resist the temptations.'

The chief rubbed his cleanly hands together. Murray did not much admire the man's principles. If his political masters had asked him to draw up a scheme to garrotte all teachers over the age of fifty, he would have produced it, and it would have been efficient. Now he took pleasure advising his subordinate, provided him with figures, inside information.

Murray, thus furnished, spent an hour of the Monday morning looking round the black, civic architecture, colonnades, impressive flights of stone steps, domes with a flash of gold. Indoors he faced a half-circle of twenty, men and two women, in solid chairs, thrones, behind polished surfaces. He sat, a cricketpitch length from the chairman who wore the mayoral chain, in a similar chair unprotected by table or desk.

For five minutes they read out his curriculum vitae, and he responded with polite words of agreement, sitting straight, arms along the chair arms, white cuffs meticulously ironed by Janet showing but not obtrusively.

Then the questioning began. No speaker named himself, perhaps that was sensible with so large a body, and for nearly an hour they quizzed him. He never replied at great length, but treated each question, even those stumbled out from prepared slips of paper, with respect. Before long, he was tying up one answer with another, sketching a system, modifying it, clearly balancing the ideal, the principle against exigencies of economics. He had identified his main opponents: a conservative barrister, who pressed him, with considerable skill, to explain why he would want to change a system which had so many strengths, a clever-looking woman who asked how he could put into operation a scheme he did not personally favour, and a quiet man, grey-haired with his head on one side, who, snatching black-rimmed glasses off, on, off, wanted to know how Murray judged value for money in educational terms. After an hour and ten minutes, it had not seemed half that time, Murray was dismissed, conscious that he had done well, had impressed, acquitted himself with distinction.

The appointment was not made until the Friday of that week, two days later, when Murray learnt that he had been unsuccessful. They had elevated a local man, a deputy, to the directorship. The letter was formal, thanking him for his attendance, and naming the successful candidate. A final paragraph informed him that his claim for expenses was already being dealt with and a cheque in settlement would be sent in due course. They were his sincerely, T. J. Bosworth (Cllr), Lord Mayor, Chairman of the Education Committee.

He passed the letter to Janet, who had read the news in the sudden pallor of his face. By the time she had looked the letter over, replaced it in its envelope, propped it against the cruet, he had steeled himself, hardened his features. She rose.

'Their loss,' she said. Her voice was granite; she picked up her plate, cup and saucer and made straight-backed for the kitchen, watched by Sebastian, six years old and ready for school, and little Janet, a boisterous three. The children sat chastened, apparently recognizing the untoward. Murray did not go out to her, though he knew what would happen.

She would stand by the sink, looking out unseeing into the garden. Two or three tears would force themselves on to her cheek; then she would sniff, perhaps twice, dab her face dry with the corner of her apron, bob to the one small mirror to check her appearance, and return. He hated the dismissive committee more for her sake than his.

Janet had come back, prepared Sebastian for school, dressed Jane for the pushchair and marched the pair off. She said no more to him, but lifted her face for a kiss. He, as usual, had cleared the table, packed the dishes for her attention, and had driven to work, racked, a divided man, with the letter in an inside pocket.

How he did his morning's work he did not know, though his secretary would have pronounced him as efficient as always. His mind tumbled back to the letter, to his dashed hopes, to Janet's wounds, to his failure. The director was out that morning, but on his return at three o'clock promised to make inquiries for him. Murray cleared his desk, left early.

He and Janet had discussed the prospects, and combed the interview together. He invariably took pleasure in recalling for her exactly what had been asked, and why, and how he had answered. She herself posed nothing awkward, merely lifting her neat head to say, 'How did they receive that?' or 'That was good, Alistair,' her Scottish accent the stronger, the sweeter in this simplicity.

The committee had not accepted him, had disbelieved his claims, and this led him to judge, then condemn himself. He was a hypocrite, a timeserver, a second-rate bureaucrat, unimpressive in public, unsupported by his superiors. He knew that in his profession such doubts only handicapped, that he would be brushed off for a thousand and one reasons unconnected with his ability. He fumed himself out of his depression within days but he had only to think of Janet straight-backed at the sink, eyes wet and blind, to be thrown momentarily down.

He had considered the experience to be invaluable. Four

months later almost to the day, after a less impressive performance at the interview, he had been appointed to Hertfordshire against a much stronger list of candidates, and ambition was satisfied, temporarily. From his chief he had learnt that he had lost the first post not on the opposition of those who had pressed him most strongly, the barrister and the clever-looking lady, a professor of psychological medicine, but on the votes of Labour councillors who'd said nothing, but who knew that their appointee would carry out the comprehensive reorganization they had already agreed on. He had learnt his lesson, Murray thought. These Toms, Dicks and Harrys, these butchers, bakers, candlestickmakers in their navy Sunday suits had no means of judging the qualities of a candidate, not even the basic requirements of the job. They had done as they were told, by their leader, a man ignorant as they were, but fluent with cliché and certain he knew what was needed. 'The best lack all conviction, while the worst are full of passionate intensity.' Now he was inoculated for ever against their foolishness. He would use them.

Today at Eleanor's news, in the centre of a city, within sight of his old quarters as assistant director, he thought of dead Janet, neat-haired at the sink, and clenched his fists, feeling the nails in his palms. He swore out loud, then looked about him. Nobody had heard the obscenity.

Eleanor could not be accused of choosing out of ignorance.

Nor Janet of weeping because another woman had rejected him.

His wife had said nothing to him about remarriage. Her death had galloped at her, within a month or two. She who had hated smokers and smoking died with cancer of the lung. Diagnosis and death seemed barely separated. Nagged by him she had presented herself and her cough at the doctor's surgery, the consultant's suite, the hospital, the pay-bed wing after an operation from which she survived for a few weeks only. How long she had hugged the symptoms to herself he did not know; she had borne pain with stoicism, without hope, in a kind of Presbyterian atheism. Once as he sat at her bedside, she whispered, 'I don't believe in the afterlife.' It was an apology. 'Do you?'

'I don't know.'

'You believe in God?'

'I think so. Yes, I think I do.'

'Good boy,' she had said, and had patted his hand distantly. 'Boy.' She had never called him that. Imminent death made her privileged. He had not dared to ask if she believed. She was honest, would have bared the truth, but even forty-eight hours from the end felt the necessity to protect him.

There was one to be admired.

His thoughts jumbled, tangled, uncontrollable, jagged as nightmares. People passed him; colours in the attractive shop windows faded, blurred unnoticed. Eleanor, Janet, failures, setbacks, frissons of cold on his skin, pain hollowing his eyes, his sinuses erased consciousness. If he had a serious thought it was that his life had been wasted, that he had achieved nothing, but it did not present itself in so plain a form. Had it done so, it might have found him ready with argument, but this morning, the raw wind cutting, found him soulless, brain-numbed, capable of nothing but black incapacity. His well-soled feet met the flagstones in miserable, ungraspable silence.

Turning to cross the road he noticed a bus which had started from one of the bays and was making towards him, gathering speed. His estranged mind signalled action; his head dropped giddy and he lurched down the kerbstone into the path of the vehicle. He sought it out. Dizzy, unhinged, he wanted that. His legs gave from under him. A hand hit the ground; his head was banged, not hard, but un-adultly, a clip, and lying crumpled on the damp ground he saw clearly again.

The bus whirled past, yards in front of him.

As Alistair tried to struggle to his feet, a strong hand hauled him up, set him on the pavement. Voices murmured advice. Women stopped, congregated. Fingers brushed mud marks off his coat. Still his arm was firmly gripped, but he no longer needed help.

'Are you all right, then, sir?' A policeman came forward.

'Thank you.'

131

'Would you like to sit down for a minute?' The man on his arm, loath to relinquish his grip. 'In a shop?'

'No, thanks.' Alistair breathed in, deeply. 'I must have tripped.' His voice told the lie with commendable steadiness.

'These kerbs are as slippy as glass once they're wet.'

'I shall be fine, thank you.'

He straightened himself, breathed deeply, found he could look round the knot of people without embarrassment.

'Thank you all very much.' His voice sounded as Scottish as his father's, thanking some choir, or church officials at the end of a service he had successfully conducted.

Alistair moved away.

His wrist ached and he limped slightly, but he could hold his hatless painful head high, above the people.

12

Alistair Murray tried in the next few days to come to terms with what he had done.

Bruises darkened, strained muscles ached. He cleaned his suit to his satisfaction, but could not clear his head. He remembered that momentary decision to stumble under the bus, but after that, confusion. If he could have recalled some counterorder he had issued to himself he would have been quieted, but he could not. He had blundered out into the road, but an accident, a fainting bout, a small stroke, an inbuilt urge for bodily self-preservation had downed him into the gutter. It was as if his organs, his limbs, his nervous system had displayed a firmer grasp of morality than the totality of his person.

He hated himself.

Sensibly, he visited his doctor, to give him an account of the fall, but without a mention of suicide. A thorough medical examination revealed nothing.

'You've not been overdoing things?' the doctor asked, delivering a favourable verdict.

'Why, is my blood pressure up?'

'Not really. Have you, now?'

'No. The opposite, if anything.'

'And that doesn't suit your book?'

'I've got used to it.'

'It's no use talking to you about cruises, is it? It's not uncommon for widowers to take to the boats with remarriage in mind.' The medico, another son of a Scot, played with the gold signet ring on his wedding finger, serious jollity in his voice.

'No, thanks.'

'One can make mistakes, admittedly. But there's something to be said for partnership.'

Robertson, the doctor, pursued it no further, but talked about his son's medical course, and made some inquiries about Sebastian's programmes on Scandinavia.

On arrival home, Alistair rang his daughter, Janet, Jane.

'What's wrong?' she asked.

'Nothing.'

'Why are you phoning?'

'I hadn't heard from you for some time, and I thought . . .'

'That's not troubled you before, has it? Are you all right?'

'Yes.'

The short passage had made him uncomfortable. Jane had been his favourite, a loving dancing child. Ten years ago, at the age of twenty, she had thrown over her university course in modern languages at Bradford to marry a man thirty years her senior, a disgruntled, withered lecturer whose wife had left him to care for two strapping boys of fourteen and sixteen.

'Finish your degree,' Alistair had advised. 'You've only fifteen months to go.'

She had refused, determined to help her husband full time with his children. Her father thought her not unlike her namesake and mother; she also knew her mind. Nothing could deter. The parents attended the register-office wedding, were received with suspicion, if not overt hostility by Selby Warren, who five years Alistair's junior, looked older, with his thin hair wetly streaked across his bald pate, his bookie's sportscoat, his baggy-kneed trousers, his goatee. Jane, with her own two children born within four years, took her lead from her husband, refused tactful offers of financial help, made it as awkward as possible for the grandparents to see the youngsters, contented herself with a card at Christmas, did not encourage her brood to acknowledge birthday presents. There had been ice-cold, feral rows between Jane and her mother, he had guessed, from which he had been excluded. Jane made one visit to Janet during the last weeks in hospital, but did not come up again for the funeral, nor send flowers, nothing beyond a pawky note of sympathy, badly expressed, on cheap notepaper.

The Warrens were not hard up.

Selby had been appointed to a headship of department, in a London polytechnic, with the rank of principal lecturer, and had published a surprisingly good book on Brecht, but still held his parents-in-law at arms' length. Janet at first had tried to keep in touch with her daughter, had made visits that were obviously unwelcome, kept up to the end a one-sided correspondence. Her daughter's approach was invariable: we're all right; we'll tell you if we aren't; otherwise, don't interfere because it only makes it worse at this end. When Janet died, nothing altered. The one visit to the deathbed was uncomfortably brief and unfeeling. Now Mrs Warren knew that her father would not bombard her with grim goodwill as her mother had done, and was silent.

Alistair had no idea whether his daughter was happy. She made no attempt to see Sebastian or Francesca; possibly she was jealous of their success. Perhaps she felt she had acted wrongly in disregarding her parents' advice. Then she was fully occupied, or the early habit of taciturnity and the cold shoulder had hardened into normality. Why he had rung Jane and not Francesca he did not know.

The conversation was not prolonged.

Yes, her Edward and Sarah made progress, seemed happy at school; no details: Selby's boys were both out and away now, one on an archaeological dig, the other as a house surgeon. No, it wasn't too likely she'd be in Beechnall; they were spending a week at Easter on Exmoor. No, she hadn't seen the Sebastians, but that wasn't surprising. Yes, Selby was well. He'd soldier on another five years until he was sixty-five; he'd just published an anthology of modern German short stories. What was he working on now? Hugo von Hofmannsthal, she thought. She didn't know if there was a book in it. He didn't either. They were going over in the summer. The whole family. Yes, she was well. She'd had headaches. Perhaps she needed specs. She'd been to the doctor, yes. She was working two days a week now in a florist's. Yes, it was quite interesting, and it got her out of the house.

By the time the conversation petered away, Jane sounded indignant and he, discouraged, was thrown back into the internal, ravelled, banal argument about what had happened on a slippery kerbstone in the city centre.

He telephoned Sebastian's number, and found nobody at home.

Jane was not her mother's girl, he reasoned, but more like him, and yet she acted in this defensive, loutish way. Their conversation had seemed interminable. First, he'd ask a question, and that would be followed by silence as if his daughter turned the question over and over for snags. The pause stretched out to such length that twice he had begun to speak again thinking she had not heard him or understood. He wondered if Jane realized now that she had made the wrong choice. Selby showed no public affection either for his wife or children, but grumbled bleakly in company about maladministration or the stupidity of students.

Alistair took to the piano, found no comfort there and decided he would hoover the house. Three minutes later he found himself standing in the kitchen where he had gone to retrieve the vacuum cleaner quite without an idea what he was doing there. In limbo his crippled consciousness disappeared. It occupied time, but he recalled his errand, and spent the next three hours, interrupted by an impromptu lunch, meticulously collecting dust. Carefully he probed every corner, lulled by the mechanical hum of the cleaner; he pushed furniture around, polished knick-knacks, determined to afflict himself. This was all he was fit for, a skivvy's life. Outside an east wind kept spring at bay under greyness. The exercise had been, he discovered, sufficient to calm him so that he could sit with a book, or at the keyboard, without fidgeting.

Next morning after breakfast he telephoned Francesca, but made no contact.

Though it was cold outside, he decided he would walk over to Eleanor's flat. He had not been near the place since he had received her news.

Wind cut through his topcoat, reddened his ears. The high stone walls of the gardens rose colourless under dull light. In the open-front gardens of new houses he noticed clumps of daffodil stalks, closed crocuses, snowdrops.

He let himself into Eleanor's flat, found no letters or circulars in the hall, where he stood for a moment. The place smelt warm, occupied. He opened the living-room door, was surprised to find a bunch of spring flowers, tulips, daffodils, iris, freesias, on the table. Mrs Mills took her duties seriously. He thought he could hear a radio; he grew certain; it played Elgar's *Salut d'Amour*. This was not one of Mrs Mills's days.

Back in the hall, he listened, shouted.

'Hello, there.'

Burglars would not entertain themselves with Elgar.

'Hello,' he called again. His voice trembled.

'Is that you, Alistair?'

Eleanor's voice. His heart banged; breathing locked itself.

'Yes.' He managed the word in the end, waited. He found the silence uncomfortable, but could drum up no message to bawl through a closed door. He concentrated on a small picture, no more than postcard size, but heavily gold-framed, which hung by his head. A pen and ink sketch, brown on old, browning paper, unsigned. It did not look like a print. Some insignificant country scene, a cottage, with trees, palings, water. Eleanor would never be foolish enough to hang an original Rembrandt so close to the front door. He did not know; his attention wandered.

There was a noise from the bedroom. Footsteps preluded the drawing of curtains, the switching off of the radio. It was amazing how clearly he heard those sounds, but no whisper of voices. Eleanor had lain in bed there with her David, and now she had struggled out, straightened her face, prepared to make an appearance. Alistair braced himself, strung words together for his first sentence. He wondered what David made of the interruption.

The door opened, and Eleanor moved towards him, in a kimono. Apart from a slight untidiness of the hair she might have been dressed for morning coffee with friends on the patio.

'I didn't know you were back.' He spoke his sentence.

'I came yesterday morning.'

She ushered him into the living room, ordered him to sit down before gliding out to splash in the kitchen. Neither spoke until she returned with two mugs of coffee. Alistair had crouched in discomfort, crossing and uncrossing his legs, wrenching himself from ham to ham. Eleanor settled in front of him, picked a small pile of mail from the table and glanced through it. She made no attempt to open any of the envelopes.

'I suppose,' he began awkwardly, having to clear his throat, 'that it's in order to congratulate you.'

She smiled vaguely, again picked up the top envelope, tapped her open left hand with one corner.

'Well, no,' she said.

He made a sour face; she relinquished her hold on the letter. No further information was offered.

'I don't quite understand you.' He cleared phlegm again from his vocal chords.

'No.' Eleanor did not appear distressed. She yawned, prettily covering her mouth. He waited. Her coffee steamed on the table. 'I have done a silly thing, Alistair.'

'Oh?'

Now she picked up her mug, warming her hands round it.

'The engagement to David Digby is off.'

'I'm sorry.'

She looked sharply at him. 'There's nothing to be sorry about. I don't think I acted very sensibly.'

Alistair kept silent, but now she sipped her coffee. He reached for his mug, but the liquid scalded his tongue. Outside bottles jingled on a milk float.

'It wasn't very sensible.'

She might have been answering a question on the price paid for vegetables; her features mirrored thought not trouble.

'You won't want to talk about it,' he said.

'I don't mind; really I don't. He asked me to marry him, almost as soon as I got there. I didn't accept there and then, but told him I'd have to consider it.' She hesitated. 'We slept together, and it was good. The next morning at breakfast I said I would, and we went out to celebrate over lunch. By the time that was over, I knew I was wrong.'

'What happened then?' He gently inserted the question into her pause.

'Happened? Nothing. David was nice, as he always is. He

138

wanted to go out straightaway and choose the ring, but I made some excuse, said we'd concentrate on the lunch. He didn't argue. We did have champagne before we went.'

She fooled again with her coffee.

'We went up to the West End, had lunch at Dorati's, came back to his flat.' She returned her mug to the table. 'He opened another bottle. We made love again. I wasn't altogether sober.'

He turned his head away, in embarrassment, closing his eyes, unwilling to look at her. For all he knew, she might have been boasting. Then he determined not to ask the next question.

Eleanor rose, fiddled with the flower arrangement, walked across to the window where she stood with her back to him.

'Just before I set off for Bournemouth,' she did not turn, 'I heard Ned had died.'

'Suddenly?'

'Yes. There was a postmortem. A heart attack. The funeral is tomorrow. Will you go with me?'

'If you want me to.'

She wheeled, dashed herself back into her chair.

'Somebody from the hospital phoned just before I was setting off. I was annoyed rather than anything, because it was so inconvenient. They told me about the postmortem, and that Ned's brother would make funeral arrangements when it was all settled. I was,' Eleanor paused pulling at her kimono, 'excited at the thought of going to David's. I had been seeing him. He wrote nearly every day. I knew he would propose.'

'And that's what you wanted.'

'I thought so.'

She lifted her head; her left hand came up with it. She gasped.

'David is not as old as I am. He's only fifty.'

'Has he been married before?' Alistair decided on a social question.

'He's a widower. They had no children.' She waved helplessly in his direction, as if both to keep him silent and maintain flagging interest. 'Then when all the celebration was on, Ned's death . . . I . . . I can't . . . While I was getting my clothes together, and all the rest, he had this attack. His

139

cleaning woman was in, it appears. They got him into hospital, but he died.'

'Wasn't he under the doctor? This post –?'

'He seemed better. The doctor hadn't been in. I couldn't bear it. It was like a mugging. I went to pieces. I told David I couldn't go on with it.' She writhed. 'Oh, he was nice. Calm. Said it was the shock. That I musn't upset myself. He was very good to me. But he was just conventional, Alistair. I wanted more than that.'

'The poor chap wouldn't know what to say.'

'Why not?'

'One minute you're celebrating . . .'

'I see.' She interrupted him, furiously cold. 'You mean I wasn't rational. That I . . .'

'I wasn't there.'

'What's that got to do with it?'

'I'm in no position to judge how you acted or talked, or how it seemed to him.'

She cowered in her chair, as if he offered violence, but recovered and reached for her coffee. Silence lengthened awkwardly.

'What time shall we start tomorrow?'

'9.30. It shouldn't take two hours.' She answered gratefully. 'We'll go in my car if you don't mind. Driving's good for me. It settles me down.' She stood. 'I want you to go now, Alistair. Thank you for coming. I would have rung you later, to ask, to ask you, you know.'

'Will you be . . .?'

'Yes. I want you out of the house, Alistair, out from under my feet.'

'Very well. Shall I ring you later?'

'If you must.'

'I'll finish my coffee,' he said with impudent rationality. She did not argue. When he had pushed himself from his chair and held out his hand, she took it.

'Thank you,' she said.

'I'll ring this evening.'

She nodded, mouth smiling, mind elsewhere. He slunk out.

140

13

Ned's funeral was well attended, and a large, loquacious company assembled after the service at his house. His brother had called in a firm of caterers, and this arrangement proved admirable. People ate heartily at the buffet lunch, shouldered their way over to Eleanor to speak becoming condolences; most were middle-aged or elderly, wore token mourning at least, but after ten minutes they gave the place the air of a captain's evening at the golf club. Eleanor, who had broken down in the church, now seemed aggressively cheerful.

The brother took Alistair by the elbow, led him to a window seat.

'Ned left the house and contents to Eleanor,' he began without introduction. He was neat as Ned, younger, smaller, better preserved.

'Does she know?'

'Yes. It was always understood. We're not a large family. I've no children. My sister has one girl, who gets some money, as I do. But Elizabeth furnished the house, set it up, and it's only proper that her sister should have the lion's share. I'm not poor.'

'I don't suppose Eleanor is.'

'I never thought so.' Affronted. 'But she'll have to decide what she's going to do. It's a fine property, and in good repair. It could be let on favourable terms, but I don't suppose she'll want that, any more than she'll want to live there.'

The man discussed possibilities with a kind of dry relish, tapping the carpet with the toe of a polished shoe. Alistair was reminded of children outlining the rules governing some game which would occupy less time than the initial preparations. He watched the rubicund cheeks, the oiled grey hair, the stiff cuffs.

'The reason that I'm talking to you about this,' Cedric

Lennox-Smith leaned forward, 'is that Eleanor, on the two occasions I have spoken to her on the telephone, seemed unduly distressed.' He looked across at her, where she stood, wine glass in hand, making some much appreciated point to two well-dressed business executives, by appearance, and the rector. 'She'll need to discuss it with somebody.'

'If she raises the matter with me, what would you think the most sensible arrangement?'

'To take out what she wants, and then sell.'

'I see.'

'It would present her with the least trouble. That's the important thing. On the other hand, I don't want to see her a party to a bad bargain. And both at Liz's funeral, and in these last days, I haven't found her, well, you know, very steady. She'll need somebody to hold her hand. I'll do my bit, at this end, but I'm a busy man, especially just now.'

'I'm sure she'll trust your judgement,' Alistair said.

'We'll see. I mean, do you agree with me?'

'About what?'

'Eleanor's state of mind. Is that how you've found her?'

'I'm not sure. She's . . .'

'Well, I am.'

Lennox-Smith extracted an easily given promise that Murray would assist Eleanor. Suspiciously, he mentioned this on their way back. Eleanor, much at ease, drove swiftly, overtaking with judgement, chatting. She had, if one could use such words, enjoyed the occasion, had met some interesting people.

'For instance?'

'That tall man, with the pale, thin wife, played cricket for Lancashire.'

'Did he tell you so?'

'No, he didn't. Cedric did. And the rector is an expert on Jane Austen. He's written a book.'

'Are you interested in Jane Austen, then?'

'No. Nor in cricket. But you'd expect him to know about Habakkuk or Ezekiel.' She accelerated with silent power around two lorries, surprising Murray with these two names out of the hat.

He mentioned Cedric's proposal which silenced her for a few hundred yards.

'You know why he said that, don't you?'

'No.'

'He thinks all women are incapable.' The speedometer trembled past seventy. 'Henry bought and sold a lot of property you know. He talked to me about it, took me round sometimes, showed me architects' plans.'

'So what are you going to do?'

'I don't know.' She laughed, pleased with her insouciance.

He heard nothing from her over the next fortnight, during which northeast winds choked inroads into spring. Deliberately he decided he would not interfere in her affairs. One cold day he baby-sat for the Montgomeries; he refused to lecture at a northern university on 'the educational administrator', met Mrs Mills with her husband in the street, walked every afternoon about the draughty parks amongst buffeted daffodils, late hedgerows and grass that looked green only in sheltered corners. He watched Sebastian ruffle the Secretary of State for the Environment one evening, and drove the next day out into the north of the country, where long lines of small red and white bollards by the roadside marked the scene of confrontation between police and flying pickets at the entrance to a colliery. The weather was wintry, with mist, grey cloud, bone-searching cold. He was pleased to come in at four o'clock and crouch in front of his gas fire. The next day he took himself off to the county library to spend the morning among the vagrants, the sleepers, the drama-club secretaries, the searchers after truth in literary magazines or philosophical journals. It was too hot, inside; his mind wandered. He took up a heavy *Country Life* and read with amazement the prices asked for properties similar to Ned's; he could live easily on the proceeds.

On his return he found a card through his front door telling him that Eleanor had called, and inviting him in two days' time to accompany her again to Shropshire 'on the final visit'. He telephoned his agreement, and she in return told him she had just spent a couple of days in the house. She was taking Cedric's advice to sell the place up, but needed one more trip to cut down the number of objects she wanted to keep for herself. 'I want a dry, rational, level-headed old cynic like you to tell me not to be so sentimental.'

'Wouldn't Cedric do?'

'He's not dry. He's dead.'

She sounded pleased with herself.

The Shropshire house was tidy, undusty; a cleaning woman came once a week, and the central heating turned itself on for a couple of separate hours each day.

'Now,' Eleanor ordered, 'sit down for a minute and think.'

'About what?'

She hurried to the kitchen, not answering. She returned with coffee, reporting she had set the heating higher and, laughingly, that he'd be able to take his raincoat off before long. Sheepishly, he removed it.

'First,' she said, 'we'll just walk from object to object.'

He stood in the drawing room, where the mourners had chattered, which was large, square, well lit by mullioned windows. The furniture was darkly suitable; chairs and settees did not match, but sat beautifully, expensively on the huge Axminster carpet; the surround was dark oak, glistening.

'This is a beautiful room.'

'Liz had a good eye.' Eleanor tapped the wide ornamental frame of a Victorian landscape with water and reflected cows. 'Just the right spot on the wall. Light or dark.' On the way out she touched the grandfather clock, Welsh, eighteenth century; it showed, he checked, exactly the right time. Somebody at some time had taken trouble.

The panelled dining room was smaller, so that the table and its ten chairs occupied almost half the space. The sideboard loomed massively, while the moulded ceiling with its chandelier shone clear white.

'They took their meals in the kitchen.'

'This was a showpiece?' he asked.

'Liz always acted sensibly,' Eleanor answered. They examined the wide, light, modern kitchen, the breakfast room, the butler's pantry, the flagged larder, the store closets and then they made their way out into the hall in preparation for the inspection upstairs.

'This is the only part of the house I'd criticize,' Eleanor said.

'Why?'

'It's too dark.' It was true that the front door, in sombre stained glass, and the diffused light from a gothic window upstairs left the parquet floor, the white area above the oak panels, and the heavily decorated ceiling in shadowed dimness this clouded day. 'Crepuscular.' She laughed at her word.

'Cool in summer, warm in winter,' he ventured.

'You've a good word for everything and everybody.'

He toiled upwards slapping the solid balustrade.

'What's the date?'

'Eighteen-eighties.'

'Retired businessman?'

'Do you know, I've no idea.'

The five large bedrooms, bright compared with the rooms below, did not occupy them long. With a merciless show of efficiency Eleanor slapped open and shut the doors of the wardrobes. All had been emptied.

'Oxfam's done well,' she said, teeth clenched.

They looked out from a back window to the garden, with its shaped lawns, its shrubberies, and at the far end a stretch of woodland.

'Beautiful,' she informed him. 'Not very difficult to maintain.' She pointed to a discreetly placed shed. 'Ned kept his equipment there. He had a seat on his mower.' She shook her head, as if this saddened her. 'He was very proud of it. Liz called them his toys. "Go and play with your Meccano," she used to say.' Again she laughed, nervously, a neigh or a bray. 'They didn't have a very happy life.'

'Even in this beautiful spot?'

'Their daughter was killed. She led them a dance before that. They were both very conventional. But, then, nobody's very happy. You weren't, were you?'

'I don't know about that. Happiness is relative.'

She left it as they stood at the window; daffodil clumps offered dabs of yellow; small irises were mistily purple.

'Would you like to live here?' she asked, not turning.

'I like the house, except that it's too big. Too much of my income would disappear on upkeep.'

'I'm not asking you to buy it.'

'And besides, I don't know anybody *in his partibus infidelium.*' She stared outwards. 'I don't think I'd have been well suited in retirement in alien Bournemouth or wherever.'

Eleanor was rapidly tapping a windowpane with the nail of her right forefinger. He wondered if she knew what she did, as the woodpecker rattle continued.

'What I meant was,' she said, and broke off. Her voice faltered, strangulated. The nail rested. She lifted her head. 'I meant: should we marry and live here?'

Murray barely understood for a few seconds before his heart lifted, momentarily, and then caution reasserted itself.

'I feel very honoured,' he began. It sounded silly; too formal with some other man speaking.

She moved, very quickly, a shimmy, a half shuffle from the Charleston, frightening herself and him, not abandoning her position by more than six inches.

'Errh?' Her question croaked.

'You don't mean it, do you?' He spoke gently.

'Why shouldn't I?'

'You've just released yourself from one engagement. Another entanglement hardly seems in order.' He tried to suggest a humour he did not feel.

She nodded, biting her lip. Outside the green garden lay unaltered; branches of trees were motionless, shiny with damp. Daffodils snagged the eye. The couple stood in silence avoiding an exchange of glances.

'Must the two go together?' he asked.

'What two?'

'Marriage and living here?'

'You don't want either, do you? There's no need for you to answer.'

'I'm too shaken to be able to think properly. It's only a week or two since you told me you were getting married, and I had to adjust myself to that. You'd be going; our friendship would wither away. Then you break the engagement. I was pleased, irrationally, perhaps, but I was pleased, I can tell you. And not only because you were strong enough to take the decision. But it set me back again.'

'Did you hope, Alistair?'

'I'm not sure. I didn't want your throwing yourself away. No, that's stupid. I didn't know David.'

'Do you see yourself as capable of marrying again?'

'I hadn't considered it seriously.'

'Not even when you met me?'

'Why should you want to marry me? I'm an old dull stick.'

Eleanor sat down, rested her right forearm along the dressing table as she leaned sideways to consider her appearance in the mirror.

'You were the first man I fully loved.'

'Thank you.'

'I shall never forget it. I suppose to you I was a raw, silly schoolgirl throwing myself at your head?'

'No. That's not how I remember it.' He shook his head. She prodded some blemish on her cheek. 'I treated you badly. I wonder you want anything to do with me.'

'I didn't, at one time. I wanted my own back on you. I think I got it. With Harry, and other men. But not now. What happened when I was eighteen seems more important than what happened at twenty-four.' The age she married Henry Franks.

'Why?'

'How the hell should I know.' She stood. 'Let's go down.'

'You're not angry, are you?' He touched her arm.

'What do you think?' She shook herself free, went rapidly out of the room, down the stairs, straight from hall to kitchen where she swilled their cups under the tap.

He followed her, bemused, inattentive to all except inchoate, tumbling thoughts.

'Eleanor,' he began. He had no idea what he wanted to say.

'Don't witter on.' Her voice snapped, but seemed withdrawn, delivered, as it were, through a crippling migraine. 'You've given me your answer, and that's sufficient.'

'Had you planned to ask me? Before we came?'

'What does that matter now?'

'Had you?' He persisted for no good reason.

147

'No. It was on impulse.'

'Which you regret?'

'I very soon shall. I can see that.'

She had finished at the sink, and opened two cupboard doors to find a teatowel.

'I will tell you something,' he said.

Her shrug, as she returned to dry the pots, was theatrical, badly acted, a flounce, infantile.

'When I heard that you were getting married, I was so depressed I think I tried to commit suicide.'

'Say that again.' He did so, and she appeared to take no notice, busily plying the teatowel. Alistair pulled up a stool, and after a considerable interval she laid down her work, went outside, returned with two glasses and a new bottle of sherry. She poured, handed him a glass, but her face showed no emotion, rather old, crumpled over the elegance of her dress. They sipped.

'You only think?' The voice had regained something of a brassy scepticism.

He gave a low succinct account of the stumble at the kerbside, emphasizing nothing, explaining nothing. She chose a stool, but perched on its edge, tiptoe to the floor, his equal in discomfort.

'I don't think you should have told me that, Alistair.'

'Perhaps not.'

'Why did you?'

He cleared his throat.

'You seemed to think I didn't care for you. It's not the truth. As to the other thing, perhaps I tripped, or fainted, or had a little stroke, and that was all. But I was confused, and in a way I didn't like, and I connected it, right or wrong, with what you had told me, your engagement.'

'Alistair, you're not making this up, are you?'

He tried to laugh, but choked into coughing.

'Oh, God,' she said. 'We are in trouble.' She straightened her back, her hands grasping the stool between her thighs. She had hooked her heels into a crossbar. 'I left the Mayors in Portugal where I thought I was going to enjoy myself. Then this contretemps, this fracas with David. Now you and

148

I are, are wrestling.' The word trickled from aphasia. 'I'll see to this, Alistair. I'd made up my mind to do so in any case. But it seemed a kind of chance.'

'To do what?'

'To try again, redeem myself. You've always frightened me because you seemed certain of yourself, grown-up. When we first knew each other, I was terrified you'd make me pregnant. You wouldn't have accepted responsibility, I knew that. Your mind was elsewhere. You wanted to get on in the world. There were more important things in your life than sex with a randy schoolgirl in a hedgebottom. Don't think I didn't know. Even then. I did, but I still wanted you to have me, and teach me love.'

Eleanor was weeping now, not loudly, but with a wildness the more poignant because of its limits.

'What can I do?' he asked.

'Nothing. Nothing.'

He put his arms round her, and she sobbed herself into quietness on his pullover.

'I think we'd be wise, now,' Alistair said, 'to go out, and I'll treat you to lunch.'

She went upstairs to doctor her face. They ate well at a pub of her choosing only three or four miles away, and at her suggestion set off straight afterwards for home.

'I'm confused,' he said. 'I thought you had lists to make.'

'You're not the only one.'

Eleanor as usual seemed at her most relaxed as she drove. Fast with decisions, she took no risks. He felt safe, and nodded off at least twice in the warmth of the car. What conversation they made was unimportant, about the provenance of the grandfather clock, the pub chef's idea of salad dressing, the cost of books and railway journeys, the murder outside Alistair's gate, the price of meat, the Official Secret Act. They exchanged these snippets like travelling strangers.

'You'll have to go back,' he said after she had dropped him and refused to come in.

'I don't mind.'

'I was just in the way.'

'I don't think so. In any case there's no hurry. I can well afford to hang about.'

Eleanor spoke cheerfully, hands at rest on the power-assisted steering wheel, handsome, masterful even, dismissing him but without rancour. He held on to his gatepost as she drove away, dizzy, uncertain of himself, or of what had happened. A man coming round after an operation might suffer similar dislocation, for though he could perfectly understand language, or the expression on the faces of his nurses or fellow-patients, and remember the ward, its occupants, furniture, light or dark corners, it was at a distance, with solid reality underweighed, underestimated. A sense of some more important, overriding factor, health or the imminence of pain or the success or failure of the surgery, existed, but even this was not significantly considered in present weakness. One lay capable only of vaguely noting sheets, or smiles, or bunches of flowers and waterjugs.

He didn't know whether he had refused to marry Eleanor, and began to rake round in his mind for excuses, finding none. He had not acted well, had given neither assistance nor comfort, had dithered once the proposal had been made.

In his garden there were hints of spring, but cold winds disturbed bushes, fine twigs. His calendar quoted Tennyson, 'In Memoriam', about the fading of the long last, last long (misquoted, he must look it up) streak of snow; there was more lion than lamb in this March, but he had failed again.

Eleanor had called for help, however bizarre the form of the appeal, and he had gaped his astonishment, incapably had done nothing, had done not even the wrong thing.

14

Alistair, idle with hands in pockets, watched Katherine Montgomerie bustle down her garden.

'Hello,' he called out. 'How are you?'

She stopped, and approached the talking gap with caution. 'Things are a bit better now.'

The woman looked pale, drained, but the northeasterly chilled still. He made a polite inquiry about what had been wrong.

'Jeremy had a chest infection, and then the others.'

'Was it serious?'

'I thought so.'

The answer, sharply given, put him into his place, a position of weakness, or formlessness, of unworth. She despised him, disregarded him, and he concurred with the judgement. In a few flat sentences she described their choking distress, the rack of coughing, the sleepless nights, the eyes appealing for immediate help which could not come.

Alistair mumbled sympathy. She replied that they were now improving, but still needing nursing. 'Illness spoils children,' she said.

'And mothers?'

She dismissed the question with silence.

'I always thought that a doctor's children were better off, somehow.'

'Why should that be? Francis didn't treat them.'

'But he would know . . .'

'Knowledge does not rid you of pain.'

'No. No. But he could reassure you.'

'Reassurance.' She blew out her lips in scorn. 'Besides, he's worried to death about his father.'

'Oh, I'm sorry.'

'He's a useless sort of man. And Francis's mother's in

151

hospital. With Alzheimer's disease. He feels he must visit each day, but . . . I must go in.'

'Is there anything I can do?'

She had already retreated three sharp steps, but she halted.

'You could perhaps take Jeremy in for an hour and read to him. You'd need to keep him warm. He says you're a good reader.'

'This afternoon?'

'Yes. It will give me a break.' Then grudgingly, 'He'll enjoy the change.'

She thanked him curtly and marched off, arrangements unmade. He would need to telephone. He heard her back door close, and stumbled round his garden. The morning frost had disappeared, but the weather gripped bitter still.

He peered over to the substantial modernity of the Montgomeries' house. There in that expensive structure, warmly comfortable, elegant as money could make it, children had been approached by death, at least in their mother's view, while their parents were staggering under certainties, or lurid uncertainties. Sudden death, which marked all families a hundred and fifty years ago, now fell sporadically in this favoured part of the globe, and was majestically repulsed by drugs, hygiene, prophylactic medicine, the advance of science, but it had glanced in at these large, double-glazed windows, and had altered for one woman at least, if temporarily, the shape of the world.

And while this untimely conflict had been fought out, he'd known nothing, heard nothing, had fooled in front of buses, had failed to open his heart to Eleanor, had slept, eaten and drunk, voided bladder and bowels, and touched the piano or opened unread books. The roof of that house, fine slates, rebuked him through leafless trees.

He rang Mrs Montgomerie and at 2.30 a cocooned Jeremy, carrying a small schoolbag of books, made an appearance. The boy accepted a glass of lemonade, and took a chocolate biscuit from the tin, though he did not make much show of eating it. They talked about trains; Alistair described Sebastian's set and where it ran in the house; the two went hand in hand upstairs to discuss the exact location. Janet, he remarked, had handed over rails, rolling stock, signals, the lot to some charitable organization as soon as she thought her son had outgrown such toys. Neither Sebastian nor his father had been happy, but had enough sense to keep their mouths shut.

Jeremy demanded to be taken on Alistair's knee while they were reading. Hans Andersen provided the first two tales and the man was surprised at tears which brightened the boy's eye at the troubles of the ugly duckling. He next read, or they looked together at pictures, in a publication called *Dr Who and the Daleks*, which appeared from its stains, its cracked discoloured pages, to have been lying for some months, years, on a second-hand book barrow. There Jeremy came to his own, explaining with élan, about Who, the time traveller, the changer of his body, the friendly alien.

'Is he good?' Alistair asked.

The question had never troubled the child; the doctor thrust himself into situations where oddities pursued oddity, and were thwarted.

After this Jeremy got down, and politely wondered if he could walk round the whole house. He grew excited at the sight from an attic window of a stalking cat, but talked in an adult fashion about the part of his home they could see, saying who slept where, and why his bedroom was preferable to Simon's.

'You don't sleep in the same one, then?'

'Oh, no. He wakes up and cries.'

'Unlike some we could name.'

They discussed Mr Montgomerie's latest car, of which Jeremy approved, though apparently on aesthetic grounds, and the situation of his consulting rooms. The boy showed an unexpected interest in the covers on the furniture of the two bedrooms Alistair kept out of use.

'They look like ghosts.' Curtains were drawn, a reminder of the customs in Janet's reign, against the sun, and the chairs looked both squat and insubstantial.

'Dr Who and the Armchairs,' Alistair suggested. The child giggled and began to make fiery, offhand suggestions about a story, and forgot it as soon. In the boxroom they sorted through a pile of framed pictures. Alistair had insisted that the boy wore his overcoat.

'You should put them up on the wall,' Jeremy chided.

'I haven't the room.'

'My Gran has a whole big wall covered with pictures. My Mum calls it "the museum".'

'And what does Gran say?'

'Nothing. She can do as she likes.'

When Jeremy admired a print of a mounted knight; Alistair presenting it to him was volubly thanked.

'I shall hang it over my bed.'

'I hung a picture over my bed once, when I was a student, and it fell right on top of my head.'

'When you were asleep?'

'No. I was reading.'

'Why did it fall down?'

'I hadn't knocked the nail in far enough.'

'Did it hurt you?'

'Not much.'

'Did you swear?' The boy understood the naughtiness of his question.

'I shouldn't be surprised.'

They completed the tour of the house, but Alistair vetoed the suggestion that they race together on the lawn. They made a start on 'The Tin Soldier', boiled a saucepan to cook up hot chocolate, and Alistair dispatched the boy to the fridge to bring out the plateful of sausages on cocktail sticks. Jeremy asked about the word 'cocktail', discoursed quite knowledgeably about his parents' drinking habits, before he sat to twiddle the comestible propeller-fashion. The child did not finish his drink, and managed only half a sausage and two fingers of bread in nearly half an hour before it was time to go home. Alistair wrapped the boy in scarf and overcoat, threatened him with a tweed fishing hat, marched him smartly into the street.

Back in front of his own hearth, Alistair sat down exhausted, if satisfied. Recovering, he dismantled the sausages to make a sandwich, then took to the pavements for an hour's sharp walk in cold sunshine and blocks of shadow. He returned, spent thirty-five minutes at the piano with *A Bach Book for Harriet Cohen*, and settled to reread, the first time since the sixth form, Otto Jespersen's *Growth and Structure of the English Language*. When the phone interrupted at eight he hoped for Eleanor; Katherine Montgomerie thanked him, said how much Jeremy had enjoyed himself, that the knight was already in place. Alistair congratulated her on her son, said the child must come again very soon and returned to the consonant shift, *die erste Lautverschiebung*, to philologist Grimm, and then to stress shift. Once upon a time he knew the details of these changes by heart, but they had vanished, roughly erased, like Eleanor who did not contact him.

Uncomfortably in his armchair, he questioned himself about the book. First he tried, with moderate success, to make a résumé of what he had read, and then to supply a motive for the activity. It was interesting, he believed. One felt the better for knowing that in the primitive Indo-Germanic languages the stress fell at random, whereas with the Teutonic group people had come to distinguish and so accent the first syllable, the important element. Who had decided this? And why? Some dictator? It seemed unlikely. Was there some factor in the environment that so altered the character of these Germanic peoples, as opposed to that of their ancestors in hotter India, the warmer Mediterranean, who refused such regimentation, spattered strong syllables at whim with the consequent modification of vowels.

Yes, it became more interesting, this cock-and-bull story. It had happened; it was accepted in academe. He tried, man swimming in swarf, to think up exceptions and failed. He admired these philologists whose knowledge was so vast that they could draw up improbable conclusions and have them approved by rivals, keen to pounce on flaws. The word '*ulema*' leapt to his mind; a crossword clue; Muslim theologians, doctors of the law. He wished he were one of them. Mathematicians created moderately simple equations to offer explanations of the complex workings of an infinite universe. Surely it was implausible that the essence of all-pervasive gravity could be enclosed in a volume, but there it was: in a short line. It was utterly satisfactory, and arrogant beyond belief.

Man had looked at God, and had made up a language to contain his mind. What was it Einstein had said? The Lord God is sophisticated . . . That word had shifted; it had once meant adulterated. Good for man with his spinning vocabulary, and those stiff-necked Prussian barons of early Teutonic who had decreed that stress should land plumb where it belonged, on the first, the meaningful part of a word.

He stood, in quiet excitement at his thought.

His father, the Rev. James J. Murray, MA, BD, later Hon. DD of his old university, had once surprised his son, a student at Oxford, by ripping off, like a child with a multiplication table, the sound changes governed by Grimm's and Verner's laws. He must have learned them more than a quarter of a century before as a student at Glasgow, and had retained them, sharp as steel, for future use. Here was a man who could hold such a vastness of erudition ready in his head, at his fingertips, that he could reduce it, if need be, to the simplicity of a law. Alistair, surprised at his father's knowledge, so accurate and quick, and not part of his professional expertise, the *beghadh kephath* letters in Hebrew wouldn't have come amiss now, even as a young man had dismissed such retention and recall as useless. It did not do, the administrator-in-the-making claimed, to remember everything; it was a nuisance, a clutter. His father must have had some interest aroused to keep that page full of sound changes bright for so long.

Now he, Alistair Murray, MA, MEd, sat in his chair amusing himself. For all it mattered he could have watched a television series on adultery, big money, fast women and automobiles. The intellectual content justified the pastime, but it would in no way alter his life, except to bolster his ego. These discoveries of Rask and Grimm had not concerned him in his working life; he had dismissed them while he tangled with the placing of public monies, employment or dismissal of teachers, building, rebuilding or destruction of schools, awards of scholarships and grants, funding sports complexes, educational equipment, testing of intelligence or special abilities, grants for leisure activity, for nursery schools and playgroups, for orchestras, for underprivileged or ethnic minorities, then sit-ins, classroom assaults, trade unions, provision of language, science, computer laboratories, the thousand and one headaches which made up an administrator's day. He was no longer concerned with these so he returned to the scholarly concerns which had occupied him, at least until final schools were over, nearly forty-five years ago.

He jumped up in anger, groaned at the pain in his hips and telephoned Eleanor. He listened to the signal which drubbed on unanswered. Her flat was small enough for her to walk from one room to the phone in a few seconds. She had an extension to the bedroom, moreover; she must be out. Obstinately he stood with his ear registering the monotonous double knell of his hope. He would not relinquish it; he would not.

In the end, he admitted defeat and rested his forehead on the cool wall.

He poured himself whisky, sat, rose again to splash in ice and water, slumped down a second time to stare at Jespersen, grey and neat, square, a well-cut sandwich of knowledge. It did not fill the fagend of his days. He had come round to considering it because he could find nothing more interesting. That hypothesis held no water. When Eleanor offered him marriage, he'd backed off from the decision.

There was the rub. Murray, who had been so quick at judging a situation, and then making his mind up, now wanted to be beloved of Eleanor, in an old man's daze of infatuation, but not to have to commit himself. He would like her to want to marry him, with a few months thrown in before he'd have to state his preference. He despised himself.

The phone shrilled; he slopped his drink, clumsily pushing himself up.

Was that Stanway Tyres? Wrong number. Tyres at this time of the evening? Still standing, he rang Eleanor's flat with no result. Uncertainly jigging, he replaced the instrument in its cradle, and reaching for the book looked up, dialled Francesca's long set of figures. He waited in disappointment. Nobody at home. Again he turned to the book of numbers, with its tartan cover, bought years ago by Janet at a church charity sale. L for Lennox-Smith. He carefully picked out each figure of Ned's Shropshire home; the service was good. In the dark of the evening, in Shropshire, his signal disturbed the air in an empty house. Grudgingly, then baring his teeth, he replaced the phone, made his long way back to the chair and sat conscious only of the disturbed chaos in his head. The whisky with its spilt splodges stood untouched. The dead television screen greyly reflected the lights. Outside it was dark now. After ten minutes he stood, drew the curtains, turned to BBC 1 for the news. He heard the raucous prelude, saw the shifting logo on nine, and drifted away from the careful voice, the mohair suit, the neat grey head. Fifteen minutes later he came to himself, with some short version of the Arts Council's decisions on expenditure. He turned the set off, decided on bed, but spent threequarters of an hour pottering before he finally made his way upstairs only to find he had failed to switch on the electric blanket.

Eleanor rang soon after nine the next morning.

She had been over to Shropshire again, and last night had been dining with an old friend. Her voice was forcibly cheerful; she merely phoned to see if he was well. He invited her to accompany him to the B Minor Mass on Saturday.

'Have you bought the tickets?'

'Not yet.'

'Shall we get in?'

'I expect so.'

She made a performance of fetching her diary, searching its pages before she accepted. He said he would go down to the city about the tickets that morning, and let her know. She thanked him, rang off abruptly.

He tried after lunch to report his success; she was not there. After tea he still made no contact. At 7.30 he caught her just as she was again going out to dinner, and when he commented on her full social life, she said sourly that she couldn't be expected to coop herself up all day and every day in a flat. Immediately she relented, softening her voice to say, 'I didn't know you were religious, Alistair.'

'I'm not.'

'Going to the B Minor Mass?'

'It's Bach I worship,' he said huffily.

'But your father was a parson.'

'He failed with me.'

'Oh, I'm sorry, but I was wondering about asking you to go with me to the Easter Communion at St Michael's.'

'Is that where you usually attend?'

'No. I'm not a regular churchgoer anywhere. Well, I turn up from time to time. That's why I wanted somebody with me. Will you? It's early. Eight o'clock. You think about it.'

She immediately switched topics, telling him they'd use her car for the concert.

'I'm not an Anglican, you know.'

'They don't concern themselves with such things. They're all ecumenical these days.'

'They expect a shred or two of belief, don't they?'

'Oh, I expect you can manage that.'

She said she'd be late for her dinner engagement, named the time she'd pick him up on Saturday, and ended the conversation.

This woman raised troublesome questions. First marriage, and now religion. He had been to church twice since Janet's funeral service; his wife had been an irregularly attending adherent of his father's former church. He had attended civic services by way of business, and that had been the end of it.

As far as he could remember, he had in his youth enjoyed churchgoing, the singing, the preaching of scholarly exegetics like his father. At Oxford he had continued this observance of the Lord's Day, but army duties and some wry amusement of the coupling of spit-and-polish with worship on church parades had interfered with regular attendance. On appointment to his first teaching post here he had lived with his parents, and had joined with them on the Sabbath forenoon turnout to the kirk until he found the quiet hour or two in the house on Sunday morning more than useful for the marking of exercise books and other schoolmasterly chores.

His father was not the sort to let such laxness pass unremarked, and therefore pointed out to his son, now aged twenty-nine, a university graduate and former officer in the army, that his sense of priorities was becoming seriously distorted.

'I don't want to quarrel with you, Father,' Alistair said. He could sense his mother hovering somewhere behind him; she would be privy to her husband's intentions, for he would have discussed them, and the young man's backsliding, with her to the meanest comma. She remained or presented herself on the field of conflict, to prevent either of her males hurting the other. Any wounds she would suffer.

'This is not a matter of quarrels, Alistair.' The old man needed the protection of his gown and preaching bands. 'I should not be fulfilling my duty as your father or your pastor, if I did not draw your attention to the dangerous nature of your recent Sunday practices.'

The old man stared over the top of his glasses.

'I'm more usefully employed,' Alistair said.

'This is no time for pleasantry. I am speaking seriously to you. About the deepest concerns of this life and the next. About your relationship or that of your immortal soul with Almighty God.'

Alistair waited; he was sitting, while both his parents stood.

'I realize I must be a disappointment to you, Father, but I am not convinced of the existence either of soul or of God.'

Oddly, he realized he had fallen into Dr Murray's formality of language.

'Is this atheism a new thing?'

'No. Over some years I have come to realize what I think.'

'I had never envisaged the day when my only child would make such a confession.' His father drew in a lungful of breath through his mouth, brushed at his hair with the fingertips of both hands. 'It was my pride which misled me. I would have boasted, and I use that word with bitter advisedness now, that I, and your mother, had given you a good Christian upbringing, as regards both doctrine and example. We have prayed for you, Alistair, while you were at university, and then in the armed forces . . .'

'I'm sure you have nothing to reproach yourself with.'

'The devil will often strike through the nearest, the dearest.' He spoke as if recalling an apt homiletic aphorism, now translated for himself into unpalatable fact. Again he sucked in air.

160

'I don't wish to hurt you, Father, and I realize that my absence might rouse comment amongst your congregation. But I shall not usually attend service in the future.'

The altercation, such as it was, lasted for perhaps a quarter of an hour. The older man raised no theological arguments, barely inquired about the dogmas or creeds which troubled his son. The main weight of his attack seemed to be that all this had happened by default, that Alistair had acted deceitfully by not bluntly affirming that he could no longer believe. The young man saw no point in the accusation, made no attempt to justify himself by claiming to have considered the feelings of his parents, merely said mildly that he found little relevance in the revealed truths of religion, at least as preached in his father's kirk, and therefore did not intend to spend time there. Modestly he advanced no claim to be right, said he had thought it over at some length; he spoke dryly, without heat, as he had spoken later when, director of education, he had found it necessary to dispel faulty arguments from a close ally.

His father, he considered later, had for so learned a man made a poor job at putting his case. It was not that he was unused to arguing with apostasy, but that he was a man of feeling; once his emotions were roused they interfered with the easy action of the mind. That it had taken Alistair nearly thirty years to discover that his father was not a dry old stick spoke well of his father's self-control or his mother's powers as a mediator. On this occasion, the elder Murray dropped his hands and, with a stricken face, furrowed black, turned and walked from the room, leaving the door ajar. His wife slipped out quietly and quickly after him, but not before touching her son lovingly on the shoulder.

It must have been a week before she spoke to Alistair about the matter. She was serving his evening meal, the father out at a meeting, when she stopped, having placed his coffee on the table, pulled out a chair.

'You've not spoken to your father again,' she asked, 'about churchgoing?'

'No.' He'd expected this.

'Nor changed your mind?'

'No.'

'I see.'

'I'm sorry, Mother. You could have done without all this.'

'Oh, no. You did right. Your father thinks you've broken his heart, but he'll get over it.' His mother smiled slyly. 'The minister's wife,' she said sarcastically. 'The minister's wee wifie.'

She did not stop there, though the rest of her conversation seemed superfluous. She made no attempt to change his mind, even made herself out to be in favour of his stand. Perhaps she prepared herself to answer her husband's inevitable question: Have you spoken to Alistair again?

What surprised Alistair was his own coolness. As a child he had feared, been overawed by his father, though he had learned early enough to distinguish between the strictly kind figure at home and the gowned presence who ascended the pulpit steps. He respected his father's opinions, in no way wished to hurt him privately or embarrass him in public, but he felt calm, above the battle, untouched by the exchange. Perhaps his army service had inured him to quarrel, blame, the blasting reprimand, or perhaps he had something of his mother's temperament, and was able to watch or join a dogfight without anger.

The gift, if that word sufficed, was useful to him often enough later. He could listen to people's histrionics, their powerful reiteration of principles, even their accusations of treachery or double-dealing on his part, without becoming involved emotionally. Times without number he argued, conceding or blocking, his ego intact, his self-respect not only invulnerable but unattacked. This had its drawbacks; soon he learnt to feign anger, to narrow his brows, clench his knuckles white, speak brusquely, even rudely, dismissively. He had become a man of no-feeling, an insensitive.

Two things remained in his memory from that morning. He knew the extent of his father's hurt, not by empathy, but from outward signs, and he determined to solace the old man as best he could. The second was that his private life was in rags; at this time he had been rejected by Eleanor Warrington, now completing her final year in London and already engaged twice, once to a man named Oliver Wykes and now to Henry Arthur Franks. Alistair's suffering on this account had seemed to him ridiculously strong, but that in no way relieved it. He shrank from the anguish, but perhaps the hoity-toity dismissal by this young woman who four years before had flung herself at him, been his mistress, had caused him to reject the existence of God, the scattering of his father's most cherished beliefs as mere ciphers emotionally, nothings, to be noted, taken care of insofar as that was possible, but not to be shuddered over. Even if his father, granted omniscience, had told him, 'I've prayed for you, so that Eleanor Warrington now loves you, will marry you' and Alistair had found that true, he would have still dismissed it as superstition.

Now, in an old age, when he expected little, looked forward to less, the wheel had come full circle. Eleanor had proposed marriage to him, and he had hesitated, backed off. But he could be hurt. The next few years, if he lived, and he saw no reason why he should not, would bring a toll of pain, setback, fear. Already he might have tried to end his life. He could argue against that, convince himself that if he were serious he would have made use of barbiturates and whisky not buses.

His father had collapsed at his church door after attending a service conducted by his successor and had been pronounced dead on arrival at hospital. Alistair, an assistant director in the town at the time, had not been at the kirk, and Janet his wife had been expecting Jane. They had taken his mother in for a month or two, when she decided to return to her sister's in Paisley. She had not lasted long; this quiet woman whom he expected to survive into her nineties had given up once her husband and son no longer needed her. What had appeared as a mild attack of bronchitis had carried her off three winters after James's death. She was buried in her husband's grave, wife to the above. She had instructed her unbelieving son to have added one word under her name and dates. 'Reunited'.

Alistair felt the warmth of his fire on his legs; television had progressed from news to fantasy, a film of a woman dominating a wild-west frontier town. He stared at it with amazement, as if it had been in Greek, and turned it off. The silence, or the hiss of gas jets, puzzled him as grievously. He had now lost his grip on the world; things happened, governed by cause and effect outside his knowledge. Shuffling, he crossed the room, began to prepare for bed, forgot his purpose, leant against a sideboard.

It was past eleven o'clock when he landed upstairs. Outside moonlight blanched the garden, soon to be whitened by frost. He coughed, a dry long bout, crept shivering under the electric blanket he had again neglected to switch on.

15

The crowd spilled gorgeously out for the interval into the foyer of the circle in the concert hall, Murray and Eleanor Franks among them. She wore a gold dress that suited her height; she walked imperiously, he thought, impressing herself on the assembly. Katherine Montgomerie pulled her husband towards them, and Murray made introductions. Francis seemed by no means keen to spend his time there, and blatantly, asking to be excused, withdrew in the direction of a group of notable medicos. Eleanor did not miss the slight.

'Oh, dear,' she mocked.

'Oh, dear, what?'

'We're not quite good enough for your friends.'

'He'll be sorry when he finds out whom he's deserted.' The lame sentence, accusative and all, earned him a brief, sour glance before she smiled again. Murray, head still dancing with the *'Cum Sancto Spiritu'*, felt suddenly dashed, down in the mouth.

Even if Surgeon Montgomerie did not rate them highly as conversational company, Eleanor was immediately surrounded by women dressed as expensively if not impressively as she, and their husbands, rich, grey-headed men. They talked of cruises, of some charitable affair Murray had not heard of out at one of the ducal houses, of mutual friends, but never of Bach. Again Murray felt shut out; one should walk exalted from that great dance of a fugue in the presence of this beautiful woman, but these people, friendly enough, confident of their own concerns, talked of important events he would not be invited to participate in. These exchanges seemed the *raison d'être* of the evening; the music a rather long-drawn-out excuse for their place.

A bald man with an egg-shaped head and glasses, in evening

dress, confronted, comforted Murray on the edge of the perfumed and animated scrum round Eleanor.

'That's the first time in my life I've ever heard the "*Quoniam*" sung properly.'

'It was good.'

'Its *tessitura*'s so low the horn just blots the voice out. Either this man's very powerful or the acoustics are unusual.'

'Or both.'

'Yes. I don't like to think Bach didn't know what he was doing.'

Murray shook his head.

'They tell me,' the man said, voice thin, like tissuepaper and comb, 'that before Bach fugal themes weren't particularly interesting in themselves.' He then, clean as tapwater, whistled the '*Cum Sancto Spiritu*' to prove the composer's power to change all that.

'I wish I could whistle.'

They grinned together, and Eleanor, noticing, called out, 'Leonard, I hope you're not telling Alistair things he shouldn't know.'

The company laughed; egg-head twinkled and slipped away.

Eleanor stood the central figure of her large, rather noisy group, though she herself did not seem to be leading the conversation. Magnificent in her gold, eyes flashing, she turned her head from one big-wig to another; Murray hoped that Montgomerie had noticed that the Dean of the University Medical School and two professors of surgical specialities had led their wives towards this knot which had now expanded so that it took on the appearance of a public meeting and was edged by a yard or two of space. Murray stood back, beyond this corridor, to admire Eleanor. She needed a platform now.

He was taken aback by his pride in her, but felt that he ought to have stood where he had started, at her shoulder. She obviously did not miss or look for him, received homage as her due, had possibly expected it. She was now engrossed in a *tête-à-tête* with Lady Strathvendon; the pair were so close it seemed they might embrace at any minute, and yet from their quiet exchange the energy of the whole group was generated. Murray told himself to dismiss such fancies; he could not. Clearly, Eleanor, the woman who had knocked on his door in the wind, was a personage creating power. She had not hinted as much; perhaps she took it that he knew. Those frequent dinner engagements were not wasted.

A Labour councillor, formerly chairman of the education committee in Murray's day, passed him by, not a yard away, eyes open for importance only. Eleanor and Susan Strathvendon did not glance towards the man.

'Hello, Mr Murray.'

A small, breathless voice, husky with shyness, greeted him. Blanche Twells, his former secretary, hugged her handbag to her untidy chest. They inquired about health; she looked old, though she'd not be much above fifty. He remembered that she had been a great concertgoer, she and a friend, a Miss Briggs, who worked for the Prudential, not now to be seen. He had not met Miss Twells since Janet's funeral. She made polite inquiries about his occupations, enthused over the new concert hall, looked forward to the visit next week of the Czech Philharmonic. Miss Briggs sidled up, from the lavatory to judge from her embarrassment, and was introduced. Tongue-tied, she did her best. This was an occasion for these women, to crown the music, to shake hands with an ex-director of education. Conversation dried up, but he would not move. No one would accuse him of snobbery. Miss Twells pointed out Lord Strathvendon to them; Miss Briggs, daring but *sotto voce*, said she or they did not expect, somehow, the word carried her greatest stress, peers to have ginger hair. 'For the nameless and abominable colour of his hair,' Miss Twells riposted at once from Housman. Murray decided that these spinsters had a great deal about them. A roar of laughter burst uninhibited from Eleanor's group; she smiled brilliantly. The two 'girls' looked round guiltily, or reprehensively.

'Are you here on your own?' Miss Twells asked when decorum had been restored.

'No. I came with Mrs Franks.' He nodded in her direction.

'Her husband was a millionaire,' Miss Briggs whispered. 'He financed the Trent House building.'

'She's an old friend. I've known her since I was at school.'

'Doesn't she live abroad quite a lot?' the Twells asked, then suddenly, 'Have you ever sung in the B Minor Mass, Mr Murray?'

'No. Why?'

'You always had such a beautiful speaking voice, so persuasive, I thought you might have been a singer.'

She would never have asked the question when she worked for him.

'I thought of myself as a bit of an actor once.'

The first interval bell rang. Eleanor's group slightly reshaped itself but did not notably diminish.

'We'd better be finding our way back,' Miss Twells told him, obedient to authority.

'I'm delighted to see you.' He put a fatherly hand on the arms of these women; in his office he had never once touched Blanche. They trotted away, proud of themselves and their contact.

On the second bell the crowd moved, pushing into the wide doors. Eleanor did not look about for him, continued her conversation as she moved. He trailed behind; on his arrival she was seated, fiddling with bag and programme, flushed, happy.

'I lost you,' she said.

'I didn't go far. I kept my eye on you. You know a lot of people here?'

'One or two.' She laid her fingers on him. 'Is the second half good?'

'Marvellous. The choir's expected to sing itself to death. Four, five, six, eight parts, full out.'

She smiled shruggingly to herself like a child flattered by a gift of chocolates, but he noticed that she lost interest after only a few pages. The contrapuntal frozen drama of '*Et Incarnatus*', the passacaglia of the '*Crucifixus*', the leaping trumpet brightness of '*Et resurrexit*' left her to fidget. The weight, the colossal strength, cathedral stone in music, angel-high of the '*Sanctus*' left her untouched, and Bach's fugue, Pelion on Ossa, '*Et pleni sunt coeli*' which made him want to soar, to jig upwards from his seat, left her bored. She smiled over at him once in the first '*Hosanna*', as if Bach had stum-

168

bled on a respectable idea and she'd noticed it, but the violin solo in the *'Benedictus'*, the second voice-bruising 'Hosanna', the *'Agnus Dei'* wasted themselves on her. This chafed Murray only intermittently, he was at first too immersed in Bach's succession of master strokes, but by the *'Dona Nobis Pacem'* he wanted the thing over, or, better, to whisper to her that this was the last chorus, that five minutes would see them on their way out. Eleanor had made it obvious that nothing she heard transported her; she hitched herself slightly up from her seat, altered the position of hands, or bag, or leg, searched the three pages of programme. Nothing strongly irritated her, but she found little of consequence for herself in these magnificences which he had hoped would lift her as they made a new man of him.

He helped her into her coat. She had clapped as enthusiastically as he, so that again her delight in applauding so vigorously on social grounds snagged his nerves. Who was to lay down criteria? He. Who was to say he had judgement? Smiling to himself he remembered a text of his father's: 'Search me, O God, and know my heart: try me, and know my thoughts.' He recalled these gobbets, they called them that at Oxford, with a half humour, nothing akin to the teeth-baring solemn delivery of his father in the pulpit.

Further greetings, invitations were flung around on their way out. He remembered hearing a well-known playwright tell him of his residence in Cambridge, where he'd read architecture or some other discipline unallied to the theatre, that there had always seemed some marvellous party going on but never in any place to which he had access. Eleanor had shaken hands with a bearded, distinguished man who would not relinquish his hold on her. They stood, arms almost at length, his palms doubled round her right hand, an unusual, a histrionic position, drawing attention to itself, to its originators, to the spacious stretch of carpet, pillars and fine glass, the lights reflected. A striking woman, in a Rembrandtesque bonnet, stood at the other side, giving her blessing. In the end Eleanor broke away, having introduced Alistair in tow to Professor and Mrs Flower; madame spoke with a strong foreign accent, almost as bizarre as her husband's posturing.

169

'I hate to meet them,' Eleanor confessed. 'It's like acting in a play.'

'What does he profess?'

'Fine art. He sculpts. So they say.'

The well-lit streets were cold; Eleanor took Alistair's arm as they marched smartly under the dark-toned, civic *gravitas* of the Guildhall towards the car park.

'How did you enjoy it, then?' His question had, even for him, a kind of plebeian gruffness.

'It doesn't hold my attention all the time.'

'Bach doesn't?'

'That's right. My mind wanders, or goes blank. There's something missing. It's in me, I guess, in my make-up or training. You have to give Bach undivided attention, don't you?'

'Any composer, I should think.' That sounded ungracious. 'You used to play the piano at one time, didn't you?'

'Still do. I've a cottage piano in my bedroom.'

That seemed amusing to them both so that they hung on to each other to laugh in the street, up the stone steps to their level of the municipal car park.

She dropped him at his gate, refusing to come in.

'I'll see you tomorrow morning. Quarter to eight.'

'You'll be awake, will you?'

'Waiting for you.'

She drove off, and he dallied on his garden path by the street-lit daffodils although the air chilled. Once the weather grew warmer, the cherry blossom would be out, the magnolia, the pear trees, but not yet. The traffic on the main road some hundreds of yards away seemed heavy and that meant the wind still came in from the northeast. His hall struck pleasantly warm, and he walked through to the kitchen without switching on lights. The kitchen furniture looked shabby after the grandeurs of the concert hall; banal like the ending of his day. He consulted the *Radio Times*; a police drama, football, then a film. BBC 2 offered *Coriolanus*, a play he had never come to terms with. Nor was this the time to start. He turned on Radio 3, and recognized the C Sharp Minor Quartet. He ought to move out of the kitchen where the small radio did scant justice to the work and to his music centre. He did not. Soon his own drumming thoughts had cut out Beethoven.

Earlier this evening, when he had bathed, put on a new white shirt, a Pierre Cardin silk tie, he had known real excitement; he had been alive, prickling to the finger-ends with anticipation. The B Minor and Eleanor. Friends he might meet. The cream of high living. A deep exchange of words. And that masterpiece of Protestant counterpoint to Catholic Latin. Life was good, productive, expanding, bright with promise, youthful, vernal.

Now he sat on a stool ignoring another masterpiece, noticing that he should have cleaned his gas stove, scalding his lips then forgetting the coffee. Hips ached; he was an old man. The number of times he would hear live performances of the Bach could now be numbered on the fingers of one hand. If that was the case, he could beat it, travelling up to London, staying the night in hotels or rattling home by taxi and newspaper trains. He need not sit about in mourning; inside a week, with luck, his garden might be warm, thick with blossom. The line of Housman drilled in, dropped out, painless and uncomfortable as an up-to-date dentist. 'Fifty springs are little room.' That was a young man's poem. He'd be lucky to manage fifteen.

He had accomplished nothing.

Sighing out loud, an amateur actor, he reached for his cold mug.

Even as he sat he began involuntarily to fight down his depression, not so much from desire, but from an answer inside his bones to aches and weaknesses. He swilled off the unpalatable drink, devil-may-care, and was presented with the uprush of life concentrated in the garden outside. On Radio 4 he heard a short act of worship for Holy Saturday; someone sang in English the recitative from the *Matthew Passion*, 'At evening, hour of calm and rest'; he did not listen with care, but it added to this sense of rising pleasure.

Alistair Murray checked himself.

Tomorrow morning he would present himself at Eleanor's house to attend Easter communion. Neither woman nor observance should have promised much. Eleanor had declared herself for the socialite she was, one who used the B Minor Mass as an excuse to hobnob with self-important cronies. And Easter? He did not understand the Resurrection, except in so far as something had convinced those odd disciples, perhaps in the way that his spirits now rose, against the evidence of painful hips, shortage of breath, heralding worse to come. The smooth voice on the radio, English-bland, instructed Joseph of Arimathaea: 'His body sinks to rest; go loving servant, ask thou it.' Alistair was glad to be able to remember the name, which came back to him from Sunday School instruction, though he had no idea where or what Arimathaea was. It seemed important, powerful, not against reason. Grinning, he switched his mind to the secular, said aloud, 'O Julius Caesar, thou art mighty yet!' His father's church had not made much of communion. No, that was wrong. They walked in solemnity to the Lord's Table, but he remembered his shock, as a middle-aged agnostic, when one of his understrappers had laid it on the line for him that the central act of Christian worship was the receiving of the bread and wine. His father had not seen it so, and it had rankled in him that he, without belief, had reacted to the statement in much the same way that the old puritan would have done.

His father's kirk still stood, dark now, decorated by unseen Easter flowers. And tomorrow morning there would be at service at least half a dozen faces which had been familiar to him from his childhood. Eyes which had watched his father's polished boots ascend the pulpit steps would look again round the gleaming pews, the cleansed windows, the daffodils, the narcissi that had occupied good ladies this afternoon. 'And many women were there.' 'Up to the hill of God, they say / And to his house we'll go.'

He did not forget the boredom, the earnestness, the competitive learning, the hard seats, the dull dogs, but these earned no weight. Again he subdued his rising spirit. It was not good enough to neglect his father's creed, worship God for two thirds of his life, the vigour of his days, to creep back sentimentally to it on the strength of loneliness, or J. S. Bach, or the unsatisfactory nature of Mrs Eleanor Franks. Outside his windows the world, plushy with darkness, grew colder.

In the spring the boy Alistair had been kitted out with new clothes. He followed his mother's guidance here, as did his father. Not that Dr Murray's clerical grey needed much choosing. Perhaps a slight difference of width of leg or length of jacket required, or received, the womanly voice of approbation or warning. Only once had Alistair insisted on an article of clothing: a maroon tie. And that, at the age of ten, he had been adamant about, because a boy he admired, Somebody Fletcher, a fair-haired lad a year or two ahead of him at school, who rode a bicycle with careless skill, had owned such a necktie. It seemed remarkable now. The boy had impressed him for a matter of two months, five weeks perhaps, had never been close, though they exchanged greetings, he thought, and then had dropped from his life. What had happened to him Alistair did not know. Living elsewhere, at sixty-seven unrecognizable, killed in the war, died young, again Murray could not know. And yet, at ten, he had on that shadowy figure's account, told his mother exactly what he wanted, would have no other. Now he could not even recall the boy's Christian name. Guy, was it? Guy Fletcher? He made for the phone book. Nearly twenty G. Fletchers of one sort or another, the wrong people, faced him in small print. What does one expect after fifty-five years?

Why he considered this particular piece of mental detritus he could not tell. Why not his wedding day? He remembered that plainly enough, and in detail. His father had taken a part, a sternly leading role, in the service at Janet's kirk in Glasgow, while her father, both overawed and determined not to be cowed, had kept his face straight as his black, greased hair. Mrs Brown had seemed much at home in a wooden fashion, knowing she had organized all things well, whereas his mother had stood back in ladylike idleness, a quality he did not associate with her, blurred at the edges, pliant, compliant. He knew exactly where the album was with the photographs; both Sebastian and young Jane had in their youth demanded its production, had stared wide-eyed or in mockery according to their age at the figures in their utility outfits, old-young faces set in decorous unbreathing. Alistair decided against searching them out at this time of the night.

He remembered Janet's proud expression from the photograph not from life. She had brought a prize back home in him; ridiculous as it seemed now, that was to her plain truth. For the rest of her life she had polished and enlarged the trophy. They drank no wine at the wedding; tea and soft drinks in some hall, not he thought connected with the kirk. But the trestle tables had been covered with starched white cloths, and the magnificently heavy cutlery, embellished and large enough to deal with the plenitude, a favourite word of his father, of food. Excited, he jumped to his feet, made to the window with a young man's stride, and there discovered old age again as he rested his forehead on cold glass.

Furiously he wrenched his mind elsewhere, to Sebastian's birth, after a difficult labour in a London hospital. He had no car, no telephone then. He had rung the hospital in the lunch hour; again at four o'clock under sympathetic eyes from the school office, without news. He had made himself tea, had changed into Sunday wear, not much different from his schoolmaster's subfusc, when a Mrs Randle, with round glasses, had brought the news: a boy, a big boy, eight pounds six ounces; both doing well. The two had shaken hands, more than once, and she had told him how her husband, a master decorator, had turned up at the hospital for her first in his white painting overalls. 'But when I seen his faice, I forgive him. I couldn't do ather. If I'd said to him, "Be pleased as Punch and frightened aht o' your skin at the saime time," he couldn't have dan it better.' He had been a picture.

Janet had not been nursing the baby when he arrived; she looked proud, buttoned up, slightly distant, as if she had seen what no woman should. She laid no complaints; the boy, the bairn was beautiful. Alistair had not thought so; Sebastian lay red and wrinkled, tight-eyed, infinitely small (he'd added Eliot's 'and dry' in hope next day in the staffroom, retelling it for the sixth time). He tried now to recall Janet's pinched face, but could not. She had looked at him as if she expected some clinching pronouncement, a final crowning word. He presented his congratulations, his inquiries, his paper-wrapped flowers, himself, but that did not seem to be it. She held his hand, even introduced him formally to a nursing

174

sister, but looked behind him, above his head, for a descending halo. He had felt, he could only remember his account to himself at the time, not the emotion itself, properly cut off from her; she had travelled where he could not and had not yet quite returned.

Jane had been born in the front bedroom of the house here, in the early hours, after one of his first days as the city's assistant director of education. Janet's elder sister, a spinster, had looked after them all, shaking her head suspiciously at their extravagance. She had asked him why he needed so many pictures. 'I never see you looking at them,' she accused. Even Janet had expressed relief when Elsie finally packed her bags and returned to keep the books of her father's expanding business. She had taught the three-year-old Sebastian the word 'bawbees', if not the concept of hoarding them. That poor woman had died three years later, at thirty-five, of cancer and disappointment.

Returning from his dark perch at the window, he had recalled his wooden pushchair, and a wicker cradle preserved through his boyhood in the lumber room at the manse. The first day at school; splitting his head open on holiday; the 'scholarship' oral examination where a small collection of schoolmasters and ladies in hats had questioned him on a passage from *Treasure Island*. He had not read the book since boyhood, not even to Sebastian. He ought to read more, both conservatively as well as radically.

From the shelves he lifted out Quiller-Couch's *Oxford Book of English Verse*, blew the dust from its top, trying to calculate how long it had been since he opened that volume. What was in it? Those medieval lyrics that he'd once gabbled liquidly off,

> An hendy hap ichabbe y-hent
> Ichot from hevene it is me sent,

and his father's favourite '*Rorate, coeli, desuper*', from Dunbar; and his 'Lament for the Makers'. That would be there: he did not open the book to check. Skelton, Wyatt, Daniel, Drayton, Fulke Greville, Campion, Barnefield,

Wither. He remembered the names from the period before he went up to the university, when he'd settled himself down to read something not in the Books III and IV of the *Golden Treasury* he'd studied for Higher School Certificate. Nicholas de Breton. The syllables dawdled. Who in hell was he? Not one line or phrase could be placed to his account. Southwell, Chapman, Wotton; the names in the small print of literature, as Guy Fletcher hid in the small print of life. Phineas Fletcher.

Suddenly he was hanging on to the parapet of a bridge, feet slipping on the slippery bricks under his toes, in no danger, pleasantly frightening himself, aged eight. The curved bricks at the top were smooth as glass, as was the sloping ledge on which his feet struggled for purchase. What had that to do with him now? Being brought on to bowl, uphill on the games field, and the ball trickling on to the stumps, to the boisterous satisfaction of the fielders. Taking a penalty that had gone in off one of the goalposts, a lime tree. Murray had despised athleticism, seen little sense in organized games and competitions, though he provided venues and cash for their pursuit, and now, a senior citizen, an OAP, he remembered these small, underserved sporting triumphs.

He should write his autobiography.

The thought lay solidly with him, like a brick hurled through an open window, itself, complete, not much damaged, not by chance damaging. There was no thud or crack as the idea landed; there it revealed itself, the onlooker. He had recovered his wits.

Today was Saturday, nearly Sunday. He would begin on Monday morning, a good time since his substantial Sabbath meal had leftovers lasting until Tuesday. He searched in a cupboard, amongst folders, and produced a thick pad of foolscap, slightly fading, in a ring binder, half a dozen years old but glossy black still.

After the breakfast he would sit at his desk and begin.

Ought he to make a plan? The admin man liked his slips of paper, his filing cabinet, his cards; he'd do better to invest in a word processor. He laughed himself out of that; he needed to put down what he remembered, and a pen was good enough. As to order, he could remember when he was born and that would do. In this first draft he would scribble off his recollections, trivial or otherwise. In a flash he thought of a red-faced butcher named Reid who bellowed hymns and psalms from the middle of the kirk, heartily matching the organ, outsoaring the choir. Why this long-dead portent appeared he could not understand; the Reid family would be represented on the morrow by the butcher's grandson, a dark, unsinging accountant with half-moon glasses and thin hair.

He turned out the lights, locked the doors, carried his folder upstairs and laid it on his desk in the study. With great care he washed out then refilled his fountain pen and placed it, in its perspex case, on top of the folder. All he needed was to sit, open the file and begin. The first sentence existed: 'I was born on February 21st, 1918, the day General Allenby captured Jericho.'

'Do without the history,' he warned himself.

As director of education he had attended a small celebration, given at the Council House, to a distinguished poet who lived locally and who had been awarded the Queen's Medal. The man had not wanted to come, had been awkward about arrangements, had arrogantly declined anything more substantial than a cup of tea and half an hour of his time.

They, the Lord Mayor, the Chief Executive, the Director of Leisure Services, and Alistair had talked about Byron, Kirke White and Lawrence, while the poet had looked them saturninely over, saying next to nothing. He was reported to be very learned, and it was quite possible that their collected inanities were beneath his notice, or his comment. Polite enough, he drank one small cup of tea, ate one rich tea biscuit, but at least he had donned a clean shirt, deeply white with broad heliotrope stripe and a dark suit, to answer their *obiter dicta* with his curt affirmatives, his short simplicities. Only once had he expanded into a paragraph, and that was when Murray, out of character, embarrassed by the toilsome lack of social progress, had asked the man what satisfaction he had when he looked back on his eight volumes of verse.

'Not very much,' the poet had said, but he'd straightened up in his chair, as if he'd heard a real question. 'I try, as far as I can see, to record matters which are important in my life. Not straightforwardly, of course. Metaphorically. By what Eliot called objective correlatives.' Somebody interrupted with a query, an objection, but he held up the white hand which had shaken theirs so limply. He gathered his strength. 'I cannot understand why one trivial event or another recurs as important in my memory. All I can say is that it is so, and poetry is an attempt if not at explanation, at least of exposition. My emotion is implicit in the event, and thus in the recording. I search for the words, mystery enough, but not so deep to me as this unconscious choice, this seemingly haphazard selection.'

They'd joined in then, with their own reminiscences, but the poet had retired into his dark suit and his silence.

A quarter of an hour later the damp hand was placed again in theirs, the poet had made for his Volkswagen and the officials for their offices and duties. At the time the meeting had seemed an oddity, amongst the many to which county officials lent their presence, but later the unassertive voice had been found to speak for him, to suggest his own puzzlement.

Murray rearranged the pen on its cover, moving it through forty-five degrees, then ninety, then back to its original position. As director of education he had inaugurated many schemes, nothing so radical as that of a predecessor who had cunningly, uselessly placed his new schools at the very centre of the rising housing estates, to be the community's cultural headquarters by day and evening, but all had been modified, scrapped, rethought even during that reforming genius's own occupation of the office. Alistair's strength had been that he had made things work: once a project had been adopted he had seen to it that it had a chance, was viable, was fed. 'The lad with the oilcan', he had once described himself at a teachers' banquet. They had laughed, applauded, but he overheard an irreverent headmaster's comment, 'the man with the shit bucket', not twenty minutes afterwards that same evening.

Quarter to twelve struck downstairs.

He closed the study door, set his alarm clock for 6.30. From behind a lifted bedroom curtain he stared out of the window into the shadows of his garden, then realigning himself at two photographs of Janet on the dressing table.

The first showed her aged twenty in her graduation robes. It did not flatter, that black and white wartime picture; she did not look young or pretty, but stiff, proleptically stiff, pinched, the dying woman in a metal hospital bed. The second, ten years later, did better by the mother of two, softer, less bony, hair fair and fluffed, a smile not after the achievement of some well-thought-out scheme, but of mother-hood recollected when the children were not there. He had taken that in this house, and she had been delighted with it; in his dark room he had made copies which were presented to friends and relations. 'I look almost human,' Janet had said, meaning 'attractive'. It had been one of his small triumphs, and easily managed. He had caught her looking at this particular enlargement, in its thin, dark wood, austere frame more than once. It was this photograph which had been reproduced in the local newspaper after her death. The editor had sent round a young woman to offer sympathy and ask for a suitable picture after Murray had inserted his plain announcement:

MURRAY, Janet, MA, beloved wife of A. S. McM. Murray and dear mother of Sebastian James and Janet Mary. On April 27. No flowers by request. Donations to Cancer Research. Funeral arrangements later.

He undressed. A headlight momentarily lit the jumping, dark-ened room once he had drawn back the curtains.

He pulled the covers of his single bed up to his cold chin.

16

Alistair Murray woke four times. Twice he traipsed out to
the lavatory; on all four occasions he checked with his heavy
old-fashioned alarm that he had not overslept. When the bell
rattled at 6.25 he was already alert. By five minutes to seven
and the weather forecast he had shaved and was stepping into
his charcoal-grey trousers when Radio 4 played him a verse
of an Easter hymn. He made instant coffee, put slices of bread
under the grill, cleaned his shoes, smelt his toast burning
and decided against scraping the blackened pieces. The pious
subordinate had explained to a fellow-worker that he fasted
before attending Eucharist, would not even clean his teeth.
This information had been given in the director's hearing,
and perhaps was strongly expressed for that reason, but
Alistair had turned away from what he considered superstition. Now he would compromise; a cup of coffee, but no
toast.

Outside the sun sparkled, white clouds passed at speed,
but he guessed it would be cold, and took out his still smart,
military-style short black overcoat. He had cleared the sink,
and quitted the house by 7.20, leaving himself twenty-five
minutes for a walk he could do in just over the quarter hour.

The air struck sharp as he stepped briskly, but without
signs of frost. Shadows, when the sun broke through, were
clean-cut; in the gardens daffodils grew abundantly, and
banks of aubretia thickly covered the limestone on rockeries;
forsythia began to be palely noticeable. The season was late,
because of the dry northeasters, but cheerfulness prevailed.
Alistair whistled breathily.

No traffic moved, not a milk float, nor an early holiday-
maker. The distant main road preserved silence as stringently
as this tree-lined street. No pedestrians stepped out. Nobody
took a turn in his garden; no bathwater ran; blinds were all

drawn. He found himself disappointed, though he knew a couple of lorries or a group of shouters would spoil his elation. That did not seem right; a half-dozen chattering youngsters on their bright way to church should add perfection. His footsteps echoed, clacking back from the high stone walls.

A blackbird shouted warningly as a cat flattened to its belly on its stealthy path. Foxes, he had heard, lived hereabouts, and he had seen grey squirrels. A flash of sunshine and a burst of wind hit him together. He rubbed his smooth cheeks, smelt the aftershave lotion, smiled, stuck his shoulders back. His mind seemed clear of lumber, naked to the morning's cool sunshine.

The incubus of unaccounted memory, of griefs, errors, misunderstanding that had troubled him the night before disappeared. The strongly felt pleasure of childhood, of adolescence had become his, but without its dubieties, its uncertainties. He was a boy emptying his stocking on Christmas morning, or after a fall, when the dirt had been washed away, the cut bathed and bandaged, the smell of sharp iodine still about but not threatening, and his mother on the way to fetch a sweet as a reward for his stoicism under the exigency of her treatment. The sweet would be wholesome barley sugar, but it was her word of praise that counted. He had seen the fright in her face at his screams, the gash on his kneecap, and her success, returning tear-streaked hysteria to sticky ordinariness, would be reflected there, for him, a substantial guerdon, one of his father's words, for his bravery. In those days, in spite of temper, sharp slaps, admonitory words, all had seemed under authority, examined, dealt with, cleared, certain. He remembered baths, he'd perhaps be four or five, when he had walked towards his bedroom in crisp pyjamas, hair still slightly damp, but brushed down, parted, singularly amenable.

Now the world was innocently clean.

George Herbert's lines, long dismissed, not recalled since revision for his final examinations goaded him.

> How fresh, O Lord, how sweet and clean
> Are thy returns! e'en as the flowers in Spring

> To which besides their own demesne
> The late-past frosts tributes of pleasure bring.

He'd first read that out to his tutor in a smoke-filled room in summer, not long before Schools, the trees outside massing unmoving leaves. He had been excited as his tutor had not; old Humphrey Worsley had coughed his dry approval of a well-made point by the essay writer, not at Herbert's recovery. And outside, Victorian gothic windows, walls paled mellow with sunshine, and in dry air voices carried through stillness; young people pursued their pains and pleasures, as Worsley nursed his summer cold and put his pupil in the alpha class, double minus of course, sucking at his pipe; an old bachelor, a classic by training, who had produced nothing in print, not even a school edition. He had died immediately the war in Europe ended; Alistair remembered that the obituary cutting his mother sent had reached him in Holland.

In this part of the street, sunshine was trapped, and all seemed suddenly warm. Above, in a cleft, an early wallflower bloomed. His daughter, Jane, had once named them her favourites, velvet flowers, she said, stamping her small feet with pleasure. What would she be doing this morning, he glanced at his watch, at 7.28? The children might well have roused their parents, but not to attend church. Was it at breakfast on Sunday morning that Jane and Selby Warren spoke German together, not insisting that the infants do likewise, they were incapable, the parents merely replying to questions in the language. 'You'd be surprised how quickly they pick things up,' Janet had once instructed him over the phone, 'and we spend at least one longish holiday a year in the country so they might just as well be prepared.' Every man or woman to his own religion. While Janet was still apparently well, the parents had dropped in, by arrangement, for an hour and a half, not exactly welcomed, Selby deliberately out, and his daughter had showed off abominably by playing a counting game with her two-year-old: *einundzwanzig, zweiundzwanzig, dreiundzwanzig, vierund* . . . Well, at least she had standards.

He ought, breath came shorter as he did not slacken pace

on an uphill slope in colder lack of sunshine, to have written to them. It was unlikely he would have received a reply; a postcard of Bach's Thomaskirche, Leipzig, or the Sans Souci Palace, Potsdam, had to suffice, once a year, to let him know that his nearest and dearest were still alive, or prospering, or travelling abroad. He would write.

A swoop of wind buffeted clumps of daffodils along the drive of Craigmore; the clayey earth lay dry, lumpy, but flower heads were large, products of new bulbs and compost. Well done, the television company and money. It seemed bleaker up here, breezier; round Eleanor's block, the neat lawns, double garages, neatly moulded crisp kerbstones, well-swept ingress roads were unaffected by weather. Alistair, now so near Eleanor's home, felt subdued, apprehensive, when he considered his purpose. To creep into a cold church; he felt inside his overcoat, to the top handkerchief pocket of his jacket, to make sure that the treasury note, his collection, was there. For the rest, he'd keep, stupid phrase, a low profile. In the same night that He was betrayed, took bread, blessed it, broke it. . . . A vague memory of Tolstoy's *Resurrection* stirred in him, of people kissing after Easter service, greeting each other, glad, with 'Christ has risen'. That was all he remembered of the book, except that he had read it in a World's Classic small blue edition; no names, not one; nothing else. A fat lot of good that effort had done for him. Christ has risen.

In front of Eleanor's maroon door, brass-lion knocker, he flicked sleeves back from his watch. Twenty-five to eight, ten minutes early; he'd made good time. He hesitated, wondering if he hadn't overdone smartness, but shortly, militarily, he pressed the bell. He heard it peal inside the corridor, very loud. She hadn't mentioned deafness to him, but there seemed no other explanation for the violence of the sound, unless the house was empty.

He turned his back, examined the sunny neatness of the close, ready to wheel back with an apology once the door opened. Eleanor was in no hurry; he smiled to himself, tapped toe on ground with impatience and leaned longer on the button. Again the peal vibrated. 'Get on with it, woman,' he

183

said, perhaps out loud. No sign from inside. He looked across the lawns, the small cherrytrees, frowning slightly as if he expected her to appear from somewhere in front, out of doors. Nothing. He pressed a third, heavy time.

When the door remained shut, he walked along the flagstones under the large picture window trying to peer inside. The oatmeal curtains were fully drawn; he could make out nothing beyond the row of plants on the windowsills. The second window round the corner was similarly occluded. A cloud crossed the sun, dashing the ground with darkness. He shivered, disturbed now.

Marching back to the front door, he held his finger on the bellpush. The loud sound rolled. He waited. Twenty to eight. Nothing had happened. Breath crouped jaggedly so that he put out a hand on to the brickwork to support himself. If something had gone wrong with Eleanor, how could he, where was the nearest, he must, telephone? Pulling himself up he stamped round the back, to Eleanor's bedroom window. Again the blank, expensive curtain material, properly drawn, with no revealing chinks. Presumably she had gone to bed, then. He could not guarantee that to himself, as it was utterly likely she had fixed her curtains before she set out to the B Minor Mass. She had probably left lights on, as he had. His legs trembled; cold invaded his spine; he groaned, this time for certain, audibly.

Hesitatingly he moved back to the side of the house, where he strained on tiptoe to look in at the stained-glass windows lighting the hall. They were too high. He flung back the way he had come, rounding the corner crudely, catching his elbow, passing her bedroom window, to the kitchen, uncurtained, the wide expanse of glass open to him. His eyes ached, watered, were set in concrete. The kitchen appeared tidy, with doors closed, bar light off; one glass stood unwashed on the draining board. The large tiles of the floor were swabbed clean.

He fought himself to make a decision; discomfort throbbed in head, in neck; his hands hung enlarged, engorged with blood, but achieved sensible conclusion. The windows must be checked to see if he could break in; he would rap loudly at her bedroom; at the front door he would try again to roust her out with the bell, and search the doormat, if it existed, or rockery stone for a hiding place for a key. If all these failed, as he was certain they would, he would look for signs of life, knock up another family and demand to use their phone.

Yet he did not move.

To stand by the kitchen window, locked in inaction, became momentarily proper; he thought of nothing, but convinced himself he was on the edge of some clinching move that would right the situation. He swayed backwards and forwards, using his feet deliberately, proving he was alive, about his business, to the rescue. Again he stooped, peered in at the kitchen; its tidiness warned. Death drops those who keep their houses in order. He clutched a handful of coat by his chest, pushed off. He rapped with such vehemence on her bedroom window that he feared he might have cracked the glass, desisted at once, then listened for a result. The cliché presented itself: 'enough to waken the dead'. Glancing down at his knuckles, he realized he must at some time have removed his gloves. He fiddled in his pockets, pulled out the handsome pair, rammed them back with enmity.

All windows this side were secure.

He looked about across the ample spaces of grass, trees, roads, but all rested quiet, houses blind, not a child delivering newspapers, not a cat; birds had flown.

Round again at the front door, he stared at, pressed the bell, holding the plastic button down. The peal ripped and echoed indoors. He waited, and in vain. He lifted the small, rubber doormat, found nothing under it but a precise pattern of dirt. No other hiding place suggested itself, but he forced himself to search, certain how easy it was to miss the obvious. Failure. He straightened his back, and decided that he would walk across the open area to waken a neighbour, rather than try at the door of the flat above Eleanor's.

He set off, discovering that he was capable of the exercise, not ill, not breathless now that he had started. His course was obvious. Once the police had arrived, found the body, dispatched it for hospital or mortuary, he would have to make another assessment, but at the moment he crossed the flagstones, reached the concrete road. His walk was vigorous, though he felt that his shoes were heavy, soled with thick motor tyre. As he stepped down the kerbstone, he tripped with such violence that his staggering carried him to the middle of the road, three or four yards, where he stood on two feet, muscle and nerve wrenched, twanging. Then as his body heaved, and yet appeared in its shocked energy distant from his mind, he remembered he might well be carrying in this suit the key of Eleanor's house. That was the nagging point. He pulled out his keyring; the small Yale shape glistened, one of five.

Back towards the front door, perfectly negotiating the kerb. He would find her himself, exclude the prying neighbours from gawping at her, as she slumped shamefully. The key in his hand pointed forward towards the lock as he walked. Halfway along the path, he stopped. She would have bolted her door. Eagerness drained off, energy. His chin dropped, trembling. He could manage one thing only at a time; his power to anticipate, to handle even a moderate complexity, to act competently, had gone. A scarecrow, a wooden cross inside a sagging suit, a pattern of failure in a loose, hostile world, Alistair Stewart McMillan Murray just held his ground in the morning's sunshine.

The door opened.

He did not believe eyes and ears. The key still gave direction. Eleanor held the door ajar. He stared.

She peered.

Her dressing gown hung the clayey colour of the earth in flowerbeds. Alistair screwed his eyes; to focus correctly was beyond him. Now she seemed to cower behind the smart door, her head twisted.

'Are you all right?' he asked.

She pulled the door wider.

'Come in.'

She coughed as if to apologize for her lack of volume. As he stepped across the step, she made her way along the hallway, one hand out to the wall. He followed her into the

186

darkened sitting room. She had dropped to a settee, eyes shut, head lolling backwards.

'Shall I draw the curtains?'

She did not answer, but breathed awkwardly loud.

'Are you all right, Eleanor?'

'My head.'

He pulled back one curtain a couple of feet.

'Shall I make some coffee?'

'Yes, please.'

He stumbled out to the kitchen, where he found himself in difficulty at once. The electric kettle proved awkward; he could not find the instant coffee; a quick opening of cupboard doors revealed no cups. He steadied himself, prepared himself for an exhaustive search and came across jar, crockery, spoons immediately. As the kettle boiled he heard the sound of the milkman outside and of a car driving off. The sky was heavily clouded for the moment; no sunshine escaped. He made strong coffee, put it on a tray, marched back.

Eleanor had barely stirred. He put down his tray, dragged one curtain fully back, rubbed his hands together.

'Coffee up,' he said.

Her face was muddy, dry, wrinkled; the whites of her eyes dull, cancer yellow. Untidy hair straggled thinly without nature. Not finding too much trouble she took her cup from him, lifting it by the saucer to her lips.

'Careful,' he warned. 'It's very hot.'

'What time is it?' she croaked, lowering the drink.

'Eleven minutes past eight.'

Alistair sat down by the tray, elbow on the table.

She looked dreadful, almost dirty, shapeless, unattractive. Sipping at her coffee she creaked out, 'My bloody head.'

'Can I get you anything? Aspirin? Paracetemol?'

She shook her head, screwing up her face at the effort. Alistair concentrated on his cup, observing her out of the corner of his eye.

'I took sleeping tablets,' she offered in the end. 'I couldn't get off. And some whisky. That was silly.'

'Couldn't you hear me ringing and banging?'

'I could but it seemed a long way off. I couldn't rouse

myself. It didn't seem to refer to me. And now it's this hangover.'

She made no attempt to speak cheerfully, to sit decently, to apologize. One naked leg showed under the dressing gown. With white and elegant nudity. If she noticed the direction of his eyes, she did nothing about covering herself. Alistair rose, walked to the window. A thrush pecked at the middle of her sunlit front lawn; its breast was clean, with enormous speckles. It was big enough for a mistle thrush, he thought; a stormcock. He remembered a family that had descended on their lawn when Sebastian and Janey were small. King-sized birds. Proud as nobility. This one dragged at a worm, won his tussle. Sunshine played impartially on predator and prey.

'We're too late for St Jude's,' he offered. She did not reply. 'I'm a bit relieved really. It's, it wasn't exactly my scene.' He winced at his word.

She played morosely with her coffee.

'I was relieved to see you at the door,' he began again. 'I really was. I was just off to fetch help. I thought something had happened to you.'

Sourly she paid no attention except to her cup and saucer.

'Your angina. I thought it might be something worse. I didn't know what to think.' He was scornful of his own euphemisms. 'I was all for ringing the police, getting them to break in.'

'Thank you.'

The words, plain, without irony, were pronounced with a kind of social grace, so that he looked at her and surprised himself to find her body still as crumpled. The tone of voice had denied shabbiness. She bent right over to place her two-thirds-full cup on the floor by her slippers before she lay out of true on the settee, eyes passively shut.

In an hour or two, Eleanor would have recovered, have repaired her face, and dressed to kill, the verb rankled, resurrected herself. At this moment nothing about her reminded him of the cream-skinned schoolgirl, the disdainful London miss, not even of last night's socialite in the foyer of the concert hall. She was a rag, except for that nakedness of leg, now almost covered. Her vulnerability lent no attraction; he now, in his dark grey three-piece suit, his shoes polished to his father's standard, sober tie, white shirt, neat head of iron-grey, seemed comical, a clown, a puppet to be manipulated into ridiculous poses: ringing doorbells, rapping at the window, crying at the lock, rousing reluctant neighbours, thinking to kneel, trousers hitched over straight-seamed grey socks, at the altar, a fool, not for Christ's sake, his father's text, but in his own dim eyes.

Tomorrow morning, if he staggered through the rest of this preposterous day, he would begin his memoir, that piece of egregious honesty, or fiction, and he would remember that it ended with a near naked woman in a robe as beautiful as a hessian sack and a stiff old man, in a suit, trousers' arse beginning to shine, hovering round, not a decent lungful of air between them, despising themselves through the eyes of the other.

Purposefully, he picked up his coffee, banged his spoon about in it, essayed a sip, and another. Its warmth, its bitter milkiness struck gratefully into his palate, into his chest, his soul. He perked up, nodded his head in acknowledgement that it was so. He considered the relationship of stimulants and despair, gave that up.

Not thinking, he fiddled with his cup and saucer, the only action he was capable of. The room was quiet with no sound from clock, radiators, furniture, floorboards; Eleanor did not stir. He came gradually to himself, recognized small aches in his body. Almost smiling, he reached again for his coffee. The liquid was drinkable and he swilled it down.

'That's more like it,' he said, replacing the cup on the table. 'Now, young woman, is there anything I can do for you?' The facetious vocative tumbled to his lips, from some old-fashioned novel, shop counter, fatherly *tête-à-tête*.

'No thank you,' Eleanor answered steadily. 'I shall be fine now.'

'That's good.'

She sat up, straightened her robe, looked straight at him.

'I'm sorry about all this.'

'Not at all.'

'It must have frightened you.'

'Yes.'

'I'm sorry, Alistair. It was unnecessary. I should have acted more sensibly last night.'

'Well,' he drawled the word out, 'we're none of us anything to boast about. Not these days.'

'No.'

Long awkwardness prevailed. In reply to a brisk question she refused more coffee, but her silence urged his dismissal. There ought to be suitable action, but he was incapable of thinking of it.

'We're too late for the service,' he said. She did not answer that one. He had already made the point. 'Is there anything I can do?'

'No, thank you.'

He waited; she did not move.

'I'll take these pots and wash them.' As she did not respond, he carried out his promise. When he had finished in the kitchen, he put away the crockery, closed cupboard doors, wiped clean all surfaces, straightened implements and containers. Thus occupied, he recalled his first days as a soldier, preparing the barrackroom for inspection. This time no one would check on him.

When he returned Eleanor sat with her head in her hands.

'That's done that,' he reported.

'Thank you. I feel like death.'

'Now is there anything I can do?'

'No, thank you.'

'If you're sure, then I'll be on my way.' He sounded military to himself. 'What are you going to do?'

'Either go back to bed, or get up very slowly.' She raised a wintry smile.

'Shall I draw the curtains?' He did so, and the sun bounced off furniture, mirrors, the glass of pictures so that her room was marvellously transformed to a dazzle of morning. She made no objection. 'Now, if you're going to be all right . . .'

'Yes, I am.' A stroke of ill temper.

Alistair buttoned up the coat he had not removed, shook himself straight, tried to collect his wits. The introduction of all that light had annoyed her; his best plan was to go.

'Look after yourself, then.'

He, for some reason, held out his hand and it seemed at first that she had not noticed the gesture. Then she took and pressed his fingers, face turned up to his, a half-grateful smile in the ravage of beauty.

Careful to close doors without noise, he let himself out, and was beyond the close into the main road before he recovered. His body, weakened, had enough vitality to propel him along the pavements from one stretch of sunshine through shadow to the next; his mind slopped awash with discomfort.

Reaching home he picked up the Sunday newspapers from the hall. Industrial trouble, government leaks, racist accusation occupied the large headlines. Alistair made breakfast toast and coffee by habit, ate and drank, subsided into a chair. His legs twitched; he could not rest; a spasm of nervous sneezing soaked his handkerchief; sunshine attracted him outside but he sat on.

He had followed instructions that morning, inadequately, and changing tack had been found wanting. That was not the truth, nor anywhere near it. If Eleanor had needed assistance he would have provided it, in the end. He had no recourse, conviction against his feelings. A rattled man had rung, knocked, trampled paths to rouse a woman ugly with headache and drugs. There he stood condemned. From this day forth. It might help to recall his victories, the building of the first comprehensive school, the reorganization of the secondary system, the opening of the junior school his grateful political masters had insisted on naming after him, the holiday camps for the disadvantaged, the youth orchestra's trips to Vienna and America, the athletic stadium, or the hundreds of letters of thanks he had received over the years, saved, and then put on the bonfire in the first weeks of retirement. People had pointed him out; teachers had been grateful for a nod of greeting; he had served on important committees, received an invitation to Buckingham Palace, but now enough proved enough. From this Sunday on he would walk continuously in a state of nerves round the outside of a well-appointed luxury flat and finally by his importunity rouse a woman who wanted nothing else but to be allowed to sleep on.

191

He dozed off.

Not bothering to cook a meal, he lunched from a cheese sandwich, huddled back in his armchair, nodded away again. At two o'clock he woke miserably, dizzy, and washed the dishes he had, unusually for him, left on the draining board. He removed, scrubbed his dentures, washed out his mouth, stared at the newspapers lying unopened on the side table where he had dropped them. Straightening a picture, he walked about his rooms; he picked up a press photograph, framed, of the presentation to his father on retirement of a silver salver and cheque. The old man was gorgeously, foolishly got up in his academicals; his mother wore a ridiculous hat, like a flowered Christmas cake made of concrete, straight on top of her head, a barmy crown. Alistair could raise no smile, nor condemnation. What did it matter now that those old people had dressed themselves so oddly to move out of the career that had occupied them both for so long? The son put the photograph down, turned his back on his father's sickly smile, close enough to a sneer, and decided on the garden as a last resort. He wrapped himself against the cold sunshine.

The borders were welcoming, but consisted as yet of dun earth which in two months' time would be high-hidden with summer growth. At least in this dry wind weeds stood little chance. It was warmer outside than he had expected; nooks protected him from the northeasterly. In a short time the blossom would load the amalanchier, the flowering cherries, the red crab; a little later clumps of surviving hawthorn in the city would be thick with may. It seemed just believable. He worked his way to the gate, stood with fingertips extended on its top bar, his mouth listless with disappointment.

A family approached down the hill. Alistair knew them slightly.

The father, a smart man, with brogues, cavalry-twill trousers, a British warm overcoat, was a well-to-do accountant and a colonel in the TA. He carried, swung an ash stick from gloved hands. He wore no hat, was balding in the middle of his head, but the sandy hair at back and sides curled attractively; his skin was deeply tanned, as if he had that day returned from the Mediterranean. He lifted his cane in greeting, half stopping.

'Lovely day,' he called.

His womenfolk, a mother and two daughters, paused with him. The girls, in their late teens, very like their mother, tall and pale, put on social faces. They were very beautiful, oval-featured, also like their mother, who might well have been their older sister.

'Cool still,' Alistair ventured.

'At least it's not raining.' The females all smiled with their father.

'We shall be praying for it soon.'

'Yes.' A moustache-biting monosyllable. 'I can see you're a keen gardener.' He pointed with his stick into Alistair's ground.

'Not at this time of year.'

'Is that a flowering cherry?' his wife asked.

'Yes.'

'It's a good size. I wonder how old it is.'

'I put it in myself, oh, twenty-one years ago.'

'Gracious. I'd have guessed it was much older than that from the size.'

The colonel flourished his stick; his wife inclined her head; the beautiful daughters smiled, slightly, slowly, with dark blue eyes, and the family moved away, the father's steel-tipped heels clipping on the pavement.

Alistair knew them well by sight, but could not come up with their name. They had lived at the top of the road for some years; he could remember the girls running home with a group, quite small schoolchildren. Nearly two years ago, was it so long?, their only son, a boy of twenty, an infantry subaltern, had been killed in the Falklands War. Murray had seen the photographs of the family in the paper at the time, at the memorial service, on the presentation of a posthumous MC, on the visit by the parents to the grave.

This Easter Sunday the four walked with equanimity down the road, passed the time of day pleasantly with him. Alton? was that the name? Halton? Halford? He could not remember.

They could present firm faces, at least, to the world.

The boy had been away at boarding school, Marlborough or Shrewsbury: Alistair thought he could recall him, but the recollection was all sportscoat, well-creased flannels, the uniform of his own youth, not of this denim generation. He gave up, but pushed forward to the gate to lean out. The family were still in sight, but a good way down the hill, much farther than he expected. They were not hanging about. He watched them cross the road, progress up the other side, still keeping their formation, father on the outside.

It ought to be a lesson to him. It was not.

The phone rang, and he turned only listlessly to answer it, believing that by the time he was indoors the caller would have tired of waiting.

'Hello, Dad. Where were you? In the bath?' Sebastian.

'In the garden.'

'Then it must be a damn sight warmer with you than it is here.'

'Isn't the sun shining?'

'I suppose it is.'

Sebastian sounded cheerful, reporting that he had a fortnight's 'reading leave' before he left for India. He sometimes wished, he whispered, that he had gone into academic life, where he could instruct a few well-chosen pupils, and spend the rest of his time reading and writing.

'You don't believe that,' his father chided.

'I'm not sure.'

'Look at your bank account, and that will make your mind up for you.'

'You have it on you this morning, my man.'

Alistair asked after Francesca, who was to accompany her husband to Bombay. She would take time off from her office and hostels, and had been preparing herself to look into the position of women in the subcontinent. No, she did not intend to write a book, it was all too complicated, but she'd already raised really interesting questions that his research team were engaged with. It would be a holiday for her, he hoped, but she was having more and more to do with Indian women over here. No, she was out this morning. She'd gone to see the Generals, the Fletchers, did he remember? They had visited them at Christmas. No, he was not in charge of the cooking. A sandwich at three, and dinner out at a tandoori this evening. Yes, they'd finished their jabs, cholera included. Yes, he knew it was a rotten time to go out east, the weather was just about as hot as it could be, but then everybody else went out in October.

'What's the idea of the programmes?' Alistair asked.

'We're not sure.'

'Political? Religious? Geographical? What?'

'We don't really know.'

'Then you might just as well stay at home, I'm telling you.'

'Well, we're taking Ben Weeks and his team with us. The pictures will be worth looking at, if nothing else is.'

'The sunlight at this time of year drains the colour out of everything.'

'Ben'll put it back. I'd forgotten that you'd served out there.'

'I'll tell you something else. Anybody who writes about India, or makes a programme and that means a commentary whether it's intended or not, is just asking to be cut to pieces by pundits. It's too complicated. You'll just make a fool of yourself.'

'Thanks. I'll bear that in mind.'

'Are you interviewing Mrs Gandhi?'

'That has been arranged.'

'And yet you don't know what the shape or the intention of the programme is? I don't believe it.'

'It's the truth. Cross mi 'eart. We've no end of experts all sticking their oars in, instructing me, and my masters.'

'And you'll fall between all their stools.'

'As long as I fall interestingly, that's all that matters.'

'You know that's not so.'

'I can see,' Sebastian sounded delighted with himself, 'that nothing I can do will please you this morning. Go on, you tell me what you think about India in about ten words. Father Murray's largest generalization. What's the sentence you'd dredge up?'

'There isn't one.'

'Come on. Don't be lazy. Here's your big chance to set me right, to make my name.'

'You've done that already.'

'Come on now, man. India forty years on in two sentences.'

They paused as Alistair found a distanced pleasure in Seb's high spirits.

'Silenced, then?'

'Not quite. Don't be in such a rush.'

'Thank God I'm on the cheap rate.'

'You'll be able to set it against expenses.' Alistair cleared his throat. 'The thing that struck me most forcibly about India was the effect of the climate.'

'Go on.'

'The extremes of heat, the set periods of monsoon rain made Indian character, religion, politics what they are.'

'Wouldn't that be so with our climate? Or that of anybody else?'

'Yes. To an extent. But they have this ferocious heat, overpowering dryness that we don't. But there again, the place is so large, one can't generalize. In some of the hill stations you might be in England. And in any case the pitilesss sunlight might have less effect on the natives than on some slightly ginger, freckled Scot like me.'

'I'll think about that, Dad.'

Alistair was sure that Sebastian would, or would arrange for his teams to do so. The boy wasted nothing; the father felt suddenly proud of his son's exemplary skills and that he himself was still capable of making a suggestion that was not dismissed out of hand. As the two chatted on, Alistair felt that Sebastian was trying out ideas on him, and was gladdened that it was so. When he laid down the telephone after nearly half an hour he reeled, exhausted, but capable of revival. Whistling, he fetched out a teabag, something he did rarely on a Sunday, a day for silver spoons and no half measures.

He debated with himself whether to ring Eleanor, and decided against it, proud of the decision.

Mrs Montgomerie phoned at about five to invite him to dinner later in the month. He searched and reported that the date stood empty in his diary.

'Just a few friends. Mostly medicos.'

'I see.'

'They'll talk shop and golf.'

'Oh dear.'

'You can talk to me. Or the women. They'll all want to ask about schools.'

'I'll do my best for you.'

'Would you like to bring a partner? Mrs Franks who was with you last night? Would she, do you think?'

That was it. Mr Montgomerie had realized that he had fluffed the chance to make a valuable social contact, and was now setting about the repair work.

'She is away a great deal,' he said, 'but I'll ask her.'

He felt twinges of guilt and power. Katherine Montgomerie, to give her credit, changed the subject at once, and quizzed him about the size of Bach's original choirs. He did not know, laid down the law on a subject he was conversant with, the date of the composition of the *Matthew Passion*, and promised he'd find out, if it was possible.

'I wish it would warm up,' she complained at the end of the lecture.

He asked about the children, Jeremy's rate of recovery, said he would contact Mrs Franks. When he had replaced the phone in its cradle, he scowled at it with something of his earlier pessimism. If he'd had an ounce of sense, he'd have choked the woman off. On second thoughts, he was pleased at his grace, though he had already decided not to approach Eleanor until tomorrow. Sebastian had not asked him about his 'ladyfriend', whereas Francesca would have ribbed him about his successes with the other sex. He sat in his chair at six o'clock, the day, Easter, as good as finished, though tomorrow was a bank holiday. It was either a cup of coffee or a turn round the garden; he decided on the latter.

The sky stretched bright still as he made for the front gate, to poke out into the wide world.

A couple approached; the man sedately touched the brim of a brown trilby.

'Nice evening, Mr Murray.'

Alistair had not recognized the man; his face was nondescript, thin and tanned, handsome, that of an aggressive nobody. The voice, as before, gave away the police inspector. He was, moreover, wearing a severely smart pair of glasses.

'Yes. Too cold for my comfort.'

The pair had taken three paces past when the man swung round.

'You saw we got your man?'

The woman had continued for a step or two beyond her husband, but now halted, determined to be on the edge only of this exchange.

'The murderer. It was in the local paper.'

'I didn't. When was that?'

'Saturday's *Post*. We fetched him in the day before. Arrested Good Friday.'

'I didn't see it.' On the evening of the B Minor Mass, his preparations had not allowed time for the reading of the newspaper. 'How did you manage it?'

The inspector came a step closer, back to his wife, lowering the already confidential voice.

'His woman. Gave him away in the end. Broke his alibi.'

'Why was that?'

'They weren't getting on very well.'

'Because of the murder?'

The inspector shrugged.

'Whatever the reason, she let on there was something hidden under a pile of wood in the garden shed, and there was his mac and trousers, soaked in blood.'

'Hadn't you searched the place before?'

'Apparently.' The inspector changed tack. 'They'd made no attempt to clean them up. Or burn them. Some people haven't got the wit they're born with. They could have taken them down to the launderette. But not them. Some folk aren't blessed.'

'What happens now?'

'Magistrates' court after the holidays.'

'Has he made a statement?'

'I'll say.'

They paused. The woman peered closely as if the Bulwell stone wall were about to speak to her.

'That's very satisfactory,' Murray said dryly.

'Ye'. It's not my case now. A young constable bothered and bothered the woman until she came out with it.'

'What'll happen?'

'Depends on psychiatrists' reports and all the rest. He'll get life. The judge might say what that means. You can never tell.'

'And the woman?'

'God knows. Live on social security with her kids. He'd quite a good job. Plumber.'

'Why did he . . .?'

'Drink. Hated Pakis. One thing led to another. They got fighting. Or he did. Nice, quiet little chap, the taximan.'

'And the knife?'

'A mystery. It's never been found. And he's not been known to carry such a thing.'

'Was it the driver's?'

'Apparently not. Though with some of these clients, and at that time of night, I'd want a sub-machine gun.' The policeman's face was impassive, as if to deny emotional involvement. 'Well, we shall have to get on.' He touched the brim of his hat and his wife diverted her attention towards Murray to smile. Alistair watched their progress up the road, the man ramrod straight, the wife jerking with one foot in front of the other. A good craftsman, that, walking his patch in off-duty hours, eyes open.

Murray worked his way towards the back garden where the wind rattled twigs at the top of the trees. A discernible light shone upstairs in the Montgomeries' house; one of the children being put to bed. A sparrow or two trundled the air. Some almost invisible creature, cat or fox, crossed the far boundary, patches of copper brown in the long grass. He closed the greenhouse window, noting that his tomato plants had not grown sufficiently to be repotted; they did not need watering.

At 6.37 the minister at his father's church would be drilling into the first prayer. Murray laughed at his presumption, because, for all he knew, the order of service had been utterly changed since his last regular appearances there nearly forty years before. With a small grimace of self-satisfaction, he doubted his doubt. They'd be immersed in the same ritual, rigmarole, and none the worse for that. They'd lost him, and improved the quality of their belief by so doing. His father had mounted the pulpit steps, praised God, instructed his flock, appealed for justice, mercy, forgiveness from on high, not sparing himself. His sermons had been models, scholarly, yet not above the heads of the congregation, livened with anecdote, spiced with pawky humour, yet all preaching Christ, and Him crucified. They had beginnings, middles, ends; they made plain, they could uplift, even condemn. And the preparation of these homilies was never done at the expense of pastoral work; the reverend doctor would rush off to hospital, to bereaved home, to pray with some querulous spinster, to argue with an errant son, to appear before magistrates, tribunals, to write testimonials, letters of appeal, comfort, humble rebuke. His father had made his name known, continuing into old age.

Even when he had officially retired, the old man could still be prevailed on to preach and spend time at the bedside of some ailing member. Not many weeks before James Murray's death, he'd gone out into the rain on one of these visits, refusing to take a taxi. 'I've an umbrella,' he pointed out to his wife, who failed to drum sense into him. 'And there is a public transport system that is not altogether inefficient.' Rhoda had complained to her son at the time that he had looked like a skeleton. 'He hardly eats enough to keep a bird alive.' She had appealed to her son. 'I wish you'd speak to him.'

'Wouldn't it be a waste of my time?'

It had proved so, but weakness had finally overwhelmed the old man, pinning him for days on end to his bed. He'd died suddenly and peacefully after attending morning service.

Alistair Murray, keyed up to begin a summary of his own life, saw his father's as a success. Disappointments abounded, doubtless, Alistair one of them, but the Lord's labour had occupied J. J. Murray almost to his last breath, whereas his son had kept himself away from people, at a distance from the workface, producing papers. True, he had done it adequately, but knew that though he often said that an administrator's task was to make it that much easier for students to learn and teachers to instruct, he'd too often succumbed to the temptation for the neat solution, that saved money, or cut time he and his understrappers might have to spend. Moreover he had nothing to show: those incisive minutes and instructions had long since perished in the pulping machine while upstairs was a tin trunk packed with his father's sermons, neatly typed, dated. They gathered dust, but so had Hopkins's poems or Schubert's manuscripts or the Abbé Mendel's researches.

He had been faceless, a powerful name at the bottom of official orders in staffrooms. Deliberately he had kept out of the public eye while he was at work, and when he retired he refused all voluntary committee work, pleading his wife's precarious health.

Indoors, removing his coat, he wondered how he could justify his life. He had been successful: his schemes worked; he had eschewed favouritism, been as just as his position allowed. He remembered a friend, not twelve months ago, quoting an assistant director about some sharp practice by a go-getting headmaster: 'He wouldn't have got away with it under Alistair Murray.' He hung his scarf.

The telephone startled him.

That was all he could expect now, interruptions from callers, none important, inquiries about groceries, or projected decorating, or his health, invitations to places as boring as his home. He lifted the receiver, grateful.

Francesca.

'What are you up to? Just as the phone went?'

'I was taking my scarf off.'

'Where had you been, then?'

'The greenhouse.'

He explained about his trip round the garden, gave a detailed account of his conversation with the inspector. She sounded interested. Without intending it, he described his attempt to wake Eleanor up. She listened, purring her close attention.

'That must have been awful,' Francesca pronounced.

'Not good.'

'Why don't you come down to visit us?'

'You're going to India.'

'Not this week we aren't.'

Her expression and tone wrung a laugh out of him.

'Are you sure you're all right?' she persisted.

'Don't I sound it?'

'No. You sound, oh, on the defensive.'

'I'll make a confession, then.' He spoke to no one else in this way.

'Yes.'

'Tomorrow morning I'm going to start on my autobiography.'

She did not answer at once; perhaps she straightened a picture or moved a pencil from one receptacle to another.

'Oh, I see. You didn't say anything to Sebby?'

'No.'

'Why not?'

'I like to have little secret holes and corners of my own. I'm a bit frightened of him, what he'll think.'

'But you'll tell me?'

'Yes.'

'Seb would have been very good. He's bursting with ideas.'

'I want to do it myself.'

'He'd let you do that. He's marvellous at getting out of people what they hadn't realized was there.' She laughed. 'I think it's funny that you're scared of him. I'd have said it was the other way about. There are the pair of you keeping your heads down while the other's around. But, go on, tell me about your memoir.'

'I start tomorrow.'

'So you said.'

'I just give an account of who I am, and what I've done.'

'On what sort of grounds? What sort of reader have you got in mind?'

'Antiquarian. I wouldn't say my life was all that interesting in itself, but it's always worth seeing what somebody put down about his everyday existence, however badly, in later years when there's not a great deal of evidence of that kind still extant.'

'Isn't there a lot more nowadays?'

'A lot more what?' He felt exasperation at her questions.

'Evidence. If we could come across a similar memoir from, say, Chaucer's time, that would be something, but printing's been invented, and we have newspapers and books and tapes and videos by the hundreds nowadays.'

'So there's not much point in my writing? Thank you.'

'Don't take it like that. You may be able to produce a literary gem.'

'I may not.'

'One doesn't know until one's tried.' She did not sound serious.

'It's very unlikely.'

They paused; he tried to work over the conversation of the last few minutes, which had revealed himself to himself in a bad light.

'This is really good.' Francesca began again. 'You surprise me, Alistair, from time to time.' She did not usually call him by his Christian name. 'Is this memoir of yours a justification?'

'*Apologia pro vita mea*?' He begged time with the Latin.

'Yes. Is it?'

'I've been thinking about that. It's not the way it began. I thought I'd just jot down what I could remember, discover what I could dredge up from the bran tub. That should be justification enough. Why do I remember this and not that? Why do I choose to write about this rather than that? I'd learn something about myself. Whether I'd lie, for instance, to make the story more readable. What I'd hide away, and why. That's been gnawing at me.'

'Good, good.'

'No. I'm not honest enough. At least I think not.'

'You surprise me. You really do.'

'I'm full of gall. Still. After all these years I hate the people who've done me down. But I'll plaster it over. My middle name is Soft Soap. I'm hard-faced, two-faced. Number one this savage; the second everybody's friend, Mr Sweet Reason.'

'Aren't we all like that?'

'I doubt it. You say you're surprised. I'm like the Bourbons in that I forget nothing. Or nothing unpleasant. I thought I had. Now slights that meant precious little at the time, that I shrugged past without second thoughts, fester like wounds.'

'Doesn't that say something about you now?'

'Of course it does.'

'I meant you-now rather than you-then.'

'You mean,' he growled, 'I've grown worse than I was; that's what you mean. And it's true.'

'Steady, steady,' she warned.

'I'll be that all right. I'm not capable of anything else.'

'I'm not so sure.' She paused; he could hear her breathing. 'I wish you'd spoken to His Nibs.'

'I'll consider it. Once I've begun, convinced myself I can beat inertia.'

'Are you going to let me read it? Or Eleanor?'

'I haven't considered that.'

'But won't it make a difference to what you write? I mean, from what bit you've told me you were chasing Eleanor years ago, when you were single. Now if you write about that and you know she'll be going to read it . . .? Don't you think so?'

'Well, yes.'

'It will be fascinating for her. To know what you thought of her at the time. She'll probably not agree.'

'And I'll probably not get as far as that.'

'Oh, come on now. You're not feeble.'

' "Human kind cannot bear very much reality," ' he said. 'If I can offer you T. S. Eliot.'

'He didn't mean what you do by "reality", my man. As well you know.'

'Do you know the *Four Quartets*, then?'

' "Burnt Norton", well, at least. Sebby and I read them to each other. How about that?'

'Now you surprise me. When? Why?'

'On free evenings. We'll do an hour, perhaps twice, three times a fortnight. We both like reading out loud.'

'And do you discuss what you've read?'

'Not now. We did at one time, but we never got anywhere. He thinks these are great poems, and I don't.'

'Why not?'

'Eliot's not honest with us, either.'

'Steady the Buffs.' Alistair visualized his daughter-in-law as a small, tight-lipped child, defying the adults. 'Come on, then. Explain.'

'I think, Seb doesn't, that Eliot is saying, memorably, superbly, something he doesn't know at first hand, something he'd sooner know for himself than anything else, but he doesn't. It's second hand, out of books. Hearsay.'

'Why do you think this?'

'He distances himself. It's not like somebody saying something for himself.'

'Isn't that always Eliot's method?'

'Well, he's secretive, certainly. Likes puzzles. But he's putting experiences down, an equivalent of the Bible, in memorable language, but more interested in the artefact than what he's found out by direct contact.'

Alistair argued no further. He should have reached for his copy, argued from the lines themselves, at first hand, made her declare herself on this word, or that, but he had neither intellectual muscle nor relish for disagreement at this hour of the evening. At the same time he felt admiration for the girl. Francesca, no expert on poetry, who'd read law at the university, had come to her own shocking conclusions. He had read 'Burnt Norton' as a young man, and it had sounded as high poetry, out of his class, quietly important, a glimpse of heaven on earth if only through the stately beauty of the words.

> shall we follow
> The deception of the thrush?

But this girl had looked on Eliot as a specious witness, beautifully delivering a testimony in her court that he was not entitled to give. That, and the picture of the two, she and Sebastian, a copy each in their hands, why did he think that?, mouthing the lines to each other, cutting themselves off from the presidents and principalities, the battered wives, the world-ordering conferences, the world-shattering punch in the face, silenced him. Why had he and Janet never read together like this? The family had interfered? He was certain that had they been childless they would not have offered poetry to each other. Janet would not have wanted it. Why should he blame her? Who was he to adopt a pose of superiority? His father and mother had read the Bible out loud at home. No, he was at fault, and knew it. He should have insisted, but it had never crossed his mind.

'You're very quiet.' Francesca spoke with care.

'I'm just thinking,' he said, 'that if you're going to indict Eliot for dishonesty, what sort of showing shall I make?'

'You'll be all right, because you'll put down what you saw with your own eyes.'

Alistair bit hard on his left thumb, because the answer he had just given her was false, the admin man's slickness, the bland disguising of awkwardness, angularity. He ought to have done better, especially for Francesca. What sort of honesty did that presage for tomorrow morning when he picked up his newly filled pen?

'You're away again,' she interrupted. 'Are you going to do it chronologically?'

'I'd thought so.'

'Thought?'

'I just am not sure,' he answered, 'not until I've tried. That's what I'd planned, if planning is the word for the few minutes I've spent. I only made my mind up on Saturday night.'

'Why?'

'Why what?'

'Why did you suddenly decide then?'

'I don't know. I suppose I'd considered it before. Vaguely. I'd been to the B Minor Mass with Eleanor. Perhaps I was taken out of myself.'

'Ah, Eleanor.' He could hear the laughter in her voice, the affection, tenderness. 'Now that enigmatic lady's going to play a big part in these memoirs, isn't she?'

'We'll see.'

'Did your wife, Sebby's mother, know her?' That phrase, 'Sebby's mother', had been inserted as an emollient, suggesting the closeness of Janet and himself, opposed to the flibbertigibbet nature of his love for the other woman.

'They met once or twice. They must have done so when we settled back here for good. But we made no real attempt to get together. Eleanor's social circle was different from ours. Franks was extremely rich, and hobnobbed with his like.'

'They put you in your place.'

'I don't think it ever occurred to either family to, oh, take steps to . . .'

'But now.'

Slowly, in shorthand, he recalled for her again Eleanor's visit on that windy night.

'She must have known your address.' Francesca laid down the law.

'I suppose so.'

'Then she must have had some interest in you for some time?'

'I don't know about that.'

'But when you come to write this part of your story, you'll have to decide.'

'No. I shall put down the facts and leave the reader to make his mind up.'

'But surely you see that the words you choose, the order of your sentences and paragraphs, will lay open what you are perhaps trying to hide.'

'Subconsciously. But by definition, I can't control that, can I?'

'This is going to be really interesting. I wish you'd talked about it to Sebastian. I tell you what. Will you phone tomorrow evening and say how the day's work went?'

'It's not the first day that bothers me, but the twentieth, the fiftieth, the two hundredth.'

'Yes, yes. You'll do your best for me, won't you?'

'For you?' he asked, surprised, not exactly pleasantly.

'Make me your reader. Somebody young and unshockable and interested, who's heard it all before. Then you can be honest.'

'Honest, yes. Honest.'

207

He repeated the word newly minted, as if its meaning were outlandish, foreign to his life, work, society.

How would he deal with his wife, Janet? 'Sebby's mother'?

The burden of finding facts flattened his quickening spirit.

'The more you talk to me,' he said, and bitterly, 'the less inclined I am to begin.'

'But you will.' Francesca sounded cheerful.

'The difficulties . . .'

'That's the beauty.' She might have been eighteen, or slightly tipsy. 'Like your inspector grubbing away until the truth's revealed.'

'That's what I fear.'

'What is?'

'That I shan't like the truth when I find it. You were quite right. This is a justification for the way I've lived. And I don't approve.'

'You mean,' she pressed, in a still, small voice, 'that if you had your life over again you'd live it differently?'

'I can't answer that.'

'Why not?'

'I'd be the same basic material. And even if I know what I know now I wonder if I would be able to make large changes. Perhaps it is the small decision that counts. Which pair of shoes to wear, whether to go by bus or on foot. But, Francesca, even as I'm telling you this, I wonder if it's not a sign of self-satisfaction. I've been what I have been, and I wouldn't have it changed.'

'I don't see it like that.' She sounded sane, confident, encouraging. 'You just realize that there is no possibility of change, and so it's no use worrying. Not now.'

'What about regret?' he asked.

'I expect you feel that and that you feel malice against those who blocked your path. But for them you might have been, oh, the top dog in the DES or the Archbishop of Canterbury or whatever.'

'I might have been like Sebastian, better known than either.'

'Are you jealous of him, then?' She sounded tense. 'He thinks it's fool's gold. That it's all nothing. That as soon as his face is off the screen, his reputation will disappear, and his name even will be forgotten.'

'You sound like an Old Testament prophet. New English Translation.'

'You've not lost your judgement. I must ring off. We're going out. I feel excited. For you, but for myself. You will ring tomorrow evening?' He promised. 'Goodness, look at the time.'

'Where's Seb?'

'In his study.'

'Listening to us?'

'No way.'

Now she was cheerful again, and he smiled as he put down the telephone. He squinted at it, as if it might speak. 'Balaam's ass.' He chewed mildly at his lower lip, and found himself mounting the stairs. In his study the paper lay ready, the pen, he tried it with a squiggle, capable of making marks. He knitted his brow for no good reason, the author, the contemplative man. He sat at his desk, trying or guying the new persona.

He made a tour of the closed rooms; they reminded him of nothing. Downstairs he turned on the radio. A hymn, new and popular, not a hundred years old, rolled blandly, informing God that His hand had guided His flock from age to age. Alistair Murray would put that to the test tomorrow.

A shudder of apprehension touched him as he turned the wireless down, then off.

On Saturday afternoons he sometimes accompanied his father to an allotment owned by a member of the congregation who sold the minister vegetables in season. The itinerary of father and son never varied; twenty minutes of pavements until they reached St Ann's Road, terraced houses opening on to the street on the one side, on the other the massed gardens where decent men spent their leisure time. They penetrated a high hawthorn hedge by means of a stout wooden gate, wide enough to allow a cart through, even a lorry if the driver didn't mind getting the sides scratched. That was always locked, but the Reverend James J. Murray held a key, an honorary gardener, at least in the eyes of his Mr Hopewell.

The lanes were dark between high protective hedges; nearly every patch had its hut where the owner stored tools. Some of these buildings were of brick, with fireplaces and elaborate chimneys; presumably on a winter's day one could retire to warmth, a cup of tea, companionship, a hand of cards if the weather proved inhospitable to work. Mr Hopewell's hut was of medium pretension only, wooden, tarred, a tarpaulin nailed to the sloping roof, one of its four windowpanes cracked across a corner. Here was no hearth, no candles, no oil-lamps; a backless chair provided the privileged guest with a seat; otherwise one perched on sacks or a heap of timber. The whole hut was covered, Alistair remembered, with a climbing rose, or two, with small pink flowers, and white, and ferocious prickles. The minister admired this combination of nature and art, but Mr Hopewell condemned it as a nuisance, a cause of damp.

Father and son always took up a position in front of the door to the hut, and waited. Hopewell never kept them long; he knew they would arrive as soon after 2.30 as Mr Murray's duties allowed. He, bending over spade or string or peastick, would jerk upwards, cough, and lumber at speed, the garden stood on a slope, towards them in his shirtsleeves. Arrived, he would apologize for the state of his hands, which he held out for inspection, saying they were unfit for shaking. The minister insisted in clasping the palm and fingers in his own: little Alistair was almost certain that Hopewell kept his right hand free from egregious filth for this ceremony. The boy would be solemnly greeted, and some inquiry made about progress in school. This passage included reference to Latin, for in his youth Alfred Hopewell had attended an elementary school, in Staffordshire or Shropshire, where the headmaster had given instruction to chosen pupils in Latin grammar. At this date, Alistair would be no more than nine, he had not begun the language, but he remembered when he was perhaps thirteen or fourteen meeting Hopewell in the street when the stock question was posed.

'We're doing the ablative absolute,' he had answered.

Hopewell nodded, his face a combination of envy and approval at the naming of this mystery.

'Good,' he had said. 'Absolute. Ablative absolute.' He did not require further explanation from Alistair; nomenclature sufficed.

As Murray remembered these visits to the allotment, the weather seemed always sunny. But he had been bored. Their trips followed the same procedure; a procession up the garden path while Hopewell pointed out progress of crops. Even gooseberries, raspberries, rhubarb, apples handed back failed to sweeten the boy. He tailed behind listening to the gardener's boastful flow, his father's questions encouraging further eloquence, and finally sound advice as to what was best to grace the minister's Sabbath table, and the ceremony of plucking or cutting. Alistair kicked the dirt path; nothing here for him.

And yet he remembered one occasion.

His father and Hopewell, oddly laconic, walked the length of the garden with linked arms. Murray could not remember this afternoon as stretching longer than the others. Only the vignette of clerical grey, J.J. made no sartorial concessions to Saturday, thrust through the awkward crook of rolled shirt-sleeves and sunburnt forearm, and the lack of words. That, and the sudden descent of his father's leaden hand on to his shoulder as they walked back in the shady lanes carrying the bag of greens and the sentence, 'His little boy died this week. Seven years old.' His daddy's voice was strange, strangled, near breaking so that he dared not look up. Two solemn creatures plodded home.

'As it might be you.' His father did not pronounce the words, but his son, eight years old, knew they existed, were real. His father had not prayed in the garden, nor mentioned the death, at least in the child's hearing; Hopewell had pointed with a forefinger and thumb at his produce; as the men walked the path the bored boy, aware of differences, trundled behind.

That was his morrow's task.

He sat in his chair, wasting time, remembering nothing until the telephone jolted him up.

'Hello, there.' Sebastian. 'Francesca's told me. We've just come into the restaurant. So I said I'd ring you.'

'Thanks.'

'I think she wanted me to.'

'I'm sure. But wait till I've done something. Come on, then. Be useful.' He tried bluff cheerfulness. 'What about a title?'

Sebastian thought. Two men waited, one hundred and twenty miles apart.

' "The treasure of your time." '

'*Twelfth Night*,' Alistair said.

'Exactly. Quotation?'

' "Besides, you waste the treasure of your time with a foolish knight." '

'Well done. Don't know about Sir Andrew, though. "Time and the hour." How about that? *Macbeth*.'

' "Run through the roughest day." Run? Runs?'

' "Runs." ' His son set him right with confidence. 'I'm just wishing you all the best. Francy didn't know whether she should have told me, but once she had, she hinted I ought to ring.'

'Thanks one and all. The whole world's writing this memoir.'

'That sounds ungrateful.'

'I want to sit down, day after day for a few weeks, to see what I can do. I don't need inspectors and advisers. Or, at least not yet.'

'Very good. I'll keep my long nose out.'

'Not you.'

'You'll see. But just for the present, the best of luck.'

'I'll need it.'

'I doubt, Dad, if you will. Don't forget, if you want a second opinion, about some of the events I appear in and can be expected to remember, here I am.'

'I'd sooner get it wrong on my own.'

'Uh. I see.'

'I'm sorry if I sound a bit grim and gruff.'

'You were always like that if you were about to take on anything out of the ordinary. Or even if I was. Before I took A-levels or university scholarship.'

'I suppose that was so.' He did not remember.

'Never mind supposition. The facts of life. That's what we want from you. I must be getting back to my table. All the best. Look after yourself. Fran told me to give you her love.'

As Alistair turned away from the telephone he shrugged discontent with himself. Instead of the grudging replies, he should have chattered, exchanged banter, been at his ease. If he could not manage that with his son, at a distance, then . . .? That was exactly the question to sort out tomorrow, the tomorrows of the next months, and it was well that he had realized it. He wondered if Sebastian loved him.

At that question, he barked with a dry laugh, straightening with quick dabs of the foot a ruck in the carpet, like a cat covering its faeces. The boy had listened to him in his childhood, had followed his advice, had shown admiration for this not smiling father, but his real affection had been for Janet. That hard woman, who had drawn up a map of expected success for her son as well as her husband, had exposed her love for the boy, and on the revelation, in return for it, had received his.

Alistair saw again his son, driving up at unexpected moments, to see his dying mother. Janet, whatever her pain or distress, could pull herself round, put a good face on it as soon as Sebastian arrived, announced or not. Except once, when she had been taken back into the General Hospital the morning that her son turned up just before his father set off for the afternoon visit.

The doctors had been blunt; it was a matter of weeks only now. Alistair sat his son down – he could see the very chair, the rug, the cushions this minute as he remembered – to explain this. Sebastian had been calm, intelligent, a man of the wide world, twenty-eight years old, in smart denim, styled hair, expensive, uncared-for Italian shoes.

'Is she in pain?'

'Yes. That's one reason they took her back in.'

'Can they do anything about it?'

'They say so.'

His son looked handsome, a cool giant, a faint smile on the well-cut lips, his hands large, held motionless, ready to seize, ruthlessly shake.

'Does she know?'

'What?' A father's mean spirit would force the son to speak with exactitude.

'That she is going to die.'

'I don't know. I don't think the doctors have told her.'

'And you haven't?'

'No.' That craggy, stony word.

The pair drove to the hospital in Sebastian's Mercedes. Alistair thought it would be impossible to park, but his son soon organized a place for himself. Inside they had difficulty in locating the small, single side room where she had been housed. Twice they tramped, in spite of noticeboards enormous with every piece of information except for the one they sought, the length of a busy corridor.

Both men kept their mouths shut.

A nurse was attending to Janet.

'Look here, Mrs Murray. Look who's come to see you.'

Alistair guessed that Janet, usually reticent, had been telling the sister about her Sebastian, who, though successful, was then nothing like the nationally known figure he was to become in the next year or two.

Husband and son both bent to kiss the yellow, haggard face. Janet tugged at the sleeves of her nightgown; the shattered features lit up.

'Hello, Sebastian. How are you? It's lovely to see you. You shouldn't have come specially.' The voice croaked, hoarse and thin, the accent daily more Scottish. Janet instructed Alistair about the finding of another chair, and when he had returned with that made him pour her a glass of lemonade, with which she moistened her lips.

'How are you, then?' the son asked.

'I feel a wee bit stronger today.'

'Are you in any pain?'

'Och, yes. Sometimes.' She spoke almost whimsically; the men translated for themselves: in agony all the time. The nurse, who had occupied herself at the cupboards during the initial minutes of the visit, interrupted to announce she was on her way, but that Mrs Murray was to call her if she wanted anything.

'I shall be fine,' Janet answered.

214

'Yes, you've got your men now.' Gratified, tense smiles all round.

Slowly Janet ground out questions, which Sebastian meticulously answered. He described his trips abroad, threw in the names of famous people he had met. The young man never boasted, but suited his audience exactly, aimed to fascinate. Once he looked up at his father from an entertaining account of three hours spent in the company of a royal couple to mention that on the same day he had met a very distinguished theologian who had heard his grandfather preach. Janet did not interrupt except now and again to indicate with a gesture of a talon that she needed to wet her lips from the glass.

In less than a quarter of an hour, though it seemed longer to Alistair perhaps on account of Sebastian's brilliant flatness, Janet's eyes began to close with pain or fatigue.

'How are you, Mother?' Alistair asked. Her eyes jerked open.

'Don't interrupt,' she snapped, signalling her son to continue.

Within minutes she had dozed off again, head lolling, her breathing barbed with small snatched snores. Sebastian hesitated, then stopped.

'It's weakness,' Alistair explained. 'She's worn out.'

The men watched, afraid she would topple. Sebastian's large hands lay poised in readiness on the bed as he leaned forward. Earlier, his mother had asked her one question self-allowed, about his girlfriends, and had accepted that no regular occupied his affections. He must not have met Francesca at this time, or not yet marked her down as out of the ordinary. Until six months before he had lived with a very bright young woman, another journalist, whom they had met once; Janet disapproved of the cohabitation, but said nothing to her son, and once to her husband, 'Young people don't look on these things in the same light as we do.' Now, she made a point of asking each time she saw her boy, but willingly backed away once a respectable answer had been proffered; Alistair was surprised, concerned, faintly amused.

As Sebastian watched his mother one tear, large as a marble, squeezed out from his left eye and rolled to stand on the side

215

of his nose. He made no attempt to brush it away; indeed, Alistair wondered whether he had noticed it.

Suddenly Janet opened her eyes, bright blue, living feature in a dead landscape, and fastened on the tear. Her face crumpled as she reached with both hands to claw at one of Sebastian's. Dry sobs scraped her chest. Sebastian looked across at his father, then raised himself, plumped on the bed to take his mother's skeleton shape in his arms.

Alistair, left out, understood Janet's agony.

She had made it plain to him in these last weeks that she would not be sorry to die, to be rid of her pain, weakness, distress, but now she realized that she would lose with these her son, his future, his love. That had now overwhelmed her, publicly, against her will. Her sobbing soon ended, she had not the strength for a lengthy bout, and she detached herself from Sebastian's arms to lie down, shamed, trying to hide from them both. They watched the nails of her right hand scratch weakly at the pillow by her closed eyes.

In the end, at inordinate cost, Alistair guessed, the old Janet reasserted herself. She asked to be sat up, propped by pillow and bolster, and there, dessicated, mummy-frail, demanded her glass of lemon. She spoke now and again; Sebastian described a cross-Channel jaunt in a friend's yacht, with danger from fog and tide, and she gave the appearance of attention, but could not hide relief when at the end of an hour Alistair drew the visit to a close.

'How long will it be?' Sebastian's question, his first word out of the ward, was not put until they were halfway up the sunny street where he had parked.

'They don't know. Not long.'

'In the next day or two?' The young man sounded savage. His father shrugged. It was, in fact, six weeks before she died. The shell of a body sipped at her glass, and clung to living. Sebastian visited her a further five times, and on the final occasion she was almost beyond speech.

'Why don't they put her out of her misery?'

'I'm not sure they haven't tried.'

She had drifted away finally, a breathing corpse one minute, dead the next, at a moment when her husband had slipped out to collect a special window fastening from an old-fashioned ironmonger's.

There had been no contact by word for some days, only his hand or lips touching her. Once it was over, he had staggered home, and roused himself only for the undertaker, the consolatory visits of acquaintances. He dully addressed the envelopes of printed thanks for condolences and flowers.

On the day of the funeral he had livened himself, to meet son, Scottish cousins, old colleagues. All had been surprised at his calm, his smart appearance, his youthful energy, but once the house had cleared he had fallen back into lethargy. Janet would not have approved; neither did he. He wished now he had continued at work until sixty-five, so that he could have found occupation. While Janet lived, however feebly, he had been himself, a man. On her death, he became worthless, a nothing.

Janet, unlike Alistair, had achieved what she had set her mind on, and more. She did not minutely interfere in her husband's work, but encouraged him when he was down, or chaffed him out of complacency or self-congratulation and nearer to common sense. She had landed him in the position she thought he deserved, and supported him there with relish. He had no idea now whether she was personally fulfilled; he remembered unaccountable bursts of ill temper from her, bouts of unreason, but these had never lasted more than a few days. She kept her home beautiful, spent time on the children, adequately made the social appearances his office demanded, and this with such determination he forgot, or barely remembered, the diffident red-cheeked lassie at the Palace Dramatic Society. Moreover, Sebastian Murray now existed, and the father often wished Janet had lived those few years longer to see her favourite become a national figure. Whether she would have entirely approved he was not sure; that Scottish sceptical eye would have weighed up, marked down such rapidity of success. On the other hand, she would have made an exception, a dozen or a hundred, in favour of her Sebastian. Certainly she had watched, on her small black and white set, and enthused over, her boy's first appearances on the medium.

Since her death Alistair Murray had been left to mime the part of living. He had gardened, read, attended fewer concerts or theatres than he intended, brooded, sulked his way back into steadiness. He missed her still, though not poignantly as he had in those first twelve months when, strength recovered, he would have given much to be able to wear himself out again chasing into her bedroom, cooking for her, cleaning her up, lying awake with her in the small hours. Now he had only himself to serve, and opportunities grew poorer with each week. At best he could expect a phone call to rouse him, could read an interesting article, make a note to buy a ticket. On that red-letter day, the only one in four years, Eleanor Franks had knocked at his door and demanded help, but it would not happen again. A chat in the street to a police inspector, an infrequent reading to Jeremy Montgomerie or a casual word in the garden with his mother would have to suffice. He had been wrong not to lumber himself with regular good works when he retired, though Janet's illness had patently devastated all his leisure as he had expected, and now he would become less able to occupy himself, until such time as death laid the finger on him.

These days as he replaced a battery in the quartz kitchen clock, or bought a new shirt, he hinted to himself that this might see his time out. But he did not convince himself; he was not serious.

Death must be close, but he could fob it off for another fifteen or twenty years. Eighty, eighty-five were not unusual ages. He often went, albeit rapidly, over his view of the end, but so far it had never threatened. In his early life he had endured examinations, interviews, occurrences he had found unpleasant; in his army days he had been for four or five weeks in danger of sudden death, but he had put up with all that. He'd die, like everyone else; he had no choice. When the time came, he hoped it would not be a long-drawn-out ordeal, he'd keep his head down as he'd always done. But at this distance death was not yet real.

Even the most significant events of his life: Janet's terminal illness, Sebastian's sorrow, Eleanor's haughty dismissal of his suit, his failures at work, now carried little emotional charge.

They were sketches; outline drawings, clear enough to remind him of the harrowing he underwent but not to revive it in any great degree. As with those so with death. It lacked clarity. His recent stumble towards a bus, deliberate or not, was equally vague, dulled. Whatever was to be said of his present mode of existence, it lowered the threshold of emotional pain, made all bearable by the humdrum nature of everyday routine or lack of it. Living or partly living, he told himself, had much to recommend it. Thus he would continue to struggle on, and remember without hate or love, so that the crises of his life would appear small as the molehill transactions of kitchen or supermarket.

That could not be good for his memoir.

He had claimed he could hate still. Well then, he would find out as he wrote. Dryly reminding himself that he must keep his head, never exaggerate, write from cool wits, he pushed out into the pantry for an early evening dram. There stood his refuge, one of six. Holding the opened whisky bottle to the light, he had to decide on its form: neat, with water, ice, ginger, soda, all acceptable as long as they did not delay the numbing process, the accommodation of Alistair Murray to his grey world.

Neat, he decided.

His glass pictured a thistle, had been Janet's father's, the one *objet d'art* left by Dairyman Brown. The old man had dropped dead in his backyard one winter's evening on his way to the outside lavatory. His wife had found him out there, being rained on, in the dark. She herself had not lasted long enough to start to spend the small fortune he had accumulated and would never waste on himself. There had been little of beauty in that grim house; many reminders of earlier poverty; only money in the bank, counted, untouched, prepared not for a rainy day, every day was that in Old Broon's view, but for the hurricane, the cataclysm which never appeared in his temperate Glasgow. Where the glass had come from in the first place, Janet could not guess. It had stood at the back of an ugly china cabinet, the father was a total abstainer, with vulgar souvenirs of Ayr or Troon or Edinburgh presented by holidaying children or misguided relatives, taken out only for dusting, a singleton. Murray remembered Brown, with his long face, looking old enough to be his daughter's grandfather, out of touch in the discomfort he had made for himself.

He put the glass and bottle down remembering his own daughter.

Jane resembled neither him nor her mother except in obstinacy. Her first ten years had lit his life, but after that she had made her own uncouth way. She asked no favours from him, sent the postcards once a year that just acknowledged his existence, did not need him. He wondered if she thought about him, and in what respect, even with what respect. That child had lived eighteen years in his house, and had then within a year or two married a man of his generation, and believing her parents disapproved had cut all but the most formal contacts. He ought to have made an attempt to, to do what? The birthday presents that Janet had regularly chosen, gift-wrapped and sent had ceased on her death. He made impulsively for the phone, dialled her number. Selby Warren, the husband, answered.

No, Janet (he kept to her real name) was not in; she was at church. Some of the women had a little get-together afterwards. Yes, they were all well. Warren described his own research, which went, his phrase, at a spanking pace, two new textbooks he was responsible for, an invitation to lecture in West Germany and the struggles, optimistically sketched, of his department. The man spoke cheerfully. Janet throve, the children likewise. He did not take umbrage at Murray's questions about their age. They were eight and six and both, as far as he could judge, clever, in local schools which were excellent. As usual, they had taken a cottage on Exmoor and would spend the last week of the school holiday there. Yes, Janet went regularly to church, he, Selby did not, but had gone this morning with the whole family as it was Easter Day. He spoke of this as he might have mentioned a visit to a zoo, a museum, a stately home.

'I thought you were anti-religion,' Murray said, chancing his arm.

'On the grounds that he who is not for it is against it?' He laughed, perhaps at himself. 'I'm easygoing in these matters.'

He volunteered that Janet (this preservation of nomen-clature by the pair was the only sign of antagonism) had attended church since the children had been born, suggesting that it gave her an extra hour out of the house. His sons by his first marriage were making as much progress as they ever would; they were smug Conservative voters, know-alls and kept out of his way until they wanted something. As he offered the opinion he did not seem displeased. Yes, he'd do another five years; it was a nuisance, but the children were young and the stresses weren't intolerable. He'd been asked to submit a talk on Goethe's letters, not his line really, by a friend who worked on Radio 3. Yes, life passed interestingly enough. He politely inquired after his father-in-law, seemed in no hurry to ring off, said Janet, to judge by the time, had probably gone round to somebody's house. Murray brought the exchange to an end.   ✓

He had never known Warren so accommodating, so forth-coming. He felt cheered, but had not told his son-in-law that he was embarking on a new project. The man would not have been interested. Why should he? He would just have remembered the fact long enough to report it to Jane on her return, and they would have wondered why he'd started on this so late in the day. They would not have made fun, he decided. Jane might just have pondered her own appearances; she would have no notion how much he had loved her, just as he had none about how and why that love had disappeared. He doubted whether he would find out; he'd drum up cock-and-bull fiction to please himself.

He poured three thick fingers of whisky, neat, to stave off despair, but before he had raised it to his lips had changed his mind, gone out to the tap and filled Mr Brown's glass to the rim.

It was not quite dark outside; the lights gleamed round his room. He stretched, ironically drank a toast to his image in the oval mirror. The thick, grey hair stood untidy; his face was heavy, doughlike, losing shape, outline sagging.

The telephone jostled for his attention.

Eleanor wanted to thank him. She'd had an easy day, and felt much better, and now she wanted to tell him how good he'd been, doing just the right things, leaving at exactly the right time. He had done well. She felt she had a real friend. That was a necessity to her. She had been lost last night on her own, with nothing to live for.

'But you seemed to be enjoying yourself so much at the concert hall with your friends.'

'They go. I'm left. On my own.'

'Without resources,' he said.

'Worse. Without anything. Blank.'

She talked on, unenlightening, like a supermarket conversationalist dragging it out. 'And I said to 'er, well, you know how it is, don't you?, I mean, you've had some in your time, what wi' your two, and then yourself, so I says to 'er, and d'you know what she'ad the nerve to turn round and . . .'

Eleanor's voice lacked the indigenous twang that might just attract an eavesdropper; she spoke with a kind of breathless candour, heaping praise of him on the foundation of her own worthlessness. Such were the hymns of his father's church: such were love poems.

'Say me a line or two of poetry,' she demanded. Her voice had changed, rang metallic. 'Don't stop to think. Just quote something.'

' "God pardon us, not harden us, we did not see so
    clear,
The night we went to Bannockburn by way of Brighton
    Pier." '

'What's that?'

'Chesterton.'

'Never read any.'

'A paradox expert. I haven't read much either. Don't know why I dredged that up. It's apposite to me. The Rolling English Drunkard.' He jokingly explained that he had whisky at his elbow.

She lost interest.

He came smartly out with the memoir, his ace of trumps. This did not excite her. She confected mild grammatical entities, sentences, neither catching her thoughts, nor his information.

'I expect you'll appear in it,' he said, 'if I get that far.'

'That'll be dull.'

He remembered the wild, knickerless schoolgirl in a summer field, and the elegant young woman who answered no letters, and never once was home at her lodgings when he phoned.

'Will you come over this evening?' she was asking. 'We could have a drink.'

He should refuse; he needed to be early to bed, at least, this night.

'I've one or two things I ought to . . .'

'Get them done then, and come over when you're ready. I'm lonely, Alistair.'

'Half an hour.' Weakly. 'Give me half an hour.'

Again the gush of non-coloured thanks.

Leaving the phone, he was glad. Upstairs he shaved again, put on a clean shirt. He told himself this would add a page or two to his book. He tried to despise himself, and failed. He repolished his shoes, made up his mind between two light grey suits. Aftershave and toothpaste added their nothings; his fingernails shone short, clean.

He left on lights in hall, dining room and kitchen, and Radio 4 braying loudly against burglars. More naïve deception; windows and doors were secured. His shirt collar gleamed to his satisfaction. 'Wearing white for Eastertide.' The irony did not heal, but neither did he care.

Banging the heavy front door behind him, and standing out on the path, he found the garden dark though stars punctured the sky.

> The starry darkness paces
> The land from sea to sea
> And mocks the foolish faces.

The lines comforted against their sense. He stepped off, having fastened the garden gate with useless care.

> On such a night
> Troilus, methinks, mounted the Trojan walls
> And sighed his soul . . .

Alistair Murray tried not to hurry up the gentle slope, failed again.

'I was born on February 21st, 1918, the only son of James J. and Rhoda Murray.'

BC	16/14
Bb	5/18